LOVE AT FIRST HAUNT

HAUNTED EVER AFTER
BOOK ONE

CARRIE PULKINEN

This is a work of fiction. Names, characters, places, and incidents are either the product of the author's imagination or are used fictitiously, and any resemblance to actual persons living or dead, business establishments, events, or locales, is entirely coincidental.

Love at First Haunt

COPYRIGHT © 2017 & 2021 by Carrie Pulkinen

All rights reserved. No part of this book may be used or reproduced in any manner whatsoever without written permission of the author except in the case of brief quotations embodied in critical articles or reviews.

Contact Information: www.CarriePulkinen.com

Edited by Krista Venero of Mountains Wanted

ISBN: 978-1-7347624-5-7

Originally published as To Catch a Spirit

CHAPTER ONE

"God, this place is obnoxious." A sickening feeling formed in Allison Gray's stomach as she walked across the yard toward the mansion. A row of Grecian columns lined the front porch, and the foreboding stone steps leading to the heavy wooden door made her breath catch.

Why did she let Tina talk her into another one of these swanky parties? Thoughts of a million places she'd rather be at the moment tumbled through her mind: the antique shop, the movies, curled up in bed with a good book. Hell, she'd take a pap smear over the torture that awaited her inside, but she put on a smile and straightened her spine. She could endure it for her friend…for a little while, at least.

"It's gorgeous, and selling it paid my bills for the next six months." Tina shook her fingers in her hair, giving it lift, not that it needed any help. Her thick black mane had more body than a packed beach in the summertime.

"You owe me for this," Allison said.

"Put it on my tab." Tina laughed and tugged her through the door.

The place was as obnoxious on the inside as it was on the outside. Marble floors, a grand staircase, expensive furniture…there was such a thing as having too much money, but, hey, at least the guy knew how to throw a party. The mansion was packed.

They made the rounds, Tina introducing her to every man she knew, and Allison smiled politely, shook hands, and excused herself from each inviting gaze. They were all the same: rich, handsome, and full of themselves. No thanks.

Been there, done that, couldn't afford the t-shirt.

As a tall man in black slacks and a blue-gray button-up waltzed into the room, Tina's nails cut into Allison's arm. "There's the new owner. Logan Alexander Mitchell. Isn't he scrumptious?"

Allison glanced at his dark hair and piercing sapphire eyes. His fluid movements and confident posture gave him an air of commanding influence, making her heart rate kick up. He was striking. Attractive, but no different than the rest of the high-rollers here. She shrugged. "He looks like a pretentious asshole to me."

Tina crossed her arms. "You think all men are pretentious assholes, Allie."

"That's because they are." Allison smirked and turned to survey the room. She shouldn't judge. Truth be told, she'd come very close to living this lifestyle, but having your life turned upside down by your cheating fiancé had a way of making people bitter.

She downed her second glass of champagne, needing something to dull the incessant chatter of emotions blasting her from every corner of the oversized house.

Allison was an empath, and though she couldn't *hear* the thoughts racing through people's minds, she could certainly sense them. Sex and money. That's all anyone thought about at parties like this. She rubbed her arms to wipe away the vibrating energy. "Tell me again why you hang out with these people."

"It's called networking. Every one of these jerks is a potential client." Tina smiled and leaned her shoulder against the wall, crossing her legs at the ankles. "And the men are hot. With any luck, I can get a few leads *and* get laid." She raised her eyebrows, and her gaze followed a tight butt in an Armani suit.

Allison laughed. "Slut."

Tina grinned. "Prude."

"I'm not a prude; I'm picky. I'm sorry if I don't go for the rich prick type."

"You don't go for *any* type." Tina winked and strummed her fingers against her arm.

"Go mingle. Go…find some real estate clients and your man of the hour. I'll be fine."

"Are you sure?" She put her hand on Allison's arm. "I always drag you to these parties, and I feel like I abandon you halfway through."

"You do, but it's okay. I'm a big girl. Things are pretty calm here anyway, and I can take care of myself. *Go.*"

"Love you, Allie."

"I know."

Tina pushed off the wall and slunk into the throng of people, leaving Allison alone with her champagne. She had to grin at her friend as she worked the crowd with her charming smile and quick wit. Tina played the game like a pro, and she had the income to prove it. Allison felt lucky she could pay all her bills on time, but making a career out of her psychic gift was her choice. She knew she'd never get rich from it, and she was fine with that.

Allison pressed her back to the wall and looked at her watch. Only half an hour more, and she could duck out. Tina would be fine without her.

As she made her way to the bar for another glass of champagne, trying to block out the raging hormone-infested emotions that flooded the room like hot honey, she felt a man watching her. His commanding presence startled her, but she felt something else hiding beneath the testosterone and aftershave. She felt pain, heart-wrenching loneliness. It seemed someone else felt just as out of place at this party as she did.

She dared turn to see who this intriguing aura belonged to, and their eyes met. For half a second, the mesmerizing intensity of his gaze held her to the spot. Her breath hitched.

Oh, crap.

She jerked her head down and picked up her pace. Logan Mitchell. Why would the host of the party be harboring such disturbing emotions? She shook her head. It didn't matter. The last thing she needed was to get caught up in a pointless conversation with a man like him. She was *so* not his type.

Ducking around a corner, she lost him in the crowd, but he didn't leave her thoughts. That pain, that loneliness would follow her. Allison's psychic ability was both a blessing and a curse in that respect. Unless she blocked it out, she always knew what other people were feeling, whether she wanted to or not. And Logan…the man had it all, yet he was empty. What was his story?

Ugh! It doesn't matter. This was her own fault. She allowed it in. She knew better than to let her guard down, especially in a crowded place like this, and now she knew way more about the sexy millionaire than she cared to. Forget the champagne. She needed to go home.

She scanned the crowd for Tina, hoping to tell her goodbye before she ducked out the door, but a woman on the stairs drew her attention. Her long, white nightgown flowed around her ankles, and she sat with her head in her hands, sobbing.

The woman's despair washed over her like a drowning pool. Allison blinked back tears as she approached, trying her damnedest to block out the unwelcome emotions, but they clawed their way deep inside her, tearing at her heart. This place was an empath's nightmare.

"Can I help you?" Allison spoke in her softest, most comforting voice.

Despite her best efforts to block them out, the woman's emotions overwhelmed her. Betrayal, desperation, sickening depression. What happened to her? Allison couldn't fight the tears as they streamed down her face.

"Excuse me, Miss?" She wiped her cheeks with her fingertips and choked on a sob, unable to recall the last time another person's emotions had affected her this way.

This was Logan's fault. Well, Allison's really, but she'd let her guard down because of him, and now look at her. Crying along with a person she'd never met, not even knowing why.

"Is there anything I can do to help you?"

The woman raised her head and blinked.

Then she vanished.

Logan Mitchell sighed as he worked his way through the crowd. His first night in the sprawling mansion on Grayhaven Island was supposed to be a happy one. He'd thrown one hell of a party, but his mind kept drifting to places he'd rather not visit. Places he'd moved here to get away from. He shook his head, forcing his thoughts back to the present.

His 150 party guests fit easily in the estate. It was way more house than a single guy needed, but he got it for a steal. Why anyone would want to leave such a beautiful, secluded place, he had no idea. This house was one dream he was happy to see come true.

Trent clapped him on the shoulder and surveyed the room. "Nice to have your own place again, isn't it?"

"Definitely. You can't build equity when you're renting, though leaving New York probably got me disowned."

"True."

He shoved his hands in his pockets. "Screw it. Doesn't matter." It was nice to rub a little salt in his father's wound. There was no way he was going down the path that man had so carefully carved out for him.

He was already cursed as it was.

"So." Trent flashed a grin and gestured to the guests. "Who's the lucky lady who gets to spend the night with Detroit's Most Eligible Bachelor?"

Thankful for the change of subject, Logan scanned the crowd. So many beautiful women, and any one of them would think it a privilege to go to bed with him. Just another one-night stand. That was all they'd ever be to him.

That was all *he* could ever be for them.

"You know that's going to get old eventually."

"How can that get old? *Detroit Weekly Magazine* named you this year's Most Eligible Bachelor. Not that you needed any help with the ladies before, but come on. Detroit's Most Eligible Bachelor."

"It's already annoying." Logan slapped his friend on the back and turned toward a group of women. "A bachelor's all I'll ever be," he mumbled.

"You say something?"

"Nope. It's nothing." Nothing but the fact he was destined to lead a lonely life because he couldn't afford to let anyone get close to him. Not when he knew the consequence it would bring.

The party was a way to fill the void that haunted him. The emptiness he couldn't escape, knowing he could never settle down. Surrounding himself with people helped stave off the nagging loneliness. Until the party was over.

No, he couldn't be alone tonight.

"How about her?" Trent nodded toward a brunette in a tight black dress.

"She'll do."

"Not good enough? There are plenty of women here. Take your pick."

"They're all the same." Sex and money. That was what they all wanted from him. He felt it every day of his life. Logan could read people, feel their emotions. It was a gift his father loved to exploit—already had exploited more than he wanted to think about. Yeah, getting the hell out of New York was the best thing he could've done, and yet, it seemed nothing had changed.

He looked at the brunette. She was pretty, though it didn't matter what she looked like. All he needed was a warm body to fill his bed and make him feel wanted for a few hours.

He stopped and raked a hand through his hair. What had his life come to?

He searched the room again, letting the crowd's emotions grate over his skin like sandpaper, but this time he found something different. *She* was different. Her blonde hair hung in loose waves down to her shoulders, and her fair skin looked like porcelain, fragile, with a sprinkling of freckles across her nose. She wore very little makeup, and her conservative black slacks and turtleneck sweater told him she definitely wasn't there for sex. Probably not the money either. She turned her head and caught his gaze, but then she flitted away. Without thinking twice, he pursued her.

Trent caught him by the arm. "Her? Seriously, man. You can do better than that." He tried to steer Logan back to the voluptuous brunette he was about to pick up.

"She's different. There's something…I need to talk to her."

"Since when do you care about talking?"

Logan waded through the crowd, trying to catch up to the intriguing woman. He followed her toward the bar, then stopped as she made an abrupt turn by the staircase. She didn't see him, didn't know he was watching when he reached out to read her.

Sadness. Overwhelming despair.

She crept toward the stairs and put her hand on the rail as she bent over. Was she in pain? She was talking to…no one. Her hand covered her mouth as she turned. Tears streamed down her face, and she ran to the door.

"Wait!" Logan pushed through the mass of people, but he was too late. She was out the door before he could catch up. "What the hell?"

She darted across the front lawn like she couldn't get out of the place fast enough.

"You all right, man?" Trent put his hand on Logan's shoulder. "She take off?"

"Yeah. She's gone."

"No biggie. There's plenty of other fish in this sea, and they're all waiting to be caught by Detroit's Most Eligible Bachelor."

Logan shook his head. "That's *really* getting old."

Allison fumbled with her keys as she tried to unlock her car. The crisp fall breeze sent shivers cascading down her spine. Her heart raced, and the vapors of her shallow breaths fogged the window as she cursed her remote. With trembling hands, she opened the door and shoved the key in the ignition. Her Toyota looked like a black sheep among the designer cars that took up most of the crescent-shaped driveway.

It didn't matter. At that moment, she focused on getting the hell off that island.

A ghost.

She should've known it was a spirit when the emotions overwhelmed her. She'd been psychic as long as she could remember, and she worked hard to keep her abilities in check. A living person's feelings couldn't consume her like that. Not anymore. But something about a ghost not being in a physical body made it nearly impossible for her to block them out.

She inhaled deeply to center herself and pulled out her cell phone to send Tina a text. *Headed home. Call me tomorrow.*

Hopefully no one saw her display of emotion, but if they did, her friend would let her know. Tina made it her business to know everything about everyone. As the number one real estate agent in the Detroit area, she'd sold the Grayhaven Mansion to Logan and made a pretty profit, even though it went for next to nothing. If you could call ten million dollars nothing.

With her emotions under control, Allison stomped the gas and sped back to her tiny apartment in the city.

Her emotions. What a laugh.

She wasn't the one who was so upset. It was that woman, that ghost on the stairs. Allison chuckled. Logan Mitchell got more than he bargained for in that deal.

Logan. She had to admit the guy was gorgeous, if she were going to judge him on outward appearance alone. At six and a half feet tall, his broad chest and muscular arms were enough to make women swoon. Thick black lashes fringed his intense crystal-blue eyes, and his dark chestnut hair was cut close on the sides and messy-chic on top.

Inside… To be honest, she didn't know much about him. She never read the newspaper or magazine articles celebrating his latest accomplishments. He was just another rich, arrogant, self-centered jerk like her ex, Mark, was. Like they all were. She didn't *want* to know him.

But what was that frightened loneliness about? The poor guy was screaming for help, and helping people was what Allison did best.

But he didn't ask for her assistance.

She parked her car and climbed the stairs to her third-floor apartment. Safely inside and away from the constant throbbing of human emotion, she pushed Logan out of her mind and concentrated on her nightly meditation. Lord knew she needed it after that escapade.

Logan saw the last of his guests to the door, then turned around to face the next woman he'd never talk to again. She had long brown hair and sleek curves, and she was looking at him with her best come-and-get-me eyes.

Her thoughts pounded at him like twenty-inch subwoofers on full-blast. He couldn't read her mind. It was a feeling he got, like registering another person's emotions. The hot, sticky flow of sex was offset by the sharp trill of excitement that only money could bring. That's all she wanted from him. That's all anyone wanted from him, and it was all he had to give. He sighed and led her upstairs to his bedroom.

"But, I'm your wife, Alex. Don't you love me anymore?"

Blood ran down the woman's face from the nasty gash on her forehead, and her utter despair slammed into him like a Mack truck into a brick wall. Her emotions paralyzed him. He didn't love her. Hell, he had another woman in his arms, and she was the one he loved.

"Please, Alex." Blood mixed with tears splashed on the marble floor, leaving little pink puddles around her feet. "I'm your wife," she sobbed. Then she climbed on the ledge and hurled herself out the window.

"No!" Logan screamed in the darkness. The sheets clung to his skin, wet with sweat, and he slid out from under his date's arm. She rolled onto her side, never opening her eyes.

He gazed down at her, wracking his brain to remember her name. Nothing.

What's my life coming to?

He ran his hand through his hair and padded to the bathroom. A good, hot shower would help chase the recurring nightmare away.

It was more than a dream. He knew that. Felt it. It wasn't the first premonition he'd had, but it was definitely the most fucked up. Only a handful of his dreams ever came true, but as soon as one became recurring, haunting him night after night, it was bound to happen in real life.

And this one…this was something he couldn't let happen. He'd never told anyone about his dreams, and he didn't plan to. As long as he stayed single the rest of his life, he'd never have to risk his wife throwing herself out a window.

The hot water beat down on his skin, washing away the anxiety from his vision. He scrubbed his face, washed his hair, and then moved down to wash the rest of his body. Always in that order.

The first night in his new place wasn't supposed to be like this. Hell, it should *never* be like this. That was what the woman in his bed was for—to stave off the impending doom that invaded his dreams. The vision only came when he was alone. That was how it had always been. So, why the hell did he wake up screaming?

The dream felt stronger this time too. More real than ever before. He felt the faceless women of his vision like they were right there with him.

"Mind if I join you?" The sultry female voice brought him back to reality. She slunk up to the shower, wearing

Logan's shirt and nothing else, and as she smiled, she dropped the garment to the floor. He cursed under his breath and shut off the water.

"I'm done." He yanked a towel off the rack and wrapped it around his waist as he stalked into the bedroom to his dresser. Sweatpants, socks, t-shirt. A good run would clear his head.

"Are you going somewhere?" The sting of rejection filled the air as the woman sat on the edge of the bed.

His stomach wrenched at what he was about to say. "You're a really nice girl, but I'm not looking for a relationship right now." The words left his lips sounding too rehearsed. Like he'd done this a hundred times. Maybe he had. He sat on a chair in the corner and laced up his running shoes.

"I understand." She slipped her dress and shoes on, stuffing her bra and panties into her purse. Then she strode toward him, kissed him on the cheek, and handed him a business card. "My brother has a start-up company, if you're looking for an investment. He's brilliant."

"Thanks." Logan flicked the card onto the table. "Can you show yourself out?"

"Sure."

He chuckled and shook his head when the front door clicked shut. Money. No one saw past the façade. No one really knew *him*, save for a few close friends. Reading people like he could, at least he knew who his friends were.

Quitting the family business, moving to Detroit, he'd gotten as far away from his father's life as he could, and yet here he was, right in the middle of it. The parties, the women, the transparent so-called friends. Who was he kidding?

He could see where this train of thought was going, and he wasn't in the mood for a pity party. He slipped on his shirt and headed out the door to run.

Always running.

The brisk autumn air chilled his lungs as he jogged along a path by the water. His party had been a success. He'd made a few business contacts; everyone had a good time. Well, almost everyone.

His thoughts drifted back to the blonde from the staircase. What could she have been so upset about? And what was a woman like her doing at a party like that? He'd never seen her before, and to say she stood out was an understatement. This woman was different. She wasn't the slightest bit interested in him, and that made her all the more intriguing.

CHAPTER TWO

"Good morning, Lucia!" Allison beamed as she strode into the antique shop with a nonfat latte in each hand. She put one on the counter in front of Lucia and leaned over to kiss her on the cheek.

"Good morning, Allison. Early appointment today?"

"No, I couldn't sleep."

Lucia, a robust Italian woman in her late sixties, had silver hair and a keen eye for good deals on priceless antiques. "How was the party? Did you meet any nice men?" She raised her eyebrows and smiled.

Allison laughed. "There's no such thing."

"I worry about you, dear." Lucia's thick Italian accent chopped at her words. "You need to find a nice man. Settle down. Raise a family."

"I don't think that's in the cards for me."

"How would you know that? When's the last time you had someone do a reading for you?" Lucia crossed her thick arms over her chest and shifted her weight.

Allison sighed. "Do you have anything new for me to look at?"

"I got some new pieces in yesterday." She motioned to an intricate cherry-wood vanity in the back of the showroom.

The moment Allison touched it, tendrils of sadness crept up her arm like ivy climbing a lattice. She saw a woman who'd lost a child, sobbing at the vanity. She'd cried there every night; the furniture had trapped her despair.

"It's eighteenth century," Lucia said.

"I know. It's got a lot of negative energy stored in it. I can clear it." Allison closed her eyes and took a deep breath as she rested her hands on the vanity and focused her mind. She opened herself up like a conduit, allowing the negative energy to pass through and out of her, releasing it back into the universe. She pulled a crystal out of her purse and placed it on the vanity.

"There. That should do it. I bet it'll sell quickly."

"What would I do without you?"

She smiled. "You'd have an extra room in your store."

"And furniture that never sells. Your small office in the back doesn't put me out one bit, child. I'm thankful to have you. Come on, I have another piece for you."

Allison followed Lucia as she waded past the centuries-old furniture to the back of the building. To the left of Allison's office, a double door led into the storeroom where a large oval table sat in the center. Dark mahogany wood and intricate carvings etched into sturdy legs gave it an aura of romance.

"It's beautiful," Allison said.

"It's French. Late seventeenth century. What do you think?"

Allison took a deep breath and placed her palms on the

table. Closing her eyes, she focused on the wood. An intense wave of fear gripped her throat, slamming into her body and sucking the air from her lungs. The force of the energy felt like a frying pan whopped her in the face. Her knees gave out, and she crumpled to the floor, her heart pounding and her head throbbing as she struggled to regain her composure.

"Allison! Are you okay?" Lucia knelt at her side and put her hand on her forehead.

Her vision wavered, but she sat up and looked at the table again. Stored energy had never struck her like that before. *What the hell?*

"It was really strong, but I'm okay. I can clear it. Just give me a minute to prepare."

Lucia helped her to her feet. "It's too much for you right now. You can try later. Come, our lattes are getting cold."

"No." Allison stopped and turned back to the table. "I can do it. I'm fine. Really, Lucia." She smiled at the woman and touched her shoulder.

But she wasn't fine. Allison didn't have this kind of trouble. She took care of herself, made sure to keep the negative energy out. So why was she so rattled now?

Maybe it was the spirit last night. Those overwhelming emotions had shaken her up. Normally she could avoid ghosts, but this one was so strong, she'd thought it was a living person.

Then there was Logan. She didn't mean to read him, but his loneliness struck a chord in her. His silent screams for help tugged at her heart, and her thoughts kept drifting to those piercing blue eyes. She could admit she was attracted to him. Who wouldn't be? But hopefully she'd never have to see him again.

She would have to work harder at keeping her guard up.

Focusing her attention back on the furniture, she prepared for the sudden explosion of despair that crashed into her chest. As the anguish slammed into her, she gripped the edge of the table and held on, allowing the horrid images to play in her mind, the energy to rip through her body.

"I see a woman. Terrible things happened to her at this table." Allison clamped her mouth closed as the agonizing energy invaded her. Anguish. Fear. She squeezed her eyes shut and bit her bottom lip as the woman's misery escaped her. It was too much. Too terrible to bear. She fought with all her strength to hold on, to release the energy. She felt it pass through her like a thousand razor blades slicing her soul. When there was nothing left but a soft hum of electricity, she opened her eyes.

"There. It's cleared. You might want to leave a crystal on it for a few days before you move it out to the showroom, just to make sure it's all gone." She stood up straight, and the room tipped on its side.

When her eyelids fluttered open, Allison lay on the treatment table in her office. The aroma of spiced tea wafted in as she shakily sat up and swung her legs over the edge.

"What happened?" She pressed her hand to her pounding head.

"I was going to ask you the same thing." Lucia handed her a mug of hot tea and settled into a chair. "You passed out, and I carried you in here. You're lucky you're so light, or you'd still be in there on the concrete floor."

Holy crap. That had never happened before. "The energy affected me more than it usually does. I cleared it. Then one minute I was fine, and the next I was waking up in here."

Lucia set her mug on the table and shifted her weight forward. "You're working too hard. You should take the week off. Get some rest."

"I can't do that. I have clients who depend on me."

"Well, you don't have to worry about me." Lucia heaved herself out of the chair and gave Allison a hug. "Anything that comes in this week can wait in the storeroom. Take care of yourself, okay?"

"I will. Thank you."

His adrenaline flowing from his run, Logan darted up the back steps and into his kitchen. Classic rock blasted through his earbuds as he made a pot of coffee and poured a bowl of Fruity Pebbles. There was nothing like a big mound of sugar to start the morning off right. He chuckled as he spooned the multi-colored cereal into his mouth. It had been his favorite since he was a kid, when his parents were together and his dad was still his hero.

What a crock.

How his mom had sheltered him from his father's betrayal was still a mystery. Even through all the mistresses and the verbal assaults, Logan and his sister had no idea what their mother was going through. Some called her weak for putting up with it, but Logan knew better.

His mom was the strongest woman he knew. She did

everything in her power to be sure Logan and Lisa had the best lives possible, and only when she was sure they were on their own and could take care of themselves did she leave. Now she had a good job and an apartment upstate, and her ex-husband could have all the mistresses he wanted. Logan's mom was his hero now.

He squeezed his eyes shut, trying to banish the invasive thoughts from his mind before they spun out of control, and jogged upstairs to shower and get ready for the day. He was sponsoring a benefit for the local children's hospital soon, and there was work to be done. Work he could feel good about.

He stripped, dropping his clothes into the appropriate color-coded hampers, and stepped into the shower. As he finished his cleansing rituals and turned off the water, the sound of his dresser drawer opening and closing rattled from the other room.

He paused but shook his head. *Just my imagination.*

Again, he heard the sound of wood sliding against wood and the *thunk* of the drawer slamming shut. Odd. Wasn't the housekeeper off today? The drawer opened one more time, and his keys clattered on the floor.

Holy crap. He was being robbed.

He stepped out of the shower and wrapped a towel around his waist before he tiptoed to the bathroom door. His heart pounded as he readied himself for a fight. His black belt in Tae-Kwon-Do wouldn't help him against a bullet, but he wasn't going down without a fight. He swung open the door, and his breath caught in his throat when he saw…nothing. He slipped out the bedroom door and crept down the hall, checking each room for the perpetrator.

Still nothing.

"Come on out, you little bastard." He reached out for an emotion. For some sliver of fear or excitement to guide him to the intruder.

His home was a void.

The only sensation in the air was the smell of his own adrenaline and his pulse throbbing in his ears. He searched the entire house, and still he found no one. All the locks were engaged, the windows latched.

Satisfied the house was empty, he went upstairs to get dressed. Still, that nagging feeling someone was there, watching him, wouldn't go away. He swept the room one more time, looking behind the curtains and under the bed. The dresser sat still and quiet, and he ran his hand along the drawers, opening each one to find everything in its place.

His mind was playing tricks on him. It was the only explanation.

He pulled on dark jeans and an onyx sweater and turned to the nightstand to pick up his phone. But he stopped cold when he saw his keys lying on the floor by the bed. He hadn't imagined that.

How the hell? They must have fallen off. He'd set them too close to the edge, and they fell. That was the logical answer. But as illogical as it seemed, he knew someone had been in his room. He could feel it.

He knelt by the nightstand and put his keys on the edge to see if he could get them to fall again. He leaned in close, balancing the ring on the ledge, willing them to fall so he'd know he wasn't losing his mind. His ringtone blasted out of his cell phone, and he landed flat on his ass, knocking his keys under the bed.

"Shit. Paranoid idiot." He grabbed his phone. "Hello?"

"Hey, baby brother. I didn't wake you, did I?"

"It's ten o'clock, Lisa. You know me better than that." The frustration drained away at the sound of his sister's voice. "What's up?"

"Oh, nothing. I was just checking in to see how your first night at Grayhaven went. How was the party?"

"It was good. You know, same old routine. How's the family?"

"Ben got another promotion. Oh! And Caitlyn–okay, okay. She wants to tell you herself."

A grin tugged at the corners of his mouth. "Well, put her on."

"Uncle Logan! Uncle Logan!"

"Hey, pipsqueak. What've you been up to?"

"I lost another tooth! See?" He heard Lisa in the background explaining he couldn't see her over the phone, and he chuckled.

"Wow! That's great, Caitlyn. How's kindergarten going?"

"It's good. I learned how to ride my bike too. Without training wheels or anything!"

"You are one amazing girl, you know that?"

"Yeah! Mom wants to talk to you. When are you gonna come see me again? I miss you."

"I miss you too, angel. I'll come see you as soon as I can. Bye."

"We all miss you, Logan. Especially Mom." Lisa's voice held a serious tone. "And we're worried about you. Have you met anyone yet?"

He leaned back against the bed and rubbed his forehead. "We're not having this conversation again."

"Oh, come on. You're not Dad. Your life doesn't have to be like his."

"That's exactly what I'm trying to avoid."

"How? By never settling down? Never giving anyone the chance to love you?"

He gritted his teeth. "Dad *did* settle down, and look what happened to Mom."

She sighed. "You don't have to relive his mistakes either. Just try. For me. For Mom. Okay?"

"All right, I'll try, but I'm not making any promises. Listen, I've got work to do. I'm going to try to get back out to New York soon."

"I hope you do. I love you, Bubba."

"Love you too, Sis."

He fished his keys out from under the bed, slipped on his shoes, and headed out the door.

Going back to New York was the last thing he wanted to do. But he couldn't abandon his family. Surely he could get in and out of the city without his dad tracking him down.

Hopefully.

CHAPTER THREE

What in the world was going on with her? Allison curled up in her favorite chair and sipped her herbal tea. She was on the edge of a very slippery slope, and if she wasn't careful, she might sink again. Like last time.

No. Not like last time. It's not going to happen.

There was a reason she didn't deal with spirits anymore, but how a table—an object—got to her like that was a mystery she needed to solve. She couldn't handle blacking out every time she felt negative energy.

It must've been the ghost. The dead woman's invasive emotions threw her balance out of whack.

She put her mug on the table, threw a plush, periwinkle pillow on the middle of the floor, and sat cross-legged on it. She needed to meditate, to focus on clearing out all the energy Logan Mitchell's ghost shot into her. Then she'd work on getting her shields back in place. She had hit her psychic rock bottom before, and that was not a place she was going back to.

She closed her eyes, breathed deeply, and focused.

Relaxing one muscle at a time, she slipped into a meditative state. Her Happy Place.

A soft knock on the door brought her back to coherence. She glanced at the clock. Had it really been an hour?

"Co—" She cleared her throat. "Come in."

Tina cracked the door and peeked inside. "Oh, I'm sorry. Did I interrupt your meditation?"

"It's okay. I've been at it for over an hour. If I haven't solved my issues by now, it's probably not going to happen today." Allison put the pillow on her treatment table and sat on the edge. Tina plopped onto the chair.

"Speaking of your issues…Lucia told me about your little fainting spell." She leaned forward, resting her elbows on her knees. "Are you okay?"

"She called you, huh?"

"She was worried about you, and so am I. That's why I'm taking you out for lunch and a mani/pedi. We're going to have some girl time, and you can tell me all about it."

Allison smiled and pushed off the table. "While I appreciate the offer, I'm fine. Besides, I have a client coming in this afternoon."

"What time?"

"Three."

"Well, then. That gives us four hours to have some fun. Let's go." She picked up her purse, and before Allison could object, Tina took her by the arm and led her out the door. Lucia nodded at Tina, her smile poorly masking the worry in her eyes.

"I'll have her back by three," Tina called over her shoulder as they exited the antique shop.

A gust of chilly wind sent shivers down Allison's neck, and she flipped up the collar of her jacket. Ponytails were good for windy days, but they didn't help with the cold. Just a few more readings, and she'd have enough money to get the haircut she so desperately needed.

"I feel like Chinese. That okay with you?" Tina asked.

"Sounds great." The quiet walk outdoors calmed her nerves, her tension relaxing with every step.

They found a table at China Star, a small restaurant with red vinyl chairs and matching red paper lanterns hanging from the ceiling.

"What happened in there? Lucia said you screamed, and then you blacked out. Was it like—"

"No." She didn't want her to finish the thought. "It was nothing like last time. It was just an object, so I don't know why it got to me."

The waiter arrived to take their order. Allison asked for chicken and broccoli with steamed rice. Tina ordered sweet and sour pork.

"Fried food will kill you." Allison grinned at her friend.

"Maybe so, but at least I'll go out knowing I ate what I wanted and enjoyed every bite."

If only life were so simple.

Tina put her elbows on the table and rested her chin on her hands. "Do you want to tell me why you ran out on me last night without saying goodbye?"

Allison cringed and smoothed the napkin in her lap. "Oh, that. How much did you see?"

"I saw Logan Mitchell chasing after you as you ducked around the corner. Then I saw him watch you burst into tears and run out of the house. What the hell happened, Allie? And why were you avoiding *Logan Mitchell?*" She said his name like he was royalty to be revered.

"Well, crap." She folded her hands on the table. "I didn't think anyone saw."

"Well, we did, so fess up."

"All right, I'll tell you. But you have to promise not to overreact."

Tina raised an eyebrow. "Okay. I promise."

"I saw a ghost at the party last night."

"What?" Tina leaned back in her chair, an incredulous look on her face. "I thought you were blocking out spirits."

"I was. I'm trying to, but this one was strong, Tina. So strong, I thought she was alive. She was crying on the staircase, and I walked over to ask her if she needed help. I went to put my hand on her shoulder, and she disappeared."

"Are you okay? Is that why you were crying? Because she was?"

"Yeah. I should've known what she was when I hit that wall of emotions. I don't know what happened. She was so sad, distraught, but I cleared her out of me. I went home and meditated, and I thought I got rid of all her energy. I was okay until that table at Lucia's."

"You think the ghost last night made you more susceptible to the energy in the wood?"

"It must have. I can't think of any other reason."

"Hmm…" Tina tapped her finger against her chin. "Maybe it's time to ease back into it. You were always so good at spirit work. Maybe it affected you like that because you've been out of it for so long. What's it been? Nine? Ten months? You could start off helping some happy ghosts cross over."

"It's been almost a year." Allison looked at her hands in her lap. She'd worked with the Detroit Area Paranormal

Society—DAPS for short—for years, helping to excise any unwelcome, *unliving* residents from their clients' property. While the rest of the team gathered scientific evidence of the hauntings, Allison had used her psychic abilities to communicate with the lingering spirits and help them cross over.

Until last Halloween at the abandoned psychiatric hospital. She shivered as the memories of the overwhelming depression that followed the incident crept into her mind. "Absolutely not. I don't work with spirits anymore."

Tina shrugged. "All right, it was just a suggestion. Are you okay, though? Really, Allie?"

"I'm fine."

"You'll let me know if you need anything."

"I promise."

"So then…" Tina's concerned look turned into one of curiosity. "Why were you running away from Logan?"

"I wasn't running away from him. I was walking in the opposite direction." And avoiding him in the process, but so what if she was? She'd had her fill of emotionally damaged men.

"You knew he wanted to talk to you?"

Allison smoothed her hair and crossed her arms. "We made eye contact briefly. You know he's not my type."

"Well, I'd sure like to land him." Tina smiled and shoved a piece of pork in her mouth.

"Land him? You'd be another woman who spends one night with the man and never hears from him again. I don't know much about him, but I've heard of his reputation."

"Yeah, but it would be one incredible night," Tina said wistfully. "I wonder why he's like that, though. I guess when you have that much money, you can be however you want to be."

Allison pushed some chicken around on her plate. "He's lonely and scared."

"Lonely? How could a guy like that be lonely?" Her eyes widened with realization. "Wait a minute… You read him, didn't you? You sneaky little mind slut!" She leaned forward and grinned. "What did you see?"

"You know I'm not like that. I don't go around reading people without their permission. I just couldn't help it with him. He was practically screaming it at me, but I shut it out as fast as I could."

Tina giggled. "Uh-huh. So he's lonely. I wonder why?"

"The poor guy's surrounded by people who want his money. It's got to be hard knowing the difference between a true friend and someone who's using you." Hell, Allison didn't even know when Mark started cheating on her, and she was an empath, for Pete's sake.

Okay, that wasn't exactly true. If she had trusted her gut and not closed her eyes to the signs, she'd have known right away. She was young and in love, though. She didn't *want* to know the truth back then, but she would never be so naïve again.

"Am I hearing this right?" Tina asked. "Does Allison Gray have a soft spot for the pretentious asshole?"

"Absolutely not!" *Maybe a little.* "He got himself into that situation. Why should I feel sorry for him?"

"Because you feel sorry for everyone."

"True."

Logan sat across the table from Trent at a deli in downtown Detroit, pushing black beans around on his plate. "It was weird, man. I could've sworn there was somebody in my room."

"I don't know what to tell you. Maybe the place is haunted."

Logan chuckled. "Yeah, right. Like *that* could happen."

Trent shoved a fry in his mouth then picked up his half-pound burger. "You never know. What about that chick who stayed with you last night? You going to see her again?"

"Ha. Not likely. But she did tell me about her brilliant brother who's starting up a new company…just in case I was looking for another investment." He rolled his eyes and toyed with his fork.

"I'm sorry, man." Trent slapped him on the shoulder. "But, you know, maybe you're going about it the wrong way. The kind of women who show up at those parties alone… They're not the type to settle down with."

Logan raised an eyebrow. "I know better than anybody."

"I guess you do. Why don't you try the library or a coffee shop? Maybe the vibes you pick up there will be different. I'm sure nice girls exist *somewhere,* and with your little talent, you should be able to find them."

"I'm not looking to settle down. You know that." He took a bite of his beans, chewing and swallowing before anything else touched his fork. He'd finish them all before he moved on to the sandwich.

Order. It was something he could control.

"Ah. The dad issues again. Just because your dad treated your mom like shit, it doesn't mean you're going to do it to your wife. Hell, Logan. I know you won't. You don't have it in you."

"And if I never have a wife, I'll never have to worry about it." Not that he'd ever mistreat a woman. That wasn't the problem. It was that damn vision.

Trent exhaled sharply and shook his head. "You've got some serious issues, man."

"Tell me about it." If Trent only knew the half of it.

As they finished their meals, a deep pull of doubt emanated from his friend. It probably should've irritated Logan, but it was refreshing to be in the company of someone who actually cared about *him* as a person and not just about his money. And to be honest, he was worried about himself. Hell, he was scared shitless. That vision last night felt too real.

"You got everything in order for the benefit tomorrow night?" Trent asked. "Sounds like it's going to be a good time for all."

"Pretty much. Just have a couple of loose ends to tie up. I need to call John and make sure he's still coming."

"I can't believe you got *him* to play at this thing. Well, yeah, I can. It's going to be one awesome party."

"And it's going to raise a lot of money for the children's hospital. Don't forget the most important part." Logan nodded toward the door, and Trent followed his lead. They left the deli, climbed into Logan's jet-black Mercedes, and headed back to the office.

He turned off Washington Boulevard and onto West Jefferson Avenue. "You remember that woman last night? The blonde?"

"The one in the turtleneck?"

His grip tightened on the steering wheel. "Yeah. You ever see her before?"

A knowing smile slid across Trent's face. "Maybe. Now that I think about it, I may have seen her with that smokin' hot real estate agent who sold you the house."

Logan rubbed his hand across the scruff on his face. Between the distraction of the alleged intruder and his sister's phone call, he'd forgotten to shave. He fought the urge to swing by his house for his razor. "I know the agent, but I don't think I've ever seen her friend before. Do you know her name?"

"No, man. Sorry. You interested?"

He shook his head. "No. No, I'm not."

"Well, that's good. Because she didn't look very interested in you, either."

And that was exactly why she intrigued him. If she didn't care about his money, maybe she could care about *him*. He pushed the thought out of his mind as quickly as it came in. Like that could ever happen.

"Maybe she doesn't like men," Trent said. "Maybe she's…you know…*with* the real estate agent."

Logan arched a brow. "Seriously?"

"I can't think of any other reason why a hot-blooded woman would run away from Detroit's Most Eligible Bachelor, can you?"

"Enough with the bachelor shit, man." He was beginning to regret ever agreeing to that magazine write-up.

With freshly polished nails and a full stomach, Allison strolled into Lucia's at 2:45 with just enough time to prepare for her session.

"Good afternoon, Lucia." She kissed her on the cheek and headed for her office.

"You look like you're feeling better."

"I am. I think some girl-time was just what I needed. Thank you."

"Anytime, dear."

Allison went into her office and took some deep, cleansing breaths to put up her walls and prepare herself for her client. She lit candles, connected her phone to the speakers, and turned on some soft, soothing music. After dimming the lights, she arranged the pillows just right on her treatment table, a massage bed with a pretty quilt thrown over it, and rolled her neck to stretch her muscles.

"Hi, Allison. Are you ready for me?" Stacey's flat brown hair fell into her face, covering one of her dull gray eyes, and as soon as she stepped into the room, her suffocating depression weighed heavy in the air.

Allison put up her walls to block out the emotion and smiled. "Of course, Stacey. Come on in and lie down. How have you been since our last session?"

"Better, I think. A little bit." She rubbed her arm and looked at the floor.

"Did you see a therapist like I suggested?"

"Not yet, but I made an appointment."

"That's good, and you know there's always the option of medication, if the healings and the therapy don't help." Allison practiced Reiki, an ancient art of healing through energy manipulation. Some called her a faith healer. But she wasn't a doctor, and she knew that. No matter what the problem, she always recommended her patients get medical attention and use her methods to help speed along the healing process.

"I don't want to take pills." Stacey's gaze remained on the floor. "I'll try the therapy first, though I wish you could counsel me. I trust you."

"I've got to finish school and get my therapist license before I can do that. For right now, I'll help you as best I can. Okay?"

Stacey slid onto the table and lay on her back.

"Close your eyes and try to relax. I'm going to work on unblocking some of the energy that's built up inside you."

Allison started with her head, placing her hands just above Stacey's crown. She opened herself up, allowing the energy to flow through her and into Stacey. The blocks were bad, as they were with most depression clients, but those were the ones she preferred to work with. She knew first-hand how it felt to be caught in that web of despair, and she wanted more than anything to help others break free.

She moved down to Stacey's heart, her hands hovering above her body. "Do you feel the healing energy, Stacey? It's working its magic right now."

Stacey made a soft moaning sound in her throat. Allison's clients often slipped into a meditative state during healing. She moved down Stacey's body, pausing to send in extra energy wherever she felt a block. Then she gave her one more push, visualizing Stacey filling up with loving white light.

Allison sat on the chair and curled her legs beneath her. "Whenever you're ready, you can open your eyes."

Stacey lay silent, but that was normal. The healing process was relaxing for both the receiver and the giver, and Allison closed her eyes to bask in the energy.

"Thank you." Stacey slowly sat up on the table and forced a slight smile. "I feel better already."

Allison patted her hand. "You still have some major blocks, but it's improving. The counseling will help too. Is there anything else I can do for you today?"

Stacey took a deep breath and exhaled slowly. "I was wondering. You know my grandma passed away two weeks ago?"

"Yes. I'm so sorry for your loss."

"Thank you, but I was wondering…if she's still around…if maybe you could contact her for me?"

As soon as Stacey made her intent clear, the presence of her grandmother's spirit buzzed in the room. She *was* still around, but Allison wasn't about to find out why. She slammed an iron door between herself and the spirit before the ghost could make contact, but the dead woman was insistent. She pushed harder, bowing the protective wall Allison worked so hard to perfect.

She felt the pressure. Felt the spirit seeping through the cracks, threatening her sanity once again.

Why was this happening?

"I'm sorry. I don't work with spirits."

"I understand." Stacey held her eyes wide, as if trying not to blink, to control the tears filling them.

Allison's chest tightened. She *could* contact her grandmother, but at what cost?

"You know her soul has moved on, and all that's left is energy, right? It may be intelligent. It can still have her characteristics and memories, but it's just energy."

"Thank you, Allison."

"I'll see you next week? Same time?"

"I'll be here." Stacey slid off the table and shuffled to the door.

Allison expected to feel relief when her client left the building. The spirit should've followed her granddaughter, but after Stacey left, the overbearing presence lingered. It coiled around her, squeezing like a python encircling its prey. It pleaded with her to listen.

Frantic energy pulsed through the room. Allison dropped to her knees, pressing the heels of her hands to her temples. She would *not* let this happen again. She squeezed her eyes shut.

"Please, leave me alone."

CHAPTER FOUR

Logan pulled his Mercedes into the garage and cut the engine. With his hands on the steering wheel, he took a deep breath and smiled. He had everything lined up for the sold-out benefit tomorrow night, and at five hundred bucks a ticket, the children's hospital was going to get a hefty donation. Plus, all the high-rollers were sure to pull out their fat checkbooks to hand out even more cash. Logan was footing the bill for the venue, the entertainment, and the food and drinks. Hell, he'd be pulling out his fat checkbook to make an extra donation too.

He strode to his living room and flipped on the eighty-inch television hanging on the wall above the fireplace. Grayhaven still didn't feel like home, but he'd get used to it. The house was six times bigger than the penthouse he'd rented downtown. What the hell was he thinking buying such a monstrous place? It wasn't like he'd ever have a family to fill it up.

He settled on a college football game, turned up the

volume to drown out the silence of his empty estate, and padded into the kitchen.

After opening the fridge, he pulled out a pack of ham to make a sandwich and bumped a jar of pickles with his elbow. He straightened the container so the label faced front like all the others and scanned the rest of the fridge contents to make sure everything was in its place. The meats and cheeses sat in their own separate containers, neatly labeled with the store's expiration date and the date he opened them. One percent milk sat on the top shelf next to the two-liter of Coke, both turned so the labels faced the front. Fresh fruit sat color-coded on the bottom shelf. Everything appeared in order.

He let out a breath and closed the door.

Some honey ham and Swiss on a slice of whole grain bread with mustard would hit the spot. He assembled his dinner, poured a glass of Coke, and took his meal to the table.

Picking up his sandwich, he was about to dig in when the faint jingle of a doorknob rattling drew his attention. He paused mid-bite and listened.

Must be my imagination again.

He shrugged and bit into his dinner. Then he heard it again. Louder this time, it sounded like it came from the front door. He paced across the living room to check it out, but he couldn't see anything through the damn peephole. The porch light illuminated the window, but no one was there, so he opened the front door and peered out.

"Hello?" No response. "What the hell?" He closed and locked the door, then set the alarm for good measure.

I must be going out of my mind.

He went back to the kitchen to finish his sandwich,

and he heard it again. This time, it came from the back door.

"Aw, hell!" He shot to his feet, stomped to the door, and flipped on the porch light. Nothing again. Squeezing his eyes shut, he leaned his forehead against the wall.

Get it together, Logan. It's all in your head. The house was old. These kinds of noises were normal in a place like this.

He took a deep breath, resolved to finish his sandwich and forget about it. Shaking his head, he exhaled a curse and turned around in time to see his dinner, plate and all, clank to the ground. The sturdy stoneware didn't break, but his sandwich lay in pieces scattered across the floor.

What the hell?

Now he *knew* he was losing it. Dinnerware didn't get up and move on its own. This wasn't a Disney movie.

He gathered up the pieces of food and threw them in the trash before using the broom and dustpan to sweep up the crumbs. While he was at it, he got out the mop and floor cleaner with bleach and scrubbed the spot where the sandwich landed.

Might as well do the whole floor. The housekeeper had scrubbed it the day before, and she'd do it again tomorrow, but the rhythm and order of cleaning helped take his mind off the crazy shit that was happening. He moved the mop back and forth, back and forth, counting the number of strokes as he cleaned. Satisfied with an even five hundred, he put the cleaning supplies in the utility closet and picked up the plate from the counter.

First my keys fall, and now this. That's some coincidence. What the hell was wrong with him? He was going crazy. There was a logical explanation for all of this, but he couldn't find it because he was losing his goddamn mind.

With a grunt, he chunked the plate against the back door, shattering it into a thousand pieces that clinked on the marble floor like rain on a tin roof.

He raked his hands through his hair and leaned on the table. His mind was playing tricks on him. The house was too damn big for one person to live in, and his imagination was running wild. He needed to get it under control.

But first he needed to clean up this mess. He shoved off the table and felt the unmistakable touch of a hand on his shoulder. He jerked around, his fist flying into the air. No one was there.

Shit.

He stormed to the utility closet, pulled out the broom, and cleaned up the shattered glass. Once every tiny shard lay in the trash, he headed upstairs to change into his workout clothes. He'd pump some iron. Focus on his body and forget he was losing his mind.

In his private gym down the hall from his bedroom, Logan pushed his body to its limits. His treadmill sat idle, as he preferred to do his running in the open air, but he used his weight machines nearly every day. Thick, black padding covered the floor from wall to wall. Equipment and free weights lined the perimeter, and a large mirror hung across from the window.

Exercising was a sacred ritual for him, freeing him from the distractions of the outside world and the barrage of emotions that clouded his mind. He could clear his head and focus on his body.

Pushing. Pulling. Lifting. Three sets of fifteen on each side. He worked until his muscles burned with exertion and every invasive thought drained from his mind.

Drenched with sweat, the tips of his hair hung wet, dripping on his forehead. *Now, that's more like it.* His muscles ached as he stretched, a welcome relief from the pain in his mind. He peeled off his clothes and dropped them into the appropriate hampers before stepping into the shower for the third time today. But the peace of mind he achieved in the gym didn't last. Alone, with nothing but the sound of the hot water pelting his skin to distract him, his thoughts drifted back to the crazy events from earlier.

He was out of his mind. That was all it could be, and the sad thing was, it didn't surprise him. It was just a matter of time before he lost control of it all. The visions, the emotions. They were driving him crazy, and now he was hearing things too. Hell, he was *feeling* things. He was positive someone touched him in the kitchen.

Turning off the water, he heard it again. His dresser drawer opened and closed.

Hell, I'm not even going to look.

Maybe he wasn't crazy. Maybe the house had a resident psycho living in the walls who was messing with him, waiting for the right moment to string him up by his ankles as an offering to some wicked god. Lord knew he'd seen enough horror movies with that plot; a copycat was bound to happen in real life sometime.

Or, hell, if he was going with the horror motif, maybe the previous resident had summoned a demon who was trying to gain enough strength to drag Logan down to hell.

Perhaps a Satanic cult had taken up residence in the basement. He'd only been down there once since he bought the place.

What the hell am I doing? He was already dressed in flannel pajama pants and a long-sleeve thermal, but he didn't remember doing it. He was too engrossed in his intrusive thoughts.

I've got to stop thinking about this shit.

Order. He needed order. Something to organize. It was the only thing that helped him when he spiraled like this. He raced downstairs to the living room and threw open the doors to a massive dark mahogany cabinet. His paperback collection sat inside. Hundreds of books exemplified his eclectic reading tastes. From Stephen King to Nora Roberts, Jane Austen to Truman Capote, Logan had it all. He'd read every one of them, but the words on the pages weren't what he was after now. This was his secret form of therapy.

Last time he was in the cabinet, he'd organized the books by spine color. This time, he was going straight alphabetical. He reached in and swept his arm across the shelf, sending the books toppling onto the thick Persian rug. He spread them out and set about organizing the collection, one title at a time.

Two hours later, he'd meticulously placed each paperback in perfect alphabetical order. He stepped back to look at his work and breathed a sigh of relief. His mind was finally clear. He closed the cabinet and went to his bedroom, where he popped a sleeping pill and collapsed into bed.

CHAPTER FIVE

"I can't believe you talked me into this. It's kind of last minute, you know." Allison sifted through a rack of dresses at an upscale resale shop on Grand River. "How'd you get these tickets, anyway?"

Tina held up a hot pink ensemble but put it away when Allison crinkled her nose. "I got them from Barb. She was going to take her husband, but he came down with the stomach flu, so she gave the tickets to me."

"And *you* couldn't find a date?" Allison draped a royal blue dress over her arm and examined a pale peach one on the rack.

"No, I *could* get a date. I just didn't want one. I felt like spending the evening with my best friend."

Allison arched a brow. "Right. What's the real reason?"

"You've been out of the dating scene for too long." Tina curled her lip at a lime green sequined number. "Taking a date to an event like this would be like taking sand to the beach…or a sandwich to an all-you-can-eat buffet. Why be stuck with one man all night when the place will be swarming with them?"

She laughed. "I should've known. But you better be careful, or people will start thinking *I'm* your date."

"Oohh! Maybe they already do." Tina's eyes danced with excitement. "That makes us all the more intriguing, don't you think?"

"I think you're a piece of work. I'm going to go try these on." She headed to the dressing room, with Tina on her heels.

"If these don't work out, my offer still stands."

"I'm not letting you buy me a dress. I'll make one of them work." She closed the curtain to the tiny dressing room and tried one on.

"Okay, but I feel like I owe you, dragging you into this on the day of."

It took a moment to shimmy into the tight-fitting ensemble, and then Allison stepped out in a royal blue, ankle-length gown. It had a beaded halter top that hugged her curves in all the right places and just enough glitter to make her sparkle without being gaudy.

"Wow," Tina said. "You *did* make one work. I'm jealous."

"You really like it?" She turned in front of the three-way mirror and smiled. It had been ages since she'd worn anything dressier than slacks and a turtleneck. To say Allison didn't get out much was an understatement. Hell, if it weren't for Tina, she wouldn't get out at all.

"You might want to take a stick so you can beat the guys off you. Allison, you look hot."

"This dress is gorgeous. Thank you for inviting me. I know I give you a hard time, but I'm actually excited about tonight."

Tina hugged her. "Good, and I bet Logan Mitchell is going to be excited to see you in that dress."

Her stomach fluttered at the thought. "Oh, shut up. He is *not* interested in me." They'd had two seconds of eye contact. She wasn't even a microscopic blip on his radar.

"We'll see. You know, for a psychic, you can be pretty dense."

"Gee, thanks." She slipped into the dressing room to put her clothes back on. No need to try on the other dress; the blue one was perfect.

"Now, come on. You may have won on the dress, but I *am* taking you to get your hair done. You're in serious need of a trim."

"Tina…"

"Allie, just think of it as a thank you gift for me dragging you around to all these pretentious gatherings of assholes. I'd probably be in some pretty deep shit without you."

Sprawled out on the bed, Logan thought he heard a faint rapping on the door. He teetered on the edge of sleep, slipping in and out of consciousness—barely coming to the surface, only to be pulled back under into darkness.

The knocking continued, followed by a muffled male voice calling his name. "Logan! Logan, you in there?"

His eyes fluttered open and adjusted to his surroundings as the knocking and the voice continued. He sat up in bed and glanced at the clock on his nightstand. Ten-thirty.

Holy hell. He checked his cell phone—four missed calls. He must've been out cold all night. Swinging his legs over the side of the bed, he rubbed the sleep from his eyes.

"Logan!" the voice continued.

"I'm coming. I'm coming." He trudged down the stairs and opened the front door.

"Man, what happened to you? You look like shit." Trent stepped through the doorway. "You were supposed to meet me at the coffee shop at nine. What's going on?"

"Rough night." He shut the door and followed Trent into the living room. "Sorry about that. I overslept."

"I see that."

He looked down and grimaced. He was shirtless, wearing pajama pants. "Shit. Let me get dressed."

"All right." Trent dropped onto the couch, turned on the TV, and flipped through the channels while Logan headed upstairs to change.

As soon as he reached the top of the steps, a faint voice echoed in the hallway. *"Why?"*

The hairs on the back of his neck stood on end, and he shivered. "You say something?" he called down to Trent.

"Nope."

He shook his head and continued to his bedroom. After slipping out of his pajamas, he threw on a pair of jeans and a t-shirt.

"How could you?" The voice, though faint, was distinctly female, and the sound seemed to slither around him, turning his skin to gooseflesh.

What the hell? He rubbed the back of his neck. "What are you watching?" he yelled to Trent.

"Football."

"Is there a commercial on?"

"Nah. Just the game."

It wasn't the TV. *Shit. Here we go again.* He hurried back downstairs before anything else could happen. He'd dealt with enough crazy last night, and he was not slipping into that abyss again. He didn't have time for a breakdown.

Trent sat on the plush tan sofa facing the TV, so Logan settled into the matching chair. He looked at his friend, trying to find the right words so he didn't sound like a dumbass.

"What's up?" he asked instead.

"Nothing, man. You okay?" Though Trent was short on words, Logan could feel the concern radiating from him. He could see it in his eyes.

"Yeah. Yeah, I'm fine." They stared at the TV, though Logan couldn't pay attention to the game. He *wasn't* fine. There was something going on in his house, even if he didn't want to believe it, and he had to get it off his chest.

"You remember yesterday, when I told you about the noises I heard in the shower? And my keys?" He leaned his elbows on his knees and fisted his hands.

Trent raised an eyebrow. "Yeah, I remember."

"It happened again. In the kitchen last night."

"Oh?"

"Shit, Trent. I think I'm going out of my mind. I was sitting at the table, and I could've sworn I heard the doorknob moving. It was loud. I checked it, looked out the window. There was nothing there, man."

Trent looked at him and raised his chin, a silent invitation for Logan to continue.

"Then I heard it at the back door, and when I went to look, my plate flew off the table. It *flew* off the table and crashed to the ground."

"Sounds like you've got a ghost."

Logan shook his head, wanting to dismiss the suggestion as bullshit, but a wriggling sensation in the back of his mind insisted it was true. "You really believe in that crap?"

Trent turned to face him and leaned forward, resting his forearms on his knees to mirror Logan's posture. "I don't know if I believe in it or not, but if it's bothering you, maybe you should get it checked out."

"What? Like call in some ghost busters?" He chuckled.

"Why not? At least you'd know then. Don't let it get to you, man. Seriously."

"Yeah…" Logan looked at the TV for a moment, then turned back to his buddy. "So, you ready for tonight?" Hopefully the smile on his face would signal the end of the uncomfortable conversation.

"Hell, yeah! It's gonna rock." Trent held out his arm, and Logan bumped his fist. "Hey, maybe the mysterious blonde will be there, and you can get you some of that action." He raised his eyebrows as he spoke.

"Something tells me she's not that kind of girl." Logan rubbed at the scruff on his face and thought about her silky blonde hair, how it framed her big chocolate-brown eyes. And her creamy white skin looked so soft to the touch. Did she feel as good as she looked?

"You're not interested in her at all." Sarcasm dripped from Trent's words.

"No. She's... No."

"Uh-huh… Well, I have to get going. I'm picking up my tux from the cleaners."

"I need to get cleaned up myself. I'll see you later."

Logan walked Trent to the door, then turned to head upstairs to shower and shave. He paused at the bottom of the staircase, his thoughts drifting back to the beautiful blonde. She'd been so upset, and she was talking to someone that night, though the staircase had been empty. It was puzzling as Rubik's Cube.

But that voice he'd just heard… Was it possible?

Before he hit the shower, an online search for local ghost busters was in order. Maybe the so-called experts could at least give him some peace of mind. Or prove he was indeed insane. Either way, it wouldn't hurt to try.

He passed up his bedroom and turned into the third doorway on the left. His home office. A thick, hunter-green rug covered most of the floor, and various plaques and thank-you letters from the scores of charities he'd contributed to decorated the walls. His mementos. Reminders he could use his powers for good. It always gave him a chuckle to think of it like that. Like he was a fucking superhero. *Yeah, right.*

He flipped open his laptop and typed *ghost hunters in Detroit* into the search field. The number of hits surprised him. Who knew there'd be that many groups chasing imaginary spirits? He scrolled down, skimming the titles until he reached the Detroit Area Paranormal Society. It sounded legit, so he clicked the link.

We are a paranormal investigation team dedicated to helping those in need. We aim to prove or disprove your situation with accurate scientific equipment. The site looked professional; it was well laid-out, and all the links worked. What could it hurt? Before he could talk himself out of it, he dialed the number.

"Thank you for calling DAPS; this is Richard."

"Hey, Richard. This is Logan Mitchell, and, look, I'm going to be honest with you, man. I don't believe in ghosts, but there's been some strange stuff happening in my new house, and—"

"You want to get it checked out. I understand."

"Yeah. Do you think you can help me out? I live on Grayhaven." He leaned back in the chair and swiveled to face the window.

"What's been going on?"

"I've been hearing things; stuff's been moving on its own. I swear someone touched me last night, but there was no one there. I think I'm going out of my mind."

"That sounds like a haunting, but we'll need to investigate to be sure. We'd love to help you out."

Logan breathed a sigh of relief. Richard sounded like he knew his stuff, and he was professional. A man he could do business with. "When can you come out?"

"Well, let's see… How about next weekend?"

Logan cursed under his breath. "How about tonight?"

"Uh, well… We don't usually do investigations on Sunday nights."

"I'll pay double your normal fee." He was desperate. He couldn't handle another night like yesterday.

"We don't charge a fee. We work for donations."

"How about five thousand dollars? Would that get you out here tonight?"

A thudding sound emanated through the receiver, as if Richard dropped something. "Can I put you on hold for a second?"

"Sure." Logan smiled. Though he couldn't read emotions over the phone, he recognized the excited tone of his voice and the urgency to discuss the offer with his colleagues. Hopefully it was a deal they couldn't refuse, but he was willing to double his offer if he had to.

"Thanks for holding, Mr. Mitchell."

"Call me Logan."

"Logan, I discussed it with my team, and we are available tonight. We'll need everyone off the property to ensure there's no interference with our investigation. Will that be a problem?"

"Not at all. What time should I expect you?" He'd be at the benefit for most of the night, and he could always crash at Trent's place. Spending the night somewhere else sounded pretty good at that point.

"Does six o'clock work for you?"

"That's perfect. I'll see you then. Thanks."

He hung up the phone and let out a long breath. Maybe he could take control of the situation, after all. At least he was doing something about it now. He closed his laptop and strode to his bedroom to shower. He put his clothes in the appropriate hampers—he'd worn them for less than an hour, but the thought of putting dirty clothes on when he was clean made him cringe. Then he tried to relax as the hot water beat down on his skin, loosening the tension in his tight muscles. Maybe having a ghost in his house wouldn't be such a bad thing. At least he'd know he wasn't crazy. And if DAPS could show him some scientific proof, he just might believe it.

"Thank you so much for doing this with me." Tina pulled her blue Audi A6 into the parking lot of Allison's apartment building. "It's going to be so much fun."

"You're welcome. And I'll try not to run out on you quite as early this time."

"I'll hold you to that. And if Logan Mitchell tries to talk to you again, you're *going* to listen."

She rolled her eyes as she unbuckled her seatbelt and opened the car door. "I doubt we'll have to worry about that. I'll see you tonight."

"Bye, Allie."

Allison ran her hands through her freshly cut hair and admired her beautiful new dress. Well, it was new to her, anyway. So what if it was last year's style? It looked good on her, and that was all that mattered. She folded it over her arm and jogged up the stairs to her apartment.

Rounding the corner, she looked up in time to avoid running right into an old friend. "Hey, Richard! What are you doing here?"

"Hi, Allison." Richard was a round man about five-and-a-half feet tall. His curly brown hair matched a full beard and mustache, and his tweed jacket with elbow patches and thick rimmed glasses screamed college professor. Richard worked in the Astronomy Department at the University of Michigan, but his passion was the paranormal. A passion Allison used to share.

"I'm here to see you." He pushed his glasses up his nose and smiled nervously.

"Oh. Well, come on in." Allison opened the door and turned on a lamp. "Have a seat. I'm going to put my things away." She went to her bedroom and laid her new dress out on the bed. After dropping her purse next to it, she joined Richard in the living room.

"What brings you out this way?" She didn't need to read Richard to know he had something on his mind. The nervous way he wrung his hands and glanced around the room, not meeting her gaze, gave him away.

"Well, you know, I was just passing through and thought I'd drop in to say 'hi.' It's been a while."

She smiled and sat on the sofa next to him. "Yes, it has. How have you been? How are things at DAPS?"

"All right. That's a lie, Allison. I wasn't just passing

through. I came here to talk to you. To see if you're ready to come back. We need you."

She took a deep breath and closed her eyes for a long blink. She certainly missed her friends at DAPS, but leaving the organization was her only choice. She couldn't risk another spiritual assault like last time. "You know I feel awful about leaving you guys, but…I can't."

Richard held her gaze. "Look, you're the best. That's all there is to it. We've tried other mediums, but they're all either full of crap, or they don't know what the hell they're doing. No one can clear energy like you."

"Richard, I…"

"We've got a case tonight. The guy's desperate. Says stuff's moving on its own; he's hearing voices; he's been touched. Allison, he's offered us five grand to do an investigation. Five grand! Lindsay and Gage are in. If you come, we'll split the money four ways. What do you say?"

That was a lot of money, and lord knew she needed it. She planned to take some online college courses in January to work on getting her therapist's license, and the money sure would help.

Five thousand dollars. The poor guy *must've* been desperate to offer that much money.

But Allison didn't work with spirits anymore.

"I'm not ready. I don't know if I'll ever be ready to do that again. Not after what happened." She shuddered to think about all those entities forcing themselves into her psyche. It had taken her months to clear out the residual energy the spirits left behind, and the agonizing, debilitating depression that followed almost broke her. "I'm sorry, Richard. I can't."

He took a deep breath and looked at his watch. "All

right, I understand. It was worth a shot. So, how have you been since? I mean, you're okay now? Still doing well?"

"It took me a while to get here, but I'm good now. I'm being careful."

"You mean you're scared." Richard's eyes held hers for a moment, and Allison was tempted to reach out and read his emotions. To see if her friend was still the same warm, caring guy she worked with for five years, or if money had infected his soul like it had so many others. Five thousand dollars was a lot for an investigation, and she could tell Richard was hot for it. But there wasn't enough money in the world to make her willing to go through that nightmare again.

"Yeah. I guess I am," she said.

"You're gifted, Allison. Denying your gifts is… Well, it's a shame. I thought you liked to help people."

"I do. I like to help *living* people, but I also have to take care of myself. I'm no good to anyone in that condition. You know that. Don't you remember what I went through?"

"Of course I remember. I do, but it won't happen again. We were stupid. We pushed it too hard. Going to that old mental hospital on Halloween was a mistake. We were cocky; we thought we had it under control, and it got out of hand. We've learned our lesson."

"You *don't* know that it won't happen again." She smoothed her jeans with her hands.

"Yes, I do, and I think you do too. Just consider it, okay?"

Allison huffed. She didn't like the truth slapping her in the face like that. It *was* fear that kept her from using her gift. Deep inside, she knew it was true. But it was a fear she wasn't ready to face. "Look, Richard. Even if I did decide to come back—and I'm not saying I am—it wouldn't be tonight. I'm going to a benefit for the children's hospital, and I can't back out."

Richard's frustration slipped into a smile. "Do *you* have a date?"

"Yeah." She laughed. "With Tina."

"Oh. Well, I better let you get ready. I have to meet the client at six, anyway. If you change your mind, you've got my number."

"It was good to see you again."

"Promise you'll think about it?"

"I will."

Allison shut and locked the door after Richard left. How could he even consider asking her to go back to DAPS? He knew what she went through. It had been almost a year since it happened, but that wasn't something she could simply forget about.

He was right, though. She was scared, and denying her gift was a waste. She curled up on the couch and laid her head on a pillow as the memories swirled in her head. No, it wasn't something she could just get over. Even after all this time, it was still too much to handle.

CHAPTER SIX

Logan thumbed through the guest list at the hotel. The benefit would take place in the Renaissance Ballroom, but Logan and Trent stood in a smaller meeting room making sure everything was in order for the event. "You sure you're okay with me crashing at your place tonight?"

"Yeah, man," Trent said. "*Mi casa es su casa.* You know that. Got the guest bedroom all ready for you, clean sheets and everything."

"Thanks. I appreciate it."

Concern emanated from his friend. "You think they're going to find anything?"

"I don't know, but I hope so. At least I'd know I'm not crazy if they do."

"Yeah." Trent looked over Logan's shoulder as he focused on the guest list. "Looking for someone special?"

He dropped the paper. "Nah. Just curious whom we should expect to see tonight."

Trent flashed a knowing smile and picked up the list.

"You wouldn't be hoping to see a certain blonde, would you?"

Busted. "No, of course not. You know me better than that."

"Uh-huh. You find out her name?"

"No," Logan grumbled. He didn't know anything about the woman, but he couldn't shake the feeling she was tied to his house in some way…that she was tied to *him.* It was a ridiculous notion, true, but it was undeniable all the same.

"Then maybe you should be looking for her real estate agent friend," Trent said. "You know her name, right?"

"Aw, hell." Logan snatched the paper from his hands and slid his finger down the list of names. "There it is. Tina Sanders and guest. No name for the guest. Shit."

"You can always hope."

"Or hope *not.* I don't know. There's just something about her. I can't explain it, but ever since I saw her the other night, I can't get her out of my head. Something's wrong with me."

Trent laughed. "There's nothing wrong with you, man. You're attracted to an intriguing woman. Go after her."

"I can't."

"Why not?"

"You know why."

"Ah, Logan. Listen. We've been friends for a long time, and… Well, you've got it hard enough as it is. Don't punish yourself for your father's mistakes. Live your life the way you want to live it."

"Thanks. That's good advice."

"But you're not going to take it."

"Probably not." This had nothing to do with his old man.

"All right, I'm done preaching. Let's go raise some money and maybe even have a little fun while we're at it."

Allison took one last look in her full-length mirror. Her new dress flattered her figure, and the royal blue against her pale skin didn't wash out her complexion like so many other colors tended to. With her new haircut and her makeup done just right, she had to admit she looked hot. Maybe Logan Mitchell would notice her tonight. And why not? She was as pretty as the other women in his circle.

Not that it mattered. She wasn't interested in him. So what if she found her thoughts drifting to those piercing blue eyes and muscular physique every now and again? She was a woman; she was allowed to wonder what he looked like underneath his designer clothes.

Okay, maybe she was a *little* bit interested, but it was his fault. If he hadn't been screaming his emotions at her that night, she never would have known that underneath his cocky, incredibly sexy exterior was a lonely, frightened, intriguing man.

Tina was right; she did have a soft spot for Logan Mitchell. But it didn't matter, because she wasn't about to get involved with him. Money was a disease that rotted people from the inside out. Mark had taught her that when he ran off to Vegas with a waitress and blew every penny in their shared bank account, leaving Allison with nothing. She wasn't taking any chances with men, especially wealthy ones like Logan. The wound was too raw.

Tina arrived right on time, wearing a sparkly silver gown that covered one shoulder and left the other bare.

Her matching three-inch heels clicked across the short, tiled entry on her way to give Allison a hug.

"You look beautiful!" She motioned for her to turn, so Allison did a spin to show off her dress. "Wow."

"Thanks. You look pretty hot too."

"I know." Tina grinned. "Are you sure you don't want to ride together?"

"I better take my own car. You know I don't last long at these things. Besides, what if you meet someone? I don't want to cramp your style."

She sighed. "Okay. But you're going to have fun tonight. I can feel it."

"Oh? Are *you* psychic now?" She laughed and followed Tina out the door.

Since Allison lived just outside downtown, the drive to the hotel was short. Tina pulled up to the valet, but Allison stopped a block away to park on the curb, where it was free. She had driven by the location many times, but this was her first venture inside the five-star hotel. It was typical—just like all the other luxury chains she'd stayed in with Mark on the vacations they took together before he left her high and dry.

Already unimpressed, she straightened her spine and put on her best smile as she strode into the ballroom with her friend. Soft jazz music piped in through hidden speakers, and a magnificent buffet sat against the far wall, complete with jumbo shrimp cocktail and a champagne fountain. They stopped by the bar to pick up a glass of wine before they began to mingle.

Allison knew how to play the game. The benefit was a fundraiser, of course, but she knew the real reason they did it this way. Networking and face time. Any one of these millionaires could've just as easily made a private donation to the hospital, but they wouldn't be getting anything in return. And that was what it was all about, wasn't it? You can't get something for nothing, after all. No, these pretentious assholes preferred to make their donations in a public setting, so everyone would know what great people they were.

Right.

And since Logan Mitchell financed the entire event, he fit right in with all the others.

She bit her bottom lip, silently correcting her thoughts. It was wrong to judge others, especially when she didn't know them. Holding a benefit like this *did* encourage a lot of people to open up their checkbooks. People who wouldn't have done so otherwise. Maybe she should give Logan the benefit of the doubt.

Or maybe not.

She spotted him across the room with a woman already glued to his side. She was gorgeous, with long, curly hair and a glittering smile, and she clung to his arm while he spoke to another man. Logan looked irritated, but Allison couldn't be sure if it was the woman who was bothering him or something else.

"I don't think we have to worry about him trying to talk to me tonight. He brought a date." Allison took a giant gulp of her wine. It shouldn't have bothered her. She'd never even spoken to the man, yet envy was rearing its ugly green head anyway. *Get over yourself.*

Tina pursed her lips. "I don't know. He doesn't look too happy to be with her. I bet she just attached herself to him as soon as she saw him."

"Maybe, but he's not trying very hard to get rid of her if he's not interested." A twinge of disappointment squeezed in her chest. She turned to walk away, but Tina stopped her with a hand on her shoulder.

"Wait, Allie. I think you spoke too soon."

She turned around in time to watch Logan peel the woman off his arm. He said something to her, put up his hands like he was telling her to stay, and he briskly strode away.

"She's not happy," Tina said.

Allison didn't notice the rejected female. Her eyes were trained on Logan. He looked amazing in his custom-tailored tuxedo, and he carried himself with such confidence. Almost too much confidence. He had something on his mind, though, she could tell. The woman on his arm was part of what bothered him, but he was still disturbed by something… Something else entirely.

She fought the urge to reach out and read his emotions like she'd accidentally done before. She wanted to know about more than what he looked like under his tux. She wanted to know *him*, and that scared her. One heartache per lifetime was enough, thank you.

"It's not polite to stare." Tina waved a hand in front of Allison's face. "Why don't you go talk to him? You obviously want to."

"I do not." She tore her gaze away from Logan to look at her friend. "He's not the type of guy I want to get involved with."

Tina crossed her arms. "What is he? Too rich? Too handsome? Too successful? Come on, Allie!"

"He's all of the above. Just let it go, okay? I'm not interested in him."

Tina's smile widened as she gazed across the room. "Well, I think he's interested in you."

"Thank you for helping make this fundraiser a success." Logan shook the man's hand and turned to the woman hanging on his arm. Where the hell had she come from?

"Listen, uh…"

"Jill." She flashed a seductive grin.

"Right, Jill. I need you to give me some space."

"Are you sure? I could keep you company tonight." She twirled her hair around her finger.

"I'm sure. I don't want any company tonight. Just… leave me alone." He put up his hands, then turned and walked away. He hated being rude to the woman, but she wouldn't give up. And even if he did want company, he sure as hell wasn't going to take a date back to Trent's place. What would he tell her? They couldn't go to his house because the ghost busters were working there? *Right.*

He spotted Trent and made his way through the crowd.

"Hey, man. I see you already forgot about the blonde." Trent smiled and inclined his head toward the woman Logan had just rejected.

"Shit." He laughed. "Not my type, man."

"Good." Trent smiled, put his arm around Logan's shoulders, and turned him around. "Because there she is."

His breath caught in his throat when he saw the vision of beauty in royal blue. She was stunning, her silky hair falling in loose waves over her soft shoulders. The turtleneck and slacks he saw her in last time hadn't done her justice. His stomach tightened, and his heart pounded in his chest as he watched her talking casually with her friend.

He got a different vibe from her, like she was set to a different frequency than the rest of the crowd. Even at a charity benefit, the sticky twinge of sex and money still pounded through the room. It sickened him, made him tired, so he tried to ignore it. But this woman wasn't interested in those things. He detected a trace of animosity about the whole ordeal radiating out from her porcelain skin. His fingers twitched with the urge to touch her. To feel the softness of her delicate curves. But it was more than that. He wanted to *know* her.

"Go get her, man." Trent slapped him on the back and gave him a push, but he hesitated.

"I don't know. She's…I don't know."

"She's different. Yeah, I got it. Now go talk to her before she gets away again. What? You need me to play wingman?"

Logan took a deep breath as the blonde turned and met his gaze. "Hell," he mumbled. "No, man. I got this."

Allison's lips tugged upward when her gaze met those piercing sapphire eyes. He returned the smile, and they looked at each other for a moment before he made his way toward her.

Tina clutched her arm. "He's coming over here. I told you he'd notice you in that dress."

"Oh, no." She pulled from her grasp. "I have to go."

"Oh, no you don't." Tina grabbed her hand to stop her. "You promised you wouldn't run away from him tonight, and I'm going to hold you to it. Even if I have to hold you *down*. Now, turn around and smile at the man." She held her by the shoulders and spun her around just in time to meet Logan's gaze. His eyes were even more beautiful up close.

"Hi. I'm Logan." He held out his hand, and she unclenched her fist to place her palm in his. His firm yet gentle handshake gave her a jolt, and her tension eased when his own nervousness washed over her. She wasn't trying to read him, but his emotions seemed to seep through his skin.

"I'm Allison." She looked at the floor and then at his eyes.

"Hi."

"Hi."

"Yeah, you both already said that." Tina shook her head. "I think I'll go get a drink." She walked away, leaving Allison alone with Logan.

"Umm…" He ran his hand through his hair before shoving it in his pocket.

She'd assumed he'd be smooth and fake, but he was nowhere near the pretentious asshole she'd expected him to be. He seemed sweet and a little bit tongue-tied, and the soft spot she already had for him softened even more.

"I'm sorry. I'm…nervous." He blew out a breath and looked into her eyes. "You make me nervous."

"Oh." She couldn't imagine herself making any man nervous, much less a man like Logan Mitchell. "I wasn't trying to."

"It's okay."

They stared at each other, and she wracked her brain for something to say. Anything to ease the awkward silence stretching between them. Where were the lines? He was supposed to say something witty. Then she'd laugh, and he'd make a move, and she could tell him to buzz off and be done with him.

But he just looked at her, all his conflicted emotions swirling in a mess around him. His eyes slid from her face, down the length of her, and back up again. "You're very beautiful."

"Thank you." Heat flushed her cheeks. Dozens of men had told her that before, but coming from Logan, it seemed to mean more. She could *feel* he meant it.

"I haven't seen you around much. Where do you work?"

"In an antique store downtown. I'm…" She paused as a man approached Logan.

"Hey, man. I hate to pull you away, but it's time. They're waiting for you."

He took a deep breath and closed his eyes for a long blink. "I'm sorry, Allison. I need to make a quick speech. Will you wait for me?" He leaned in and whispered against her ear, "It won't take long."

His lips tickled her skin, and her breath hitched. Unable to form a coherent sentence, she nodded.

"I'll be right back." He smiled and walked away, and all she could do was stare.

"Well…what happened?" Tina handed her another glass of wine.

Allison's heart raced, and her stomach quivered as she watched Logan take the stage. The chardonnay cooled her fingers, but she couldn't tear her gaze away from the intriguing man long enough to take a sip.

"Allie, talk to me!"

She blinked. "He, umm… Well, nothing happened, really. He had to go."

Tina beamed. "I see that. I also saw him whisper something in your ear. What did he say? Tell me everything."

She couldn't wipe the smile off her face. When was the last time she felt so giddy over a guy? She was about to answer Tina's questions when Logan began his speech.

"Welcome, friends. I hope you're enjoying my little party." He spoke to the crowd, but his eyes focused on her the entire time. "We've got some great entertainment lined up for you, but let's not forget the real reason we're here—to raise money for the children's hospital. I hope you all brought your checkbooks, because I'm going to be asking you to open them up pretty soon. But first, put your hands together for our entertainer of the evening." As the audience cheered, Logan hopped off the stage and disappeared into the crowd.

A flush of dread washed away the elation Allison had felt a moment ago. What was she doing talking to Logan Mitchell? He wasn't just out of her league; they existed in completely different universes. "I have to go." She turned to make her escape, but Tina caught her by the arm.

"He's coming over here."

"I know, that's why I have to go," Allison whispered.

"No, you don't. Quit acting like a freak and talk to the man."

She closed her eyes and took a deep breath. Logan had her heart pounding and her stomach doing flips, and that was never a good thing. But she could do this. Talk to him. Let him down easy and excuse herself to leave.

"Hi." When he smiled, the cutest little dimple formed on his left cheek.

"Hi." Her whole body warmed under his gaze.

"Sorry about that."

"It's okay." She tried to think of something intelligent to say, but staring into Logan's eyes made her mind go blank. A small sigh of relief escaped her lips when a gray-haired man walked up to shake his hand.

"Great party," the man said.

"Thanks for coming," Logan replied. He turned back to her. "Sorry. Listen, I was wonder—"

Another man with blond hair and beady brown eyes interrupted them. "Looks like it's a success, man."

"Yeah. Thanks for your support." Logan focused on her, and yet another person approached to greet him. He gritted his teeth and took her by the hand. "Let's get out of here." His frustration flowed into her as if he was willing her to feel his emotions, and he led her toward the elevator. She couldn't block him out.

Couldn't, or didn't want to? She wasn't sure which. "Where are we going?"

"Somewhere quiet so we can talk."

The elevator doors whooshed open, and he ushered her inside. He pressed the button for the top floor and faced her, taking both her hands in his. Her stomach fluttered as she took a step toward him, drawn to him in a way she didn't understand. She gazed up into his eyes, and the elevator dinged, opening into a short hallway with a door on either end. He led her to a dimly lit banquet room with an amazing view of the city below. Bright lights sparkled in the distant night sky behind the breathtaking cityscape. The exterior walls were glass from floor to ceiling, and the same soft jazz music from the ballroom below danced through the air.

She paused near the doorway. "Should we be here? What if someone finds us?"

He chuckled. "It's okay. I own the building."

"Oh." She went to the window, placing her hand on

the glass as she absorbed the scenery. "The view is incredible."

"Yes, it is." But he wasn't looking at the city below. He was staring at Allison. Her heart jumped when she looked in his eyes, and he reached his hand out to stroke her cheek. She leaned into his touch almost instinctively, and as he brought her mouth up to meet his, she yielded to him. The kiss was soft, tentative, his lips lingering over hers, so close she could feel his breath on her skin.

She could have pulled away. That would've been the smart thing to do. Just turn around and get her butt back on the elevator. But she didn't feel like being smart. In fact, all rational thoughts dissipated from her mind as she slid her hand behind his neck and pulled him to her, crushing her mouth to his.

He responded, desire flooding from his body as he wrapped his arms around her waist and slipped his tongue between her lips. The taste of him sent shivers down her spine, and she trembled as his hands slid up to the bare skin on her back.

This was crazy. She didn't make out with men the first time she met them, but there she was, wrapped in Logan's embrace and wanting nothing more than to feel his naked body against hers. To drown herself in his essence. *Damn.* How long had it been since she'd felt this way? Had she ever?

She ran her hands up his abs and across his chest, sliding his jacket over his shoulders. A deep moan escaped his throat when he shrugged out of the garment and dropped it on the floor. She felt his desire ignite as her own flames burned hotter.

With her back against the window, he leaned his body into hers, urgently exploring her mouth with his tongue.

His arousal grew, pressing into her stomach, waking every feminine desire that had long lay dormant inside her. His phone buzzed in his pocket, but he ignored it, running his hands up and down her arms and across her shoulders. The phone quieted, but the passion between them built as their kiss deepened and their bodies intertwined. The phone buzzed again, and Allison took a deep, shuddering breath.

"Maybe you should answer that," she whispered.

He pressed his forehead to hers, closed his eyes, and blew out a hard breath. Then he pulled the phone out of his pocket and put it to his ear.

"Yeah." Frustration rolled off him as he spoke to the caller. "Shit. Yeah, I'll be right there. Meet me at the elevator." He turned off the phone and dropped it in his pocket, shifting his gaze to her eyes. "I have to go. Will you come back down with me?" He took her hand, picked up his jacket, and led her to the elevator.

"Is something wrong?"

He stroked her hair. "Nothing's wrong. It's just time for me to go work some money out of these stingy high-rollers."

She smiled, her head still spinning with passion. She'd probably regret this tomorrow, but for the time being, she could enjoy feeling wanted.

"I'm sorry," he said. "I didn't mean to come on so strong. I brought you up here so we could talk, and I don't know what happened. I got carried away, and I apologize."

She put her hand on his cheek. "It's okay."

"No. No, it's not okay. You're different, Allison, and I don't want you to think that's all I want from you. I'm going to make it up to you. Have dinner with me tomorrow?"

She inhaled sharply and followed him into the elevator. Getting involved with Logan was the last thing she needed to do. "I don't think so. I—"

"Please?"

The door opened, bringing a gust of cool air from the lobby rushing into the elevator. A man stood outside the door, waiting for them.

"Come on. Where have you... Oh, hello there. I'm Trent." His gaze landed on Allison as she smoothed her disheveled hair.

"Hi."

He looked at Logan and pointed to his mouth. "You got a little lipstick there, my friend."

Allison held in a groan. No doubt she'd be the new topic of their locker room conversation now. What was she thinking sneaking out of the party with him like that? They weren't at the high school prom, for goodness' sake.

Logan wiped his mouth with the back of his hand and slipped his jacket on. Then he handed her a card. "So you can call me in case you get away, though I hope you won't go anywhere. I'm not done talking with you." He gave her one more quick kiss on the lips before Trent pulled him away.

"So, it went well, eh?" Trent asked as they made their way through the crowd toward the stage.

"Too well." What the hell was he thinking? Allison wasn't the type of woman who fell for a seduction like that, and he hadn't intended to seduce her. Shit, he was an idiot. And why the hell did he just ask her out to dinner? If he didn't want to get involved, he was doing a hell of a job. He could always hope she didn't call him, but he couldn't leave things that way. She probably already thought he was a womanizer, and that little escapade just drove the point home. He had to make things right with her.

"Aw, don't get all gloomy on me now," Trent said. "You've got to squeeze some money out of these tightwads first."

"You're right, man. You're right." Still stiff from his encounter with Allison, he cursed under his breath and adjusted his pants before he mounted the stage. He pretended to adjust the microphone as he scanned the room for her. He had to talk to her again. Why her opinion of him mattered so much, he wasn't sure, but it was something he knew he would obsess about until he could make things right.

"Hello again," he said into the microphone, still searching for Allison. "How about that entertainment? Was it awesome? Make sure you stop by the buffet and the bar too."

At last, he found her. His gaze locked with hers, and he smiled. "I hope you've been enjoying yourselves. I know I have, but it's that time of night. As our party comes to a close, I ask each and every one of you to think about how blessed you are to be healthy. To have healthy children. We should all be thankful to be standing here today. We have the power to change the world, my friends, and we can do it one life at a time. By donating to the children's hospital, you'll be saving lives. So, who's with me? Let's be the change. Let's make a difference."

Trent climbed on stage to collect checks, and Logan gave him a nod before descending the steps in pursuit of Allison. But he lost her in the crowd. He scanned the room, searching for her silky blonde hair that felt so good in his fingers. For her royal blue dress that hugged her curves the way his hands ached to. But there was no sign of her. She was gone.

Hell. What if that was the last time he saw her? What if she got in a wreck on the way home? She'd die thinking he was a pig who only wanted her for sex. What if she was mugged? Or murdered?

A sickening feeling formed in the pit of his stomach. She could get rear-ended at a stoplight and be forced into oncoming traffic. Or she might have a blow-out and roll her car over in a ditch. It was stupid. He knew it was irrational, but he couldn't stop the thoughts from consuming him. When he got like this—in this obsessive state—the emotions around him amplified. All the horny, eager, disgusting feelings of the crowd blasted at him from every direction, disorienting him until he felt like crumpling on the floor.

Leave. He needed to leave. He had to get out of that cesspool of emotions and be somewhere he could get control of his thoughts. But he couldn't go home. The ghost busters were there, and that was another problem he couldn't handle thinking about right now. He'd have to find a way to calm his mind at Trent's place.

He bolted for the door. Trent would cover for him; he'd seen Logan through plenty of these episodes. He waited for the valet to bring his car and counted the number of times he could tap his foot before the Mercedes pulled into the drive. He could not lose it in front of these people.

Trent lived twenty minutes outside the city, and the drive back was hell. He counted the stripes in the road to keep his mind off the incessant thoughts that trampled through his head. Now he was the one on the road and in danger of crashing. What if he lost control and drove off a bridge?

Shit! He had to stop thinking like that. He clutched the steering wheel in a death grip as he drove over I-75, afraid he might lose his mind and actually do it.

He pulled into the driveway and marched to Trent's front door, letting himself in with the spare key. He made a sharp right into the guest room, threw his duffle bag on the bed, and undressed. There were no color-coded hampers to put his clothes in, so instead, he folded them into neat piles and placed them on the dresser. He stepped into the adjoining bathroom, turned the hot water on full blast and stood under the shower, letting the stream pelt his body, washing away the sludge of emotions that lingered on his skin. He scrubbed his face, washed his hair, then continued down the rest of his body, relaxing with the routine.

This time's not so bad. Still, it wouldn't hurt to give the tub a good scrubbing. He pulled on some sweat pants and a t-shirt and headed to the utility closet, where Trent kept his cleaning supplies. A little Ajax with bleach on a scouring pad would get rid of the thin film of soap scum that coated the tile. He scrubbed the walls and floor of the shower, counting the movements as he went. Five hundred strokes later, he rinsed and stood back to appreciate the sparkling bathroom.

"Feeling better?" Trent perched on the counter, watching Logan work through his misery.

"Oh, hey. I didn't hear you come in." He walked the scouring pad to the kitchen sink and put the Ajax in the cabinet.

"Of course you didn't." Trent followed him through

the house as he cleaned up his mess. "You were pretty focused on that shower. You get it scrubbed clean?"

"Yeah. I'm good now." He knew it wasn't the shower Trent was talking about as he shuffled to the living room and plopped onto the couch.

"She ran out on you, huh?"

"Yeah." He raked his hand through his hair. "Can't say I blame her, though. I was an animal."

"You okay? I've never seen *this* happen over a woman." Trent gestured to the bathroom.

"I don't know what happened. I took her upstairs to talk, you know? We kept getting interrupted down there, but as soon as I had her alone…" He took a deep breath and shuddered as he recalled his evening with Allison. "It was mutual, though. She was just as into it as I was. I don't know how far it would've gone if you hadn't called."

Trent chuckled. "Sorry about that."

"No. No, it's good. I just… I can't get her out of my head. She's not into all the money and the façade. She's real. It was just me and her, and she didn't have any motives, nothing going on in her head about getting my money or marrying me to get my money. She scares the hell out of me."

"Oh, man. You've got it bad. When are you going to see her again?"

He sighed and rubbed his forehead. "I don't know. I don't even know her last name, and I doubt she'll call me after the way I acted."

"I don't know." Trent shrugged. "Sounds like she acted that way too. Did you get any other info on her?"

"She said she works at an antique store downtown. We didn't do much talking after that."

"Well, there you go. There are what? Three, maybe

four antique stores downtown? It shouldn't take you long to find her. You could do it on your lunch break tomorrow. And if that doesn't work, you can always look up her real estate agent friend."

"Now that's just creepy."

"Or romantic. Some chicks dig that stuff. You never know."

CHAPTER SEVEN

"I can't believe I did that. What was I thinking?" Allison leaned against the counter in Lucia's Antique Shop, sipping her nonfat latte. She confided in Lucia like she were her own mother, and this morning, Tina was there for the gossip too.

"You were thinking about your hot little hands on his sizzling body. What else?" Tina put her arm around her shoulders. "When are you seeing him again?"

"I'm not." Allison straightened her spine. "I'm not going to call him, and I didn't give him my number. He doesn't even know my last name, not that he'd try to find me if he did."

"Boy, you two really didn't talk much last night, did you?"

She shivered at the way his rock-hard muscles had felt beneath his shirt. The warmth of his hands against her skin. His smell. His taste. It was a night she wouldn't soon forget.

"No, we didn't, and anyway, I've told you a hundred

times, I don't want to get involved with him. He's not my type."

"Really, Allie? Because he seems *exactly* your type to me. Did you know his Mercedes is a hybrid? And I looked in his pantry at the party the other night. The guy's got color-coded recycling bins for stuff I never even knew could be recycled."

"Why were you looking in his pantry?"

"I sold him the house. I figure that gives me the right to nose around. You know, see what he's done with the place."

"Uh-huh."

"And he's got a home office with all these plaques and certificates all over the walls. They're from charities he's donated to. Stuff that never made it in the paper. The guy just gives for the sake of giving. Don't tell me he's not your type. He is *so* your type."

"Jeez, Tina. What were you doing in his office?"

A sly smile curved her lips as she glanced at Lucia and then at Allison. "You remember the tight butt in the Armani suit?" She raised her eyebrows a few times for emphasis.

Allison's jaw dropped. "Tina! You *did it* in Logan's office?"

"Oh, no. We just messed around a little. We didn't do it till we got back to his place."

"You're unbelievable."

"That's why you love me. But seriously, I can't find a single thing wrong with the guy. What's the problem?"

She sighed and toyed with a lampshade, unable to look her friend in the eyes. "You know what the problem is."

"Oh, Allie. He's not Mark. He's not going to leave you

penniless. You need to let go of your fears, live your life. I love you, but it's been four years. Stop punishing yourself."

That was exactly what she was doing—punishing herself. But she couldn't let go of the sense of abandonment, and not just from Mark. Both her parents abandoned her too. Her father had a heart attack when she was sixteen, and her mother didn't tell her about her cancer until it was too late. Allison could have helped her, but she didn't let her. Not soon enough, anyway. A sharp twinge of guilt still stabbed at her heart because of that, and she didn't know how to let it go.

Tina pulled her into her arms. "Just think about it, okay? Logan wants you to call him, and it won't hurt you to have a little fun. I have to show a house, but I have my cell if you need me."

"Thanks." She watched her friend leave the shop, and then she turned to Lucia. "You've been awfully quiet today. What do you think?"

Lucia smiled as she walked to Allison and put her arm around her. "I think Tina is right. How do you expect to be a therapist when you can't bury your own demons? Look, Allison, he is a beautiful man. He is what he is, and he is not your ex. Give him a chance."

She took a deep breath and blew it out. "I can't. I just…can't. I don't want to talk about it anymore. Don't you have some pieces for me to clear? I need to work, get my mind off things."

"Okay. I have some items going to auction tomorrow. Let's go have a look at those, yes?" Lucia paused and searched Allison's eyes. "Are you sure you're ready for this?"

"I'm ready. What do you have for me?"

Logan sat behind the desk in his downtown office, perusing the stack of proposals in front of him. In his line of work, he acted as a silent partner in promising start-up businesses. It was time to find a new investment, but this morning, his thoughts drifted far away from his job. He couldn't get Allison out of his head. He could still taste her. The feel of her smooth, soft skin lingered on his fingers, and he wanted more.

Shit. They'd both be better off if he could forget about her. Allison wasn't the type of girl he could sleep with and walk away from. He wanted more from her. He wanted to be more *for her.* But he couldn't. Not unless he wanted her to throw herself out a window. The only way he knew to keep that from happening was to never get involved with a woman. He sighed and pushed the stack of papers across his desk as Trent walked through the door.

"Hey. What's up?" Logan asked.

Trent closed the door and sat in a high-backed leather chair across from his desk. "Not much. What did the ghost busters say when you met them this morning?"

He strolled to the front of his desk and sat on the corner. "They're going to review the evidence they got, but they think they need another night in the place."

"Hmm…" He rubbed his chin skeptically. "They ask for more money?"

"No, they seem legit. Apparently, the girl in the group —Lindsay was her name, I think. She was the only one who made contact with anything, and they said it was hostile. Whatever *it* is."

"So, you've got a ghost."

"Looks like it. They want to spend another night and

see if they can figure out what it wants. Try to get it to leave me alone."

"You crashing at my place again?"

"Yeah, and thanks for keeping a lid on all this. I didn't think I believed in ghosts, but after what I've been through in that place… Well, I do now."

"I hear you, man. It's hard to deny it when it's happening in your own home." Trent scratched the back of his head and glanced at the door. "So, you, uh…talk to Allison yet?"

"No, but the ball's in her court. She's got my number."

"Since when is Logan Mitchell content to sit back and let someone else lead?" Trent pulled a slip of paper out of his pocket and offered it to him. "I did a little research for you this morning. There are only three antique stores in the downtown area."

"Hell, Trent." Logan shook his head and snatched the paper from his hand.

"The closest one's on West Fort, and there's another on Shelby and one on Bagley."

Logan looked at his friend. Should he thank him or curse him?

"You like her?"

"Yeah. But you know I can't—"

"You don't have to marry her, man. Just have some fun. You deserve it." He stood and put his hand on his shoulder. "Go find her."

Logan took a deep breath and nodded. Trent was right. He didn't have to marry her. It didn't have to go any further than he wanted it to. He could take her out to lunch, set things straight so she didn't think he was an asshole, and that would be the end of it.

Before he could change his mind, he strode out the

door to the elevator and glanced at the list of stores. *Might as well start with the closest one.* But he drove past the first shop.

Without thinking about it, he pulled up in front of the shop on Shelby and parked on the curb. Allison was there. He could feel it.

He sat in the car for a few minutes, taking deep breaths and trying to calm himself. He wasn't exactly sure what he was going to say, and his palms were slick with sweat as his heart pounded in his chest. Why the hell was he so nervous? He never had trouble with women, and that was all Allison was, right? Just a woman.

He chuckled at himself. He knew damn good and well Allison was more than just a woman, and if he thought about it anymore, he'd turn his car around and get the hell out of there. He took one more deep breath, killed the engine, and headed into the shop.

The door chimed when he walked in, and a stocky Italian woman greeted him. "Hello, I'm Lucia. How can I help you?" She had a warm smile and a look of satisfied recognition in her eyes.

"Just browsing." He pretended to examine an ornate coat rack. He needed to get himself together and just ask for her. She was there; he could feel her energy in the air.

Lucia's smile widened. "If you don't find what you're looking for out here, there's something beautiful in the back that might catch your eye."

Damn it. He might as well fess up and admit the real reason he was there. "I'm looking for Allison. Is she here?"

"Allison Gray?"

"Uh…"

"Wait here." Lucia turned and hurried through a set of

double doors in the back of the shop. A moment later, Allison appeared through the same pair of doors.

"Logan." Her eyes widened, her soft lips parting in surprise.

Christ. She was just as beautiful as he remembered. Her silky hair was pulled back in a loose ponytail, and a few wispy pieces framed the delicate features of her face. She wore gray slacks and a tight pink sweater that emphasized her feminine curves. It took all of his control to fight the urge to take her in his arms and kiss those inviting crimson lips that he remembered so well.

"Hi, Allison."

"Hi."

He took a few steps toward her, needing to lessen the space between them. "Are you busy?"

Her tongue slipped out to moisten her lips, and his knees went weak. Did she realize how sexy she was?

"Yes, I'm doing some work in the back. Lucia's got some pieces going to auction tomorrow, and I'm helping her get them ready."

"Oh." His heart sank. He shouldn't have expected anything more from her. After the way he'd acted last night, he deserved her rejection.

"Actually, Allison," Lucia said, "I think we're finished for now. Why don't you two go have lunch?" She smiled and winked at Logan.

"Would you, Allison? Have lunch with me?" He took another tentative step toward her.

"Oh…I…I really need to get this done."

"Nonsense." Lucia pushed Allison toward the door. "You have to eat. Go."

"I guess lunch wouldn't hurt." Allison glared at the woman.

"Thanks, Lucia. I won't keep her long."

"Keep her as long as you want," she called as they walked out the door.

They made it onto the sidewalk, and he stopped, turning to her. "Where do you want to go?"

She cut her gaze toward the shop before looking at him. "There's a good little Chinese place a block from here. We could walk."

"Okay. I love Chinese."

Nervous energy clouded around her, but he didn't sense any hostility in her emotions, which was a good thing. At least she didn't hate him. They walked side by side with their hands in their pockets and their eyes trained forward.

Why was he having such a hard time talking to her? He needed to say something. Anything. He sucked in a breath to speak, but she beat him to it.

"Logan, how did you find me?" She glanced at him, then shifted her gaze ahead of her.

"There aren't that many antique stores downtown, so I knew you had to work at one of them." He reached out to read her emotions, hoping she wouldn't find his persistence disturbing.

She furrowed her brow. "And you went to every one of them looking for me?"

"No, I got lucky. This is the first place I looked. Is that weird?"

A tiny grin curved her lips. "I think it's kind of sweet." She raised her gaze to his, and soothing warmth spread through his body like a soft blanket hugging his soul.

Holy hell, he was in trouble.

"Here we are." She gestured toward a restaurant with red paper lanterns hanging in the windows.

He held the door for her and followed her inside to a cozy table in the back corner of the room.

"What's good here?" He flipped through the menu and tried to keep his leg from bouncing incessantly under the table. Never in his life had being near a woman affected him this way.

"I like the chicken and broccoli over white rice. It's delicious."

"That sounds good." He waited for her to tell the server her order before making his own request. "I'd like the chicken and broccoli as well, but with the rice on the side, please. And is there any way you could put the broccoli on the side too?" The server nodded and went back to the kitchen.

"Don't like your food to touch?"

"No." He rubbed the back of his neck. "Listen. About last night…I'm really sorry. I didn't take you up there to take advantage of you." He strummed his fingers on the tablecloth, and she put her hand on top of his. Whether it was to still his nervous movements or because she actually wanted to touch him, he wasn't sure. But that simple gesture unleashed a swarm of butterflies in his stomach.

"You didn't take advantage of me. I'm just as much to blame for that as you are. Don't feel bad."

He took a deep breath and caught her hand before she could pull away. "Thank you."

She smiled and slipped from his grasp.

"How long have you worked with Lucia? She seems nice."

"Two years. What about you? You moved to Detroit recently, didn't you?"

"I've been here about six months."

"And you've already made quite a name for yourself."

The arch of her eyebrow told him she wasn't at all impressed with his social status.

"I guess." He shrugged. "I just want to live my life, help as many people as I can, and be happy. I'm not trying to make a name for myself."

Her smile crinkled the corners of her eyes like only a true smile could do, and something in her demeanor changed. As she held his gaze, he could almost feel the gears turning in her mind.

He shifted in his chair. "What?"

"It's nothing." She bit her bottom lip as if unsure what she was about to say. "You're a lot different than I expected you to be."

"In a good way or a bad way?"

"Good. Definitely good."

The server brought their food, and he waited for her to take the first bite. The way her lips parted and wrapped around the fork as she slowly slid it out of her mouth sent blood rushing to his groin. Christ, she was sexy. Just watching her eat got him worked up.

He forced himself to tear his gaze away and focus on his own food. A piece of broccoli had fallen onto the chicken, and that wouldn't do. Using his fork, he carefully slid it back into place. Since he'd already touched the broccoli, he had to start there. He ate each piece, chewing and swallowing before picking up the next bite. Then he moved on to the chicken.

Allison stirred up her food, mixing the rice, broccoli, and chicken together. He watched her, envious of the casual manner in which she ate. If only life could be that simple.

"You should try mixing the rice in with the chicken," she suggested. "The sauce helps take away the blandness."

He inhaled sharply at the disturbing thought and shook his head. "I'm good."

"Okay."

"So, you've been at Lucia's for two years?"

"Yeah. I'm going back to school in January, though. I want to be a therapist. I want to help people too."

His stomach tightened. They had something in common, and she'd pointed it out. Why did that excite him so much? "I can see you doing that. You're different than most of the people I know."

"How so?"

"You have a kind heart. You don't seem impressed by the façade of the rich and famous."

She laughed. "How could you tell?"

"I don't get that feeling from you. Most people in my circle have this hot, sticky vibe about them with a sharp twinge of greed. I don't know how to describe it. It's weird. God, don't listen to me. I must sound crazy."

He clamped his mouth shut. Shit, he was an idiot. He didn't talk about his ability like this with anyone, but she made him feel so damn comfortable, he couldn't shut up.

"No." She reached across the table and took his hand. "I understand. It must be hard for you, not knowing who your friends are. I bet a lot of people want to use you."

"You have no idea, but the thing is…I do know. And I think that's probably worse."

She smiled and squeezed his hand. The skin-on-skin contact allowed him to filter her emotions from the crowd's, and she *did* understand. He could feel it, and it gave him the insatiable urge to just lay it all out for her. To tell her everything. To let her *know* him.

"And on top of all that, my own father used me the most. I've always been good at reading people. I guess it's their body language or the way they talk, and it comes in handy for making business deals. My dad recruited me to be his partner. I worked with him for a while, but it was awful. He buys companies, like I do, but he breaks them apart and sells the pieces. People lose their jobs. He's caused entire communities to collapse, and he doesn't care. As long as it's making him money, he doesn't give a shit who he hurts."

The sympathy in her eyes encouraged him to keep talking. He shouldn't have been telling her all this. He barely knew her, but he couldn't help himself. The words tumbled out.

"So, I quit. I bought a failing restaurant chain and turned it around. I made it profitable again, and it felt good. They were about to close, and hundreds of people would have been out of work, but I helped them. So I bought another company, and then another. I turned it into my own business, and my father never forgave me. That's why I moved out here. I had to get away."

"I'm sorry, Logan. I had no idea."

"No one does. Well, except for Trent. You met him last night at the benefit…by the elevator?"

"Right." She blushed and glanced down before meeting his eyes. "I remember him. You're close?"

"He's my best friend and a hell of a lawyer too." He laughed. "You know, you're going to make an amazing therapist."

"I hope so." She let go of his hand and fidgeted with her napkin.

Good going, man. Way to scare the woman off. "I don't mean to burden you with my problems. You've probably got a great relationship with your parents, and I'm going on and on about my issues. I'll shut up now."

"It's okay." She shrugged and looked at her hands. "Both of my parents passed away."

"I'm so sorry." *Shit.* Could he screw this up any worse?

She waved off his apology. "It was years ago. My mother died of breast cancer, and my father… It was a long time ago."

"I'm sorry."

"It's okay, Logan. Really. But I think I do need to get back to work. I have an appointment I need to get ready for. Will you walk with me?"

"Of course." He paid the tab, and they headed to Lucia's, thoughts racing through his mind on the short walk back. Allison was a remarkable woman, and he connected with her on so many levels. He wanted to be with her. To get to know her.

Hell, she was someone he could fall in love with, but he couldn't let that happen. He had issues, and he didn't want to pull her into them. He sure as hell didn't want to hurt her, which he was destined to do to *someone*. But like Trent said, he didn't have to marry her. Would it be so bad to date her?

When they reached the front door of the antique shop, she turned to him. "Thank you for lunch."

"You're welcome." He tucked a loose strand of hair behind her ear and held her cheek in his hand. She took a deep breath and closed her eyes, anticipation and longing radiating from her skin. That was all the invitation he needed.

He leaned in, placing a gentle kiss on her lips. When she didn't pull away, he kissed her again, brushing his tongue to hers. She let out a soft moan and wrapped her arms around his neck, pressing her body against him.

God, she felt good in his arms. He could hold on to this woman, and that scared him to death.

She took a deep, shuddering breath and touched her forehead to his. Then she put her hands on his cheeks and stepped back. "Logan, I can't…We can't do this."

"Why not?" But he knew the answer, even if his reason was different than hers. They couldn't be together, and seeing her again would only make their inevitable end even harder.

"I like you, Logan. I really do, but I don't want to get involved with anyone. I can't."

"I understand."

She smiled briefly and swallowed hard. "I have to go." She kissed him on the cheek and turned around. With her hand on the door, she paused. He could feel her hesitation, and a glimmer of hope shot through him. Hope that she would turn around and change her mind, taking him in her arms and telling him she was his forever.

She let out her breath and stepped through the door.

CHAPTER EIGHT

Allison blinked back tears and hurried through the showroom to her office. She had a client coming in an hour, and she needed to get herself together. To get Logan out of her mind. What was her problem? Did she really just tell that incredible man she didn't want to see him again? What the hell? She knew exactly what Tina would say. She'd tell her she was batshit crazy, and she'd be right.

She lay face-down on her treatment table and put a pillow over her head. Why couldn't she let it go? Just because Mark couldn't handle the pressure of a relationship didn't mean Logan would treat her like crap. He was nothing like her ex, and she knew that. But fear was a powerful emotion. One that Allison couldn't overcome.

"Allison?" Lucia peeked her head in the doorway. "Is everything okay, sweetheart?"

She sat up and wiped the tears off her face. "I'm fine. You can come in. I'm just being a cry baby."

Lucia settled into the chair and looked at her with motherly concern in her eyes. "Didn't you like him?"

"No. I mean yes, I liked him too much. He was practically perfect. So real and sweet. God! I don't know what's wrong with me."

Lucia patted her on the knee and was about to speak when someone knocked on the office door. Her client wasn't due for another half hour.

"Come in," Allison called.

The door creaked open, and Gage's beaming smile lit up the room. "Hello, ladies."

"Gage! Hi!" Allison jumped off the table and threw her arms around his waist. His familiar, woodsy scent grounded her, helping her rein in her emotions like it always did on ghost hunts with DAPS. Gage's official assignment on the team may have been IT, but the most important thing he did was keep Allison grounded when she communicated with spirits. He was her rock, and his timing couldn't have been more perfect today.

She pulled away and smoothed his shirt. "I haven't seen you in so long. How are you?"

"I'm good. How are you?" He wiped a tear off her cheek as Lucia slipped out the door.

"Fine. Just a little emotional."

"I see that. What happened?"

She sighed. "I had a date with an amazing man, and I told him I didn't want to see him again."

He sat on the table and patted the spot beside him for Allison to sit. "Still having those abandonment issues, eh?"

"I guess I am."

"Well, I'm glad to know I'm not the only one you're turning down. But when you're ready, you know there's an amazing guy for you right here." He winked and bumped his shoulder to hers.

"Oh, stop it." She smiled. Gage was one of her best

friends, and even if she were interested in him, she'd never risk ruining their friendship. She'd explained that to him so many times, she'd lost count. Still, he'd asked her out so many times, it was hard to tell if he was serious or not anymore. "Did Richard send you here to do his dirty work?"

He lowered his gaze. "How'd you guess?"

"I'm a psychic, remember?" She tapped her temple with her finger.

"Right." He chuckled. "He asked me to try and convince you to come back. He told you about the case we worked on last night?"

"He did, but it sounded basic. Nothing you guys can't handle without me."

"Oh, we can handle anything." A cocky grin slid across his face, and she laughed. Gage never lacked self-confidence. "But it would be a lot easier if you were there. This one's hostile. We think it's a female entity, but we don't know what she wants. She seemed pretty pissed about Lindsay being there last night."

"What happened?"

"We did our usual thing. You know, going around asking questions, trying to see if we could pick up anything on the recorder. We were heading up the stairs, and when Lindsay got to the top, something pushed her. If I hadn't been right behind her, she would have fallen down the steps."

"Is she okay?"

"Yeah, but that wasn't the end of it. In the kitchen, where the guy said he saw objects moving on their own, we put a plate on the table to see if we could get the spirit to knock it off, recreate the event. She didn't just knock it off; she threw it right at Lindsay's head. And in the living room, the damn thing scratched her arm. She's still got the marks."

"Wow. That's insane. It only messed with Lindsay? Not you or Richard?"

Gage shook his head. "Just Lindsay. What do you think about it?"

"Could be a jealous lover. I wouldn't know without actually being in the house, though." She rubbed her arms as if she had a chill. She knew where this conversation was heading.

"We're going back tonight. Will you come?"

"I can't. I'm not ready."

"I totally understand. I told Richard to give you some more time, but he thought I could change your mind. He thought you might be able to make contact, figure out what's wrong with the spirit, and help it on its way. The owner's freaked out, and I can't say I blame him after last night."

She took a deep breath and closed her eyes. Her instinct to help both the owner and the entity was strong, but her fear was stronger. "Go back tonight, and see what you can do. If it's bad, call me. I might be able to help out if you really need me. I trust you to know the difference."

He held her gaze for a moment. "I'll let you know what we find out, either way." He gave her a quick hug. "You take care of yourself, okay?"

"I will. It was good to see you again."

"Yeah. It was." He walked out the door, and her mind reeled.

It was easy to tell strangers she didn't work with spirits anymore, but when her friends needed her help, she couldn't ignore it. Maybe it was time for her to face her fears. Whoever heard of a professional psychic who was afraid of ghosts, anyway? She laughed at herself to think of it that way. She was afraid of ghosts. How absurd.

She could start small, like Tina suggested. She sure as hell didn't want to face the hostile spirit Gage talked about without some experience. It had been almost a year since she communicated with a ghost. Where could she start?

Of course! Stacey. Her client asked her to contact her grandmother, and she did feel the spirit's presence before she shut it out. That would be perfect.

If she could make this work, if she could get over her fear and get back into ghost hunting, it would be a great distraction. She could forget all about Logan and his mesmerizing eyes. She missed her friends, and spending more time with Gage and the rest of DAPS was just what she needed. She dialed Stacey's number.

"Hello?" Stacey's voice was strained and thick with tears.

Her stomach dropped at the sound. She remembered all too well the hopelessness and desperation depression triggered. "This is Allison. Are you okay?"

"No. Not really."

"Oh, Stacey. I'm so sorry. Why don't you come in and see me? Maybe I can help you…and I thought about your request. You wanted me to contact your grandmother? I think I'd like to do that for you."

Shuffling sounded on the other end of the line before Stacey responded. "Really? You'd do that for me?"

"Yes. I'd like to give it a try. What do you say? Can you be here in an hour?"

The hope in Stacey's voice drained away. "I don't get paid till next week. I can't."

"Tell you what. This one's on me. I haven't communicated with spirits in almost a year, so you'll be my guinea pig."

"Oh, Allison, thank you! Thank you so much! I'll be there in an hour." Hope again washed through Stacey's voice, giving her desperate tone a slight lift.

"Great. I'll see you soon."

Allison hung up the phone and checked her reflection in the mirror, wiping off the makeup that smeared her cheeks. She felt better. No, she felt great. She was going to help her client and face down her fear of ghosts.

Logan pulled into his garage and leaned his head on the steering wheel. What the hell was his problem? Allison was everything he was looking for in a woman. Only, he wasn't looking. She just showed up at his house in this perfect little curvy package that he couldn't wait to unwrap. He wanted to know her inside and out. Every inch of her body. Every thought in her head. Every emotion in her heart.

And he'd let her walk away.

She said she didn't want to get involved, but he knew better. He felt the indecision mixing through the air as she hesitated by the door. She was scared. What on earth did a woman like that have to be scared of?

He killed the engine and went in through the back door. There was no sense in returning to the office; he couldn't keep his mind on work. He'd spend a little time in the weight room before heading to Trent's place for the night. The ghost busters would be there at five, and he'd have to clear out by then.

He stopped in the kitchen and poured a glass of water

from the filtered faucet in the sink. The taste of Allison lingered on his tongue, and though he relished the sweet sensation, he had to wash it away. He needed to forget about her before his heart got caught in a tangled web of emotion he didn't know how to untangle.

He stood there, lost in thought, and stared out the window overlooking the river. They weren't obsessive thoughts. Not yet. But he knew how easily he could slip into that abyss of fixation. Better to stop it before it started.

He took one more swig of water and nearly choked when he felt a pair of arms slide around his waist. He froze, dropping his glass in the sink as a body embraced him from behind like a lover.

Holy shit.

He took a deep, steadying breath and spun around. There was nothing there.

"What do you want?" he yelled into the empty house. "Why won't you leave me alone?"

He rinsed his glass and put it in the dishwasher before jetting up the stairs. As soon as he reached the top, he heard the same voice from a few days before.

"Why?"

"Leave me the fuck alone!"

Forget the weights. He wanted to get the hell out of that house. He changed into his running clothes as fast as he could, threw his dirty clothes in the appropriate hampers, and darted out the front door.

The jogging path along the river gave him the sense of being away from it all, even though he was only minutes from his office downtown. Trees lined the gravel path, and his feet pounded it in a crunching, soothing rhythm. If he was close to spiraling into one of his episodes, he'd count the steps as he ran. But he was okay. His mind was clear enough to think rationally, and he knew he had to get rid of that spirit. Surely the ghost busters would take care of it tonight.

His muscles burned to the point of exhaustion, and he headed home to brave the specter. Opening the front door, he slipped inside.

"Hello? If you're still here, I want you to leave me alone. I'm going to shower, and then I'm leaving. Just please…leave me alone." He felt like an idiot talking to his empty house, but what else could he do? He had enough stress in his life without adding a deranged ghost into the mix.

He made it upstairs with no sign from the spirit, so he relaxed in the shower, letting his cleansing ritual soothe his mind and his body. When he finished, he got dressed and packed his bag.

The bell rang at exactly five o'clock, and he opened the door to find Gage and Richard with their arms full of gear. Cases with cameras, audio recorders and other odd devices weighed them down, and he stepped aside for them to enter.

"Lindsay didn't make it tonight?" he asked as the men unloaded their gear.

"She's here," Richard said. "She's going to wait in the van for a while, so Gage and I can try to make contact on our own. Your ghost wasn't thrilled about her being here, and we need to figure out why."

"Okay. You're the professionals."

"Have you had any more trouble today?" Gage pulled a pack of Twizzlers out of his pocket.

"Yeah." He slung his bag over his shoulder. "This is

going to sound crazy, but I think it hugged me in the kitchen."

"That's not crazy," Gage said. "Any info you can give us helps. What did it feel like?"

"You know when a woman hugs you from behind? When she slides her arms around your waist and presses her body against your back?"

Gage nodded.

"That's what it felt like."

Gage looked at Richard. "We'll set up some extra cameras in the kitchen. Seems to be a lot of activity in there." He turned to Logan. "You said you hear the voices at the top of the stairs?"

"Yeah."

"We'll do some EVP work up there. See what we can catch."

"What's an EVP?"

"Electronic Voice Phenomenon," Gage explained. "We use digital audio recorders to catch the voices of spirits we can't hear with our ears. We ask the ghost questions, and sometimes, when we play back the audio, we hear answers."

Logan chuckled. "That's just weird, man."

"Yeah, it is."

"We need to get set up before dark, so, uh…" Richard said.

"I'm on my way out. The housekeeper gets here at six a.m. Will you be done by then?"

"That's perfect," Gage said. "We'll just be packing up."

"All right. Thanks, guys." Logan shook both their hands and left them alone to bust his ghost.

On the way to his car, his phone buzzed in his pocket, and excitement fluttered in his stomach at the thought that it might be Allison. Maybe she was calling to say she changed her mind. He pulled out the phone and checked the caller ID. His excitement faded when he saw his sister's number on the screen.

"Hey, Lisa."

"Hi, Baby Brother. How are you?"

"I'm good. What's going on?"

"I'm going to be in Detroit tomorrow working with a witness, and I thought you might want to have dinner with your favorite sister."

He laughed. "You're my only sister."

"That makes me your favorite."

"Doesn't that also make you my least favorite?"

"All right. I see how you're going to be. So, are we going to have dinner or what?"

CHAPTER NINE

Allison finished her healing session with her client and stared at the clock as she waited for Stacey. Her leg bounced up and down, her heart racing as the minutes ticked by. Was she crazy? She swore she'd never work with spirits again, yet here she was preparing to communicate with one. Maybe she should call Tina and let her know what she was doing. Just in case.

No, Tina would want her to hold off until she was there, and Allison didn't want to keep her client waiting. She rearranged the pillows on her treatment table to keep her hands busy and glanced at the clock just as Stacey knocked on the door.

"Come in."

Stacey's eyes had swollen into thin slits, and tears stained her cheeks. Her mousy brown hair was a tangled mess, and she kept her eyes focused on the floor as she entered the office.

"Hi, Allison." She tucked her hair behind her ears. "Thank you for doing this. It means so much. My grandma…she was everything to me."

Allison smiled and settled into her chair while Stacey sat on the treatment table. "You're welcome, but like I said, I haven't done this in almost a year. I won't be keeping the channel open for long. I'll do the best I can."

She closed her eyes and took a deep breath. The buzzing energy of Stacey's grandmother indicated her presence, so she slowly and carefully let down the wall she'd spent nearly a year constructing.

"She's here." Allison opened her eyes.

Fresh tears streamed down Stacey's cheeks as she brought her hand to her mouth. "Will you tell her I love her?"

"You can tell her. She can hear you."

"Oh, Nana! I love you. I miss you so much. Why did you have to go?"

Allison didn't so much *hear* Nana speaking. She felt her. Her empathic ability allowed her to feel the spirit's emotion and to receive Nana's thoughts. "She says she misses you too, and it was her time to go. She wants you to know she wasn't in any pain. Her passing was peaceful."

"Oh, thank goodness."

"She knows you worried about that, and she worries about you. She knows…" A sickening feeling formed in her stomach as she received the message from Nana. Death of loved ones struck a personal chord with Allison, and she fought to protect herself from falling into that cycle of emotion. She took a deep breath and exhaled slowly. She would *not* lose control.

"She knows what you were about to do when I called you, Stacey… You're welcome, Nana. She's thanking me for calling when I did."

Stacey's gaze dropped to the floor, and another tear slid down her cheek. "I'm so sorry, Nana. I just don't know what to do. I want it to stop. I want the pain to stop."

"She says you're a special girl, and she loves you very much. She wants you to promise that next time you get that low, you'll get help. Go to the hospital."

"I promise, Nana. I promise." Stacey folded over, sobbing into her hands. The emotion was too much for Allison to bear. Too close to home. She couldn't shut out Stacey and stay open for Nana when they were both feeling so strongly. Tears welled in Allison's eyes as she felt herself slipping into Stacey's depressive state. Pain ripped at her heart. Destructive. She had to close it out before it consumed her.

"Stacey, I'm going to have to shut it down now. Is there anything else you want to say to Nana?"

Stacey sat up straight and wiped the tears from her eyes. "Just that I love her, and I promise I'll try to get better. I'm going to see a therapist tomorrow."

"That's good, but she wants you to spend the night with your sister, Jenny. She wants me to call her. Can I do that for you?"

"Yes. Yes, of course."

"Okay. She says she loves you, and that she's going to stay around for a while to watch over you. You can talk to her any time you want, okay?"

"Thank you."

Allison took a deep breath and slid her wall back in place. Relief washed over her as the emotions from the two women drained from her body. She was herself again, and surprisingly, she was okay. She smiled and looked at Stacey. "Are you all right?"

"You saved my life."

She sat on the table and put her arm around her

client. "Remember there are people who love you, and even when you feel like their lives would be better with you gone...they wouldn't. You'd hurt them more by taking your own life than by anything else you could do."

Stacey took a deep, shaky breath and nodded. "I'll try to remember that."

"Now, what's Jenny's number? I'll call her to come and get you."

Allison called Stacey's sister and waited for Jenny to pick her up. A conflicting mix of emotions swirled in the air as Jenny embraced Stacey—relief, worry, love, disappointment. Stacey was in good hands now.

"Thank you so much." Jenny hugged Allison. "How can I ever repay you?"

"Just take care of her. Make sure she gets some professional help."

Allison watched the two sisters leave the shop, and she smiled. *It's funny how things work out that way.* It wasn't a coincidence she decided to give spirit work another try at the precise time Stacey needed her. The universe worked in mysterious ways, and Allison wasn't one to question it.

"How did it go?" Lucia moved from behind the counter to stand in front of her. "You're okay?"

"I'm great, actually. I mean, I started to get a little overwhelmed toward the end, so I had to shut it down, but I did it. I shut the spirit out, and she was gone. I did it, Lucia." Allison bounced on her toes as excitement flooded her body.

"I knew you could. And you feel better now, yes? You conquered your fear."

"I guess I did." She laughed. "It was so natural, like nothing had changed. The past eleven months of hiding from my ability just slipped away."

"I'm proud of you, dear, but you should take it slow. Why don't you go home early today and relax?"

"Oh, I can't. I didn't finish clearing your auction items." She looked longingly at the door. An afternoon off sounded so appealing, it didn't take much pushing from Lucia for her to accept it.

"It can wait," Lucia said. "The truck isn't coming for them until noon tomorrow."

"I'll get here early in the morning to finish up."

"That will be fine. Now, go take care of yourself."

"Thanks, Lucia"

She left through the back door, climbed into her Toyota, and took the short drive to her apartment. She felt good. No, not good…exhilarated. Overcoming her fear of spirits had been so easy. She chuckled at herself. Of course it was easy. All she had to do was focus her intent on what she wanted. She told her clients that all the time, but sometimes it was hard to take her own advice.

The sun shone high in the cloudless sky, and the crisp fall air nipped at her arms as she sprinted up to the third floor. It was a perfect afternoon for a run. She changed into her jogging clothes—lavender pants with a matching jacket and sports bra—and sat on the edge of the bed to lace up her shoes.

She glanced at her nightstand. Logan's business card sat by her phone. *Jesus.* She'd been so distracted by Stacey and her grandmother, she hadn't thought about him since their lunch date. Why on earth did she have to leave that card right by her phone? Was it the universe working its mystery again?

Her fingers twitched with the urge to dial his number, but she couldn't do it. She needed to stay away from him. She'd conquered one fear today; she didn't need to push it.

Maybe one day she'd be open to letting a man into her life, even one who reminded her of Mark, but this wasn't that day.

She headed outside with her phone strapped to her arm and The Eagles blasting in her ears. Sunlight streaked the sky in shades of red and orange as she jogged up Rivard Street. Two blocks ahead, just across East Jefferson Avenue, her favorite trail awaited her.

She needed some more upbeat music first, though, so she focused her attention on the screen on her arm. Flipping through the albums, she searched for some tunes to match her mood. Never breaking her stride, she pounded ahead and crashed face first into the hood of a stopped car.

Logan took the side streets on his way to Trent's house. The freeway would've cut fifteen minutes off his drive time, but he wasn't in a rush. Trent wouldn't be home from the office yet, and a long drive might help clear his mind.

He could always sell the house, but that would be giving up. And he was anything but a quitter. No, he'd have to tough it out. Figure out a way to get rid of the ghost.

Then there was Allison. Christ, he wanted that woman, and she wanted him too. He could feel it. But she was better off without him; that was for sure. He had to stay away from her, for her own good.

He turned onto East Jefferson Avenue and stopped at a light. A jogger approached on the sidewalk, her gaze trained on the phone attached to her arm. Without even hesitating, she ran smack into his car and bounced off the hood, landing on the pavement.

Holy shit!

He threw it into park and jumped out of the car to help the woman. She was just getting to her feet when he rounded the front of the Mercedes.

"Allison?" His eyes widened. "Are you all right?" Fear shot through his system that she might be badly injured, but his tension eased as she cursed under her breath and dusted off her pants. Her hands were scraped, but she was on her feet and coherent.

"Logan?" The surprise on her face dropped into an embarrassed grin. "Yeah, I'm okay. You…hit me with your car?"

He chuckled. "You ran into *me*, actually. I was stopped at the light. What were you doing?"

She picked a piece of gravel out of her palm and winced.

"Jesus, you're bleeding. Here, get in, and I'll drive you home." He led her to the passenger door and opened it for her.

"I don't live far. I could walk." She protested, but she got in the car anyway.

He smiled and shook his head. So much for staying away from Allison. "Where do you live?"

"Two blocks ahead. The apartments on the right." She pointed to the complex, and he drove into the parking lot.

"Wow, you didn't get far, did you?" He put the car in park and killed the engine. They looked at each other, and an awkward silence stretched between them.

"Well, thank you for the ride. I better get cleaned up." She hesitated with her hand on the door handle. He could feel the indecision rolling off her again, and he wasn't about to let her get away this time.

"Can I walk you up?" Without waiting for an answer, he got out of the car and opened her door. "Your hands are scraped up pretty bad."

"Yeah. Concrete's a bitch."

He laughed and followed her up the stairs. What the hell was he doing? Hadn't he just decided to leave her alone? He wasn't good for her. He knew he shouldn't get involved with her. Not with the visions that haunted his dreams. But right then, the only thing he could focus on was the way those lavender pants hugged her curves as she climbed the steps. Maybe he could spend a *little* time with her.

"Well, this is it." She stood by her door and played with her keys, that same indecision swirling around her. She wanted him as much as he wanted her, but she hesitated. Clearing her throat, she glanced at the ground before lifting her gaze to his eyes. "Do you want to come in?"

His heart pounded. He wanted to. God, did he ever. But he shouldn't. "Yeah. If you want me to."

"I do." She slid her key into the lock and pushed the door open.

He followed her into the small living room and admired her as she turned on the lamps, filling the simple space with warm light. A small television, a bookcase by the window, mismatched coffee and end tables. Her modest possessions were few, but they definitely had character. She smiled at him as she turned on the last lamp, and his chest ached at her beauty.

Even in leggings and a ponytail, she had his heart racing. She walked past him, lightly brushing his arm with hers as she made her way to the kitchen. Shivers ran down his spine, and he couldn't help but follow her. He watched silently as she scrubbed the scraped skin of her hands. The bleeding had stopped, and she dabbed at the raw flesh with a dish towel before turning to him.

"What were you doing in this area?"

"I was headed to Trent's place. Just thought I'd take the scenic route."

She put the towel on the counter and glided toward him. "Oh, do you need to go?"

"No." Her body was inches from his, and he could feel the roller coaster of emotions emanating from her. She was nervous, not quite sure what to make of the situation, but she was excited too. He could almost feel her heart pounding in her chest as her eyes held his gaze. "I guess you didn't see my car."

She flashed a sheepish smile and brushed past him. "I was messing with my phone, not paying attention to where I was going."

"Obviously." He grinned and followed her into the living room.

"I'm embarrassed enough as it is. Don't make it harder on me." She sat on the couch and patted the space next to her, inviting him.

"I'm sorry." He laughed. "It's not every day your car gets hit by a pedestrian."

"There's a first time for everything."

"I guess there is." He sat next to her, so close his thigh brushed hers. "What now?" His gaze traveled from her eyes to her lips and back again as he slowly leaned in, the memory of her taste lingering on his tongue.

She responded, drifting toward him until their lips almost touched. "I don't know," she whispered against his mouth. Then she kissed him. Slowly, tenderly, her lips parted as he tasted her.

He cradled her face in his hands and drank in her sweet essence. Her kiss was better than he remembered, and he couldn't get enough. He moaned softly as his tongue brushed with hers.

She laughed and pulled away. "We're not doing a very good job of not getting involved, are we?"

He took her hand and gently touched her bruised palm. "No, we're not."

Who was he kidding? There was no staying away from this woman. He wanted her more than he'd ever wanted anything in his life, and if it wasn't for that stupid vision, he would have told her right then.

"Do you believe in destiny?" he asked.

She tilted her head. "Of course I do."

"Do you believe you can change your destiny? Take a different path than what you're meant to?"

"True destiny? No, I don't think you can change it. Whatever the universe wants to happen is going to happen, no matter how hard you try to stop it."

He bit his bottom lip and looked at their hands in his lap. That wasn't the answer he wanted to hear.

"But," she continued, "I also think people get confused on what it actually is. We're not meant to know our destiny. If we were, that would make life a little too convenient. Don't you think? You have to live your life and let whatever happens happen. You may get off course from time to time, but if it's meant to be, it will be. Nothing is a coincidence."

"So you running into my car wasn't a coincidence?" He slid his hand up her arm, resting it on her shoulder.

"I don't think so."

"Is that why you invited me in? Because the universe wants us to be together?" The words should have sounded crazy coming from his lips, but for some strange reason, they didn't. They sounded…right.

She put her hand on his cheek and stroked it with her thumb. "I invited you in because I wanted to invite you in. Isn't that reason enough?"

"Works for me." He wrapped his arms around her, taking her mouth in another kiss as she roamed her hands over his back, her painfully intimate touch awakening masculine urges inside him. He unzipped her jacket, sliding it off her shoulders to reveal nothing but a sports bra beneath. Good lord, she was beautiful.

She tugged at his shirt, pulling it over his head, and her soft fingers traced the patterns of muscle on his stomach and chest, raising goose bumps on his skin. Desire rolled off her in waves, tangling with his own emotions until he couldn't tell where hers ended and his began.

"I want you, Allison. I want you so badly, I can hardly breathe." He slipped the band out of her hair and twisted his hands in her silky mane.

"Then take me, Logan. I want you to take me." She rose from the couch and grasped his hand, leading him to the bedroom. She slipped off her bra and slid her arms around his waist, pressing her chest against his. The feel of her bare skin on his tightened his stomach, sending blood rushing to his groin.

She kissed his neck, trailing down to his pecs, where she playfully lapped at his nipples, hardening them with her tongue.

"God, woman. You're driving me crazy."

"The feeling is mutual." Her mouth found his again,

and she popped the button on his jeans. She undid the zipper and slid his pants over his hips, licking her lips as her gaze locked on his dick. Slipping out of her running clothes, she stood before him, beautifully naked.

He took in her feminine form and tried to memorize every delicate dip and curve of her body. As his eyes met hers, she held him with a sincere gaze, the purity of her intentions swirling in the air around her. She wasn't after his money, didn't care about his status or what he could do for her. She wanted *him*. Plain and simple.

"Oh, hell." He took her into his arms and crushed his mouth to hers. The feel of her soft skin pressed against his was enough to make him lose control. They fell to the bed, and he spread her legs with his hips. His desire overwhelmed him, and he wanted nothing more than to please her. To taste every inch of her body and watch her squirm with pleasure.

He trailed the tip of his tongue down her neck and across her chest, taking her breast in his mouth. He teased her nipples, reveling in the soft moans that escaped her throat. He worked his way down, kissing and tasting her, grazing her delicate skin with his teeth as she whimpered with desire.

Settling between her legs, he kissed down one thigh and up the other, relishing the breathy sound of his name on her lips. He tasted her, bathing her sensitive nub with the warmth of his tongue, slipping his fingers inside her and driving her closer and closer to climax. Her scent. Her sounds. Her taste. Everything about this woman made his head spin. Her hips bucked as she cried out in ecstasy, trembling with her release.

"Logan, I need you inside me." She reached for him, pulling his face to hers as she whispered, "Please."

"Do you have protection?"

Chill bumps rose on her skin. "In the nightstand."

He found an unopened box of condoms in the drawer and rolled one down his length. Holding her gaze, he slid inside her, shuddering as her wet warmth enveloped him. For the first time in as long as he could remember, he was there, in the moment, making love to Allison because he wanted her. No other reason. She held his gaze as he moved in and out, letting him know she was there too. Mind, body, and soul.

He couldn't hold back anymore. Letting need consume him, he thrust harder and faster, sending her over the edge again. She was all he wanted. Everything he needed. He climaxed, calling her name as his trembling body found its release.

This is how it's supposed to be. He rolled onto his side, and she curled up in his arms as he stroked her hair and kissed her. He definitely could not stay away from this woman. No fucking way.

Allison wrapped herself in the warmth of Logan's embrace, snuggling into his chest as he stroked her hair. She felt safe in his arms, a feeling she wasn't used to. What had come over her? It was so unlike her to be as aggressive as she was with him. Of course, she hadn't been with a man in so long, it was no wonder she couldn't control herself. That box of condoms had been sitting in her drawer for almost two years. Thank goodness she hadn't thrown it out.

And the way he touched her, like he knew exactly what she wanted, what she was feeling. Everything about him felt so right. She smiled and raised her head to look at him.

"Hi there." He gazed at her with hooded eyes, and an intoxicated smile slid across his face. He stroked her cheek with the back of his hand and placed a tender kiss on her lips.

"Hi." She laid her head on the pillow with his, so close she could feel the warmth of his breath on her face. "That was…"

"Incredible."

"Yeah." She lay on her side facing him, their legs intertwined beneath the sheets. His heavy gaze seemed burdened, like he had something on his mind. Something he wanted to tell her. She was tempted to read him, to see what he was feeling, but she wouldn't do that without permission.

She knew about his reputation with women. Could that be the issue? Maybe he was looking for a way out. Deciding which line to give her so he could slip out the door and never call her again. That might not be such a bad thing.

"If you need to go, I understand. You don't have to make an excuse."

He stared at her in silence for a moment, searching her eyes before taking a deep breath and exhaling slowly, taking her hand in his. "I don't want to go anywhere, Allison. Unless you want me to leave." He kissed her hand, his eyes never leaving hers.

"I want you to stay. I just thought…"

He smiled and propped his head on his hand. "You thought since I had my way with you, I'd be done with you?"

Heat flushed her cheeks at the truth in his accusation. "I didn't mean…"

"It's okay. I don't have the best reputation, do I?"

"No, you don't."

He pushed into a sitting position, leaning his back against the headboard. "I wish I could say it wasn't true, but it is. I've never had a meaningful relationship."

She sensed the fear and loneliness emanating from him, though she wasn't trying to read him. It was the same feeling she got that first night at his house, and he was desperate for her understanding. She sat up and put her hand on his shoulder.

"You can talk to me."

"Christ, Allison. I know I can, and that's what's so scary. I've never wanted to be in a relationship."

"I don't believe you."

"Why not?"

She ran her hand through his hair and gently clasped the back of his neck. "You're lonely and scared. What are you afraid of?"

He chuckled and shook his head. "Well…*you* for one thing. I'm terrified of getting close to you."

"And yet, here you are in my bed."

"I know. I can't stay away from you. I don't *want* to stay away from you."

"But you keep everyone else at arm's length. You don't let anyone get to know you. You're a beautiful person, so why do you hide?"

He laughed cynically and leaned his head against the wall. "If you could feel what I feel. If you could read people like I can, you'd know. Ninety percent of them aren't worth my time."

She smiled. Logan wasn't aware of her gifts. She never

told him she was a psychic. "And what about the ten percent who are?"

"I'm afraid I'll end up just like my dad. He cheated on my mom so many times I've lost count. Treated her like shit too." He took a deep breath and blew it out hard. "I went into business with the man. I don't want to be any more like him than I already am."

She folded her hands in her lap and looked into his eyes. "I'm sorry. I didn't know. But you *won't* be like him. I don't think you have it in you." There was no way this kind, sensitive man could purposely hurt someone.

"I don't either, but I—" He clenched his fists as he stared at the ceiling.

"There's something else, isn't there? Another reason?"

"I don't want to talk about it anymore." He took her hands and looked into her eyes. "I like you, Allison. I like you a lot, and it scares me to death. But right now…at this moment, we're together, and I don't want to think about anything else."

"I'm sorry." She stared at their joined hands. She was pushing him too hard, and if she didn't stop, she'd probably push him right out the door.

He lifted her chin with his hand, forcing her to look at him. "Hey, don't be sorry. It's me, okay? I have issues. I'll figure it out."

"Okay."

"Come here." He pulled her into his arms and kissed her. "You're so beautiful." He slid his hands into her hair and pressed his lips to hers. She opened her mouth to let him in, and desire pooled below her navel. Everything about this man called to her.

His cell phone rang from the floor, and he pulled away, cursing under his breath. "It's probably Trent wondering where I am. Can you hold that thought?" He placed a finger on her lips. "I need to answer it."

"Sure."

He slid out of bed and walked across the room to answer the phone, and man, oh man, was he a sight to see. He was built like a Roman god, each muscle skillfully carved out of perfect stone. He was so confident, so comfortable in his nakedness, he didn't try to hide his body. *What a view.*

He dug the phone out of his pants pocket and checked the caller ID. "It's my sister." He put the phone to his ear, and his face lit up when he heard the voice on the other end. "It's my niece," he whispered.

Resting the phone on his shoulder, he picked up his pants, folding them and placing them on the nightstand. "Hey, pipsqueak. What are you up to?"

She watched in amusement as he folded the rest of his clothes and then moved on to hers.

"Another tooth? That's great, Caitlyn!" His voice raised an octave when he spoke to the little girl; he was obviously enamored of her. "Okay, sweetie. Tell the tooth fairy 'hi' for me."

By the time he ended the phone call, all of their clothes lay in neat piles on the table. She glanced at the stacks and then at him.

He followed her gaze to the nightstand. "Sorry about that. It's a habit."

"How old is your niece?"

"Six. She wanted to tell me she lost another tooth."

"That's sweet. Do you see her often?"

He sighed. "I used to, when I lived in New York. I don't see her nearly enough now." A grin stretched across his face, and he ran his hand through his hair as he stared into her eyes.

She crawled toward him on the bed. What was it about this man that created such an insatiable lust inside her? She licked her lips, and his cock twitched.

"Let me call Trent real quick, so we don't get interrupted again."

She said nothing as she rose to her knees, sliding her hands up his bare chest.

He sucked in a deep breath. "Real quick. I promise." Sitting on the edge of the bed, he dialed Trent's number as she explored his body with her hands. His muscles were firm, his skin soft, and she couldn't get enough of him. She wrapped her arms around his chest and trailed kisses up and down his neck.

"Hey, man. It's Logan... Yeah, sorry… I'm with Allison."

Her hands slid down his stomach, and he let out a whimper as she wrapped her fingers around his length. His hardness grew in her hand as she stroked him.

He stifled a groan. "I'm good, but I don't think I'm going to make it tonight. See you tomorrow."

Logan tossed the phone onto the nightstand, took her in his arms, and made love to her again. As she lay there, nestled in the warmth of his embrace, her chest ached. She could fall in love with this man if she wasn't careful.

CHAPTER TEN

*L*ogan held the faceless woman he loved as the other woman cried out to him. She wore a long, white gown, and blood dripped down her featureless face. He clung to his lover with resolve, feeling nothing for the woman in white as her desperation drove her to the window ledge.

"I'm your wife, Alex. Don't you love me?"

"No. I love Allison." The one in his arms rested her hand on his cheek, and he gazed into her eyes. Allison's eyes. Relief washed through him as he held her to his chest. Then he turned to face the other woman.

"Alex?" Her features slowly began to take shape in his dream, and he gasped as he stared into Allison's eyes again. How could it be, when he was holding her in his arms? He looked back and forth at the two versions of Allison, and the woman in white dove head-first out the window.

"No!" He shot up in bed, clutching the covers and gasping for air. "Allison." He stared around her room, felt the cotton between his fingers. Her bed. Her sheets. But where had she gone? His vision had taken an unexpected twist, and now he was confused as hell and worried about her safety. He stumbled out of bed and padded down the short hallway where a light emanated from the bathroom.

Running water and hot steam mixed with Allison's sweet scent wafted out through the half-open door. She stood in the shower, not crumpled on the pavement below. Could Allison really be the woman from his vision? If so, which role did she play? She couldn't be both.

He stood there for a moment watching her, the half-open door a clear invitation. He could've gone in and joined her in the shower. The thought of his hands on her body, slick with soap, as the hot water rained down on them was more than appealing. The silhouette of her perfect form through the translucent shower curtain had him cursing himself and his damn peculiarities. Showering was a ritual, and he'd never been able to overcome his obsession with the routine.

Shit. He stomped back to the bedroom and cringed at the thought of putting on his dirty clothes from yesterday. His bag was still in the car, with fresh clothes and everything else he needed to get ready for the day. He could go down and grab it. Get ready at Allison's.

But what would she think about that? How would he explain that he was planning to spend the night at Trent's place? Grown men didn't have slumber parties.

He couldn't tell her about the ghost; she'd think he was nuts. No, he'd just have to bite the bullet and put on his dirty clothes. Then he could swing back home and clean up there. He gritted his teeth as he pulled on his jeans, but he completely forgot about the grimy feeling his imagination rendered when Allison walked in the room wearing nothing but a soft blue robe loosely tied at her waist. Her damp hair was combed back away from her face, and her cheeks were still pink from the heat of the shower.

"Hi." Her smile made him weak in the knees.

"Hey."

She slid her hands up his chest and laced them behind his neck, pulling his face to hers. He took her mouth in a soft, tender kiss.

"I tried not to wake you. You were having a fitful sleep. Nightmares?"

"Something like that." His vision had him so confused he didn't know his ass from a hole in the ground. He wanted to tell her, but he'd never told anyone. It was too damn weird.

She sat on the bed, and her robe gaped open ever so slightly at the top, revealing the sensuous curves of her breasts. His hands twitched with the urge to touch them, but he balled them into fists and sat down next to her.

"Do you want to talk about it?" Her smile was soft, her voice reassuring. She made him feel so damn comfortable, he'd tell her his whole life story if she'd listen. But not this. Not now.

"I'm good."

She shrugged. "Okay. I promised Lucia I'd go in early to finish clearing her auction items. You're welcome to use my shower if you want." She hesitated, then stood and went to her closet.

"Do you think people can see the future in their dreams?" As soon as the words came out of his mouth, he wished he hadn't said them. She was going to think he was a nutcase.

She turned to face him. "Sure I do. Premonition is a powerful psychic ability if you can control it."

He laughed. "I'm not psychic."

"I am."

She looked at him with such sincerity, he believed her without question. Why hadn't she told him before? Maybe because he never asked her what she did. All she told him was that she worked at Lucia's, and he was too wrapped up in burdening her with all his issues to even ask her about it.

What an ass.

"I feel like that's something I should have known by now. I spend way too much time talking about myself."

She slipped on a pair of tight jeans and pulled a purple sweater off the hanger. "It's okay. I have that effect on people. It's part of the reason I want to be a therapist."

"And I still think you'll make a damn good one." He pulled his shirt on over his head. "What do you do as a psychic? And why do you work in an antique store?"

"It's a long story."

"I have time."

She put on the sweater and leaned against the doorway. "Lucia took me in after my mom died, helped me get back on my feet. She gave me some space for an office, and in return I clear the negative energy out of the furniture she sells."

"What do you mean?"

"Things can absorb energy, and over time, the buildup can affect even non-sensitive people. You won't realize what it is, of course, but you might always get in a bad mood when you sit in a certain chair, for instance. I clear it out, and it helps her sell the items."

"Interesting. What else do you do? That pays the rent for your office, but what do you do *in* the office?"

She grinned. "I give psychic readings. Look into people's psyches to help them figure out what makes them tick. What their true desires are. Would you like me to read you?"

"I'll pass." His answer came quickly and for good reason. He was fucked up in a hundred-fifty different ways, and if she looked into his soul, she'd probably bolt for the door and never look back.

Her eyes narrowed. "Are you sure? Most people jump on that offer."

"Every romance needs a little mystery, don't you think?"

"I guess you're right." She pushed off the door frame and stepped toward him. "I'm also an energy worker. A healer."

He furrowed his brow as he tried to comprehend what she was saying. "You mean like a witch doctor?"

She laughed. "No, I'm not any kind of doctor. I work to unblock people's energy, get it flowing again to speed up the healing process. I practice a form of energy healing called Reiki. It's very common in Japan."

She never stopped surprising him. He walked to her and swept her up in his arms. "You are truly an astounding woman, Allison."

"I guess. But in answer to your question…I don't have premonitions. Not in dreams like you're talking about."

He slid his hands down her arms and laced his fingers through hers. "That wasn't exactly my question. I think I have them. Some of my dreams come true, and lately I've been having the same one over and over again."

"Really? Will you tell me about it?"

Christ, what was he doing? He didn't tell *anyone* about his visions. Not even Trent or his sister. And now this woman came along, whom he'd only known for a few days, and he was ready to tell her everything. Well, almost everything.

Before he could talk himself out of it, he did it. He told her about the dreams. About the woman in white diving out the window when he told her he loved someone else. He told her everything, except the part about both women in the dream being her. That was something he'd have to mull over for a while before he shared it. *If* he ever shared it at all.

Allison looked at him sincerely. She didn't laugh or order him out the door, like he was afraid of. Instead, she pursed her lips and nodded thoughtfully. "That's interesting. She said she was your wife?"

"Yeah."

"And that's why you never let anyone get close to you. Because you're afraid if you let someone love you, and you get married, she'll end up killing herself." She said it as a matter of fact, though he'd never said it outright. God, this woman knew him already.

He half-smiled and gave her an apologetic shrug. "Crazy, huh?"

"Not really. A premonition like that would be terrifying, and it's a natural reaction to try and keep it from happening. But sometimes visions aren't literal."

"What do you mean?"

"It could be symbolic of something. Overcoming fears, letting go of something you've held on to for way too long. It could mean a lot of things."

"Or it could mean I'm going to cheat on my wife, and she's going to kill herself over it." He sat on the bed and put his head in his hands.

"That's a possibility, but not very likely. You don't strike me as the cheating type." She perched on the edge of the bed and put her arm around him. The warmth of her touch relaxed the tension from his muscles, and for a moment, he started to believe her. But…

"I've been having this dream for years. I can't let go of it that easily."

"Why do you think she called you Alex?"

"I don't know. It's my middle name. My dad tried to get me to go by Alex when we went into business together. He said people would respect me more if I had a more common name."

"But you didn't go for that?"

"No, it's ridiculous. I've been Logan all my life. I'm not going to change my name because he thinks it would be better for business."

She sighed as she rubbed her hand across his back. "So, where does this leave us? If you really believe your vision is literal, what are we going to do?"

He looked into her eyes. "I like you, Allison. A lot. But…"

"But you don't want me jumping out of a window over you."

"Exactly."

"Well, then. Why don't you go home and think about it for a while? Give it a day or two for it all to soak in, and then decide if you want to see me again."

"I do want to see you again. Again and again. I just don't…"

She put her hand on his cheek. "It's okay, Logan. Fear is a powerful emotion. Believe me, I know. I don't think your vision is literal, but it's *your* vision. If you think it is, then you have to deal with it. I can't make up your mind for you."

"Have I told you what an incredible woman you are?"

She grinned. "A few times. Now go home and think about it, and come see me when you decide what you're going to do."

She walked with him through the living room and opened the door. His heart slammed into his throat as he took her face in his hands and pressed his lips to hers. He didn't want to leave. She was the most remarkable woman he'd ever met, and he was about to walk out with no promise of returning. He was insane for leaving her, but the fear was too strong.

She pulled away from his embrace and kissed him on the cheek. "Goodbye, Logan."

Allison closed the door and leaned her back against it. She was falling for Logan. Falling hard, and she just let him walk away. She *told* him to leave. A small part of her secretly hoped he wouldn't come back. Then she could return to life as usual and not have to worry about getting close to a man. But that was a very small part. The rest of her ached to be in his arms again. To feel his tender touch and his not-so-tender kisses.

Tears welled in her eyes, and she ran to the bathroom to blot them away. She'd made a promise to Lucia, and she intended to keep it. She had to get ready for work, but putting makeup on a tear-streaked face wasn't easy.

"Get it together, Allison," she told her reflection. "You're twenty-eight years old; you don't cry over boys."

She dried her tears enough to apply a little makeup and be on her way to the antique store. Even if she never saw Logan again, she'd have the memory of their night together…and what a night it was. Focusing on the good was the way to go with this situation, and that was what she intended to do. She pulled into the back parking lot and took a few deep, cleansing breaths before going inside.

"Allison, you look radiant today." Lucia stood in the storeroom labeling her pieces for the auction. "Your afternoon off was good?"

Her cheeks warmed as she thought about her night with Logan. "Let me put my purse away, and I'll tell you all about it." She dropped her things off in her office, and when she returned to the store room, Lucia looked at her with a knowing smile.

"You saw him last night."

She tucked a piece of hair behind her ear. "How could you tell?"

Lucia laughed. "It does not take a psychic to see you're glowing. What happened?"

"It was a chance meeting, serendipity. I ran into him while I was out jogging, and he came home with me."

Lucia put the last tag on her auction items and dusted off her hands. "You had a good time, yes?"

"It was amazing. *He* is amazing." She rubbed the goose bumps on her arms. Just thinking about him made her heart race and her palms sweat.

Oh, yeah. She had it bad.

"I'm so happy for you, dear. When are you going to see him again?"

"I don't know, Lucia. I just don't know."

CHAPTER ELEVEN

Logan parked in his garage but went around to the front door, avoiding the kitchen entirely. It would take the ghost busters another day or so to go over all their evidence, and he wasn't in the mood to deal with the spirit.

He turned the lock and pushed open the door. "I'm going to shower and change, and then I'll be out of here. Leave me alone."

His heart sprinted as he jogged up the stairs and slammed his bedroom door behind him. Not that a closed door would stop a ghost.

This is ridiculous. He shouldn't have to be afraid in his own home. He peeled off his dirty clothes and put them in the hamper before getting into the shower. His ritual immediately relaxed him, clearing his mind of thoughts about the ghost and allowing him to focus on the more important issue—Allison.

What was he going to do about Allison? Maybe he should tell her everything. She'd been accepting of him so far, so she might not think he was crazy. Hell, she might even be able to help him. But did he want to risk it? What if the vision really was literal? He'd be signing her death warrant if he pursued a relationship with her.

How could it be literal, though? If Allison represented both women in the dream, it couldn't possibly be. But what could it mean? His shoulders tensed in frustration as he shut off the water and wrapped a towel around his waist. He could see where he was headed, and he didn't have time for another episode.

He flipped on the light to his walk-in closet and relaxed a little more with the order of his organization. His clothes were arranged by color, with shirts on the left and pants on the right. He picked up a pair of black slacks and a lavender dress shirt. The same color Allison had worn the night before…

Who was he kidding? He couldn't stay away from that woman.

He made it out of the house without a sign from the ghost and went back to work, where he had some control. Order and control kept him sane. He spent the morning alone in his office researching potential investments, but staying focused was easier said than done. His thoughts kept drifting to Allison's soft skin. The way she felt pressed against his body. A smile tugged at his lips as he thought about the way she teased him when he was on the phone with Trent.

A knock on the door brought him back to the present, but he was still smiling when Trent walked in the room.

His friend paused in the doorway and shook his head. "I've got some bad news for you, man."

"What's up?" Logan walked around the desk and leaned on the edge.

"You've got that dreamy look in your eyes. You're falling for her." He plopped into a chair.

Logan rubbed his forehead. "I know. This is exactly the situation I've been trying to avoid for God knows how long."

Trent chuckled. "It's about time you found a woman worth holding on to."

"You're one to talk."

"Hey, at least I've had girlfriends that stuck around for a while."

"Uh-huh."

Trent leaned his elbows on his knees and squared his gaze on him. "How did it happen, anyway? I thought she said she didn't want to see you anymore."

"She ran into me while she was out jogging. Literally. I was stopped at a light, and she ran right into my car." His smile returned as he thought about the fortunate twist of fate.

"No kidding?"

"I drove her home, and she invited me in, and…" He shrugged and grinned.

"Man, talk about your crazy coincidences." Trent leaned back in his chair. "She was okay, though?"

"Just a few scrapes."

"So…how was she?" He leaned forward again.

Logan's smile returned. He could still feel her in his arms—her warmth, her scent. "She was beyond words."

"Yeah? And you said she's an antiques dealer? That's cool."

"Actually, she just has an office in the antique shop." He scratched the back of his neck and took a deep breath. "She's a psychic."

"A psychic?" Trent arched a brow.

"She does some kind of energy clearing and healing. She's going to school to be a therapist too." He held his breath as he waited for his friend's reaction.

"I don't know much about all that, but if you're cool with it." He shrugged his approval, and Logan let out his breath.

"I am. She's incredible."

"When are you going to see her again?"

Logan shook his head and looked at the floor. That was the million-dollar question, wasn't it? "I don't know."

"You've got some serious issues."

"Yeah." He chuckled.

"Don't wait too long, or you might lose her." Trent stood and walked to the door. "Seriously, don't blow this. It sounds like she's good for you."

"I don't know how good I am for her," he mumbled as his friend left the room.

Alone in his office again, Logan couldn't concentrate on work. His thoughts kept drifting back to Allison. Damn it, he needed to see her.

He flipped open his laptop and did a search for Reiki, the type of healing she told him she practiced. He browsed a few of the sites, soaking in the information. It was fascinating. *She* was fascinating. And she probably knew a lot more about his premonitions than he did.

He glanced at the clock. Was it too soon to tell her he'd made up his mind? She'd told him to take a day or two, and it had only been four hours. But four hours was all he needed.

Allison watched as the movers loaded the last auction item onto the truck. Then, she signed the paperwork and pulled the heavy back door closed.

As she walked into the showroom, the front door chimed and her stomach fluttered at the sound, just as it had done every time the door opened this morning. It was silly to hope Logan would come back so soon, but she couldn't help herself. She padded to the front of the store, and her hope deflated again when she found Tina waiting by the counter.

"Hey, girl. Ready for lunch?" Her friend wore a heather gray skirt that hit her at mid-thigh and a matching jacket. Three-inch pumps completed the outfit that was a staple in Tina's wardrobe.

Thank goodness Allison didn't have to dress up for her occupation; she was much more comfortable in jeans and a sweater. "I'm starving, but I have to wait till Lucia gets back. She had to run some errands. Anything new and exciting in the world of Tina?" Allison curled into a nineteenth-century cigar chair, and Tina sat in the matching one next to her, crossing her legs at the ankles.

Tina sighed. "Not really. I'm showing a house at two today, but other than that, my life is dull."

"Hardly."

"What about you? You look good today, by the way."

Warmth flushed her cheeks. Did she really look that different, just because she slept with a man? "Thanks. I had an interesting night."

"Really?" Tina's face lit up. "What happened? Wait… Don't tell me. Let me guess… Okay, I don't know. Just tell me."

She laughed, and her heart skipped a beat when the door chimed again.

"Good afternoon, girls. Allison, thank you for watching the store for me." Lucia shuffled in carrying a big brown paper bag in her arms.

"Anytime. We're going to the sandwich shop on Washington. Do you want me to bring you back anything?"

"I ate while I was out. Thank you, though." Lucia ducked behind the counter to put her packages away, stacking the reels of register tape in a cabinet.

"Okay. I'll be back in an hour." She followed Tina out the door.

"Well, are you going to tell me or not?" Her friend bounced with excitement on the sidewalk.

Allison bit her lip, a giddy sensation bubbling in her core. "I saw Logan last night."

"What?" Tina squealed and grabbed her by the arms. "What happened? Did you do it? Please tell me you did it. How was he? Tell me!"

"Jesus! Calm down. Let's get our food, and I'll tell you all about it."

They entered the deli and walked up to the counter. Allison ordered a turkey and swiss on rye with baked chips, and Tina got her usual burger and fries.

"It was true serendipity." Allison settled into a chair in the back of the restaurant, and Tina sat across from her. "No, it was fate, so I couldn't fight it. After lunch yesterday, you know I told him I didn't want to see him again. Oh, and I contacted a spirit for a client, but I'll tell you about that later. So Lucia sent me home early, and I went for a run. I didn't get past East Jefferson Avenue when I ran into Logan."

Allison told her the story, pausing for her friend to laugh out loud.

"You must have been mortified. I know I would have been."

"Gee, thanks."

"Obviously you're okay. So, what happened next?"

"Well, he took me home, and then one thing led to another…"

Tina jumped in her seat, clapping her hands. "You did it! I knew it! You finally did it! How was he? Was he as good as I imagined?" She rested her elbows on the table and leaned forward as she spoke.

Allison sank in her chair. "Will you calm down? I don't want the whole world to know."

"Sorry," she whispered. "I'm just so excited for you! How long has it been? Three or four years?"

"A while. God, I don't know what came over me. I was an animal. I couldn't get enough of him."

"Four years of celibacy will turn anyone into a beast. I'm sure he enjoyed it." She wiggled her brows.

"I know I did." Boy, oh boy, did she ever.

"I guess he wasn't the pretentious asshole you thought he would be?"

"Not at all. He was sweet and kind and *real*. He's nothing like the image he portrays." She sighed and traced the patterned tablecloth with her finger.

"Oh my God." Tina gaped.

"What?"

"You're falling for him."

She straightened her spine and crossed her arms. "No, I'm not."

"Yes, you are."

"Okay. Maybe I am. What am I going to do?" She slumped in her seat and put her hand to her temple.

"You're going to keep seeing him."

She opened her mouth to protest, but Tina crossed her arms. "You are. And don't give me any crap about not wanting to get involved."

"Tina."

"No, Allie. No crap."

She sighed. "I don't know if he wants to see me again."

"Why do you say that?"

"It turns out I'm not the only one with commitment issues."

"Uh-huh."

"He's got some stuff going on, so I told him to take a few days to think about it, and to let me know what he decides."

"I see." Tina shoved a fry in her mouth and stared at Allison as she chewed.

"I know that look. What are you thinking?"

"Nothing. I don't know the situation. I don't know what the *stuff* is, but I do know that I wouldn't have let him go that easily."

"I know, but there's nothing I can do about it now. I *already* let him go, and it's probably better this way. I didn't want to get involved either, remember?"

"You *didn't* want to get involved. But now…"

She tucked her hair behind her ear. "I think I'd make an exception for him. If he ever comes back."

Tina beamed a smile and sat up straighter in her chair. "Do you mean that? If he walked through the door right now, you'd go out with him?"

"I would. I really would." It was time to let go of her past and start living her life again.

"Well, good." She bubbled with excitement. "Because he's here."

"What?" Allison's eyes widened.

"He's coming over here."

She turned in her chair to see Logan striding across the restaurant. His eyes met hers, and he grinned his adorable crooked grin. In his hand, he held a single red rose, and her heart sprinted in her chest as he approached their table.

"Hi, Allison."

"Hi." She held his piercing gaze and took the rose he offered. She'd been anticipating—hoping for—this moment all day, but she didn't expect it to actually happen. He came back to her, and the look on his face said he was here to stay.

He ran his hand through his hair. "Hi."

"Hi."

"You two really need to work on your conversation skills," Tina said. "Why don't you have a seat, Logan?"

He glanced at Tina as Allison scooted over to let him sit. "Hi, Tina. Thank you."

He slid into the seat, and his knee brushed against hers. Her stomach tightened at the contact. The warmth of his body next to hers, his musky, masculine scent… Simply being near him made her head spin.

"What are you doing here?" Allison asked.

"I looked for you at Lucia's, and she told me where you were. I hope you don't mind."

"Of course not." Heat rose in her body. "I didn't expect to see you so soon."

He took her hand under the table, lacing their fingers together. "I thought about everything you said. Will you have dinner with me tonight?"

The butterflies in her stomach turned into a lump in her throat. She bit her bottom lip as she stared at him, unable to answer. He came back. She was diving into this head first, and she needed to reply so he knew she was all in, but she couldn't make her mouth form words. *Answer the man, Allison.*

"Of course she will," Tina answered for her.

She nodded, and he grinned. The way the corners of his eyes crinkled when he smiled had her heart doing back flips. All he had to do was look at her, and she was putty in his hands.

"Great," he said. "I'll… Oh shit. Damn it, I forgot I'm meeting my sister for dinner tonight. She's only in town today."

"That's okay." She finally found her voice. "We can do it another time; I know you don't get to see her much."

He pressed his lips together, narrowing his eyes as if considering his options. "Come with me. Come meet my sister."

"Oh, I don't know." The lump tried to return to her throat, so she swallowed it down. Dinner with the family already? She couldn't decide if the idea excited or nauseated her. "I don't want to intrude. She's not expecting me."

"She'll be thrilled to meet you."

The heel of Tina's shoe came down on her foot. "Ow!" She glared at her friend before looking at Logan. It wasn't like he was asking her to meet his parents. She could handle his sister. "Are you sure?"

"I am. Absolutely. I'll pick you up at seven."

"Sounds great."

"Oh, and the restaurant has a dress code. Nothing like the benefit, but dressy."

"Got it." She nodded. "I promise not to embarrass you."

He put his hand on her cheek. "I wasn't worried about

that. I like you in your jeans and sweaters, but the *maître d'* wouldn't let you in."

"I'll be ready."

"Great." He drifted toward her, hesitating slightly, and brushed his lips to hers.

She leaned into him, deepening the kiss before her inhibitions kicked in and she remembered she had an audience. Pulling away, she glanced at Tina, who looked like she was going to explode with excitement. "I'll see you tonight."

"I'm looking forward to it." He kissed her on the cheek and rose to his feet. "Bye, Tina."

Allison couldn't help but admire his tight backside as he left the restaurant. When he walked out the door, she turned to her friend and mouthed the words, "Oh my God."

Did that actually happen? She was going on a date with him?

"Allie! Oh my God! He wants you to meet his family. That's serious."

She shook her head. "It's just his sister. Don't make a big deal out of it, or I'll change my mind."

"Still, that's so exciting. What are you going to wear? It sounds like a perfect event for a little black dress. Do you have one?"

"I think so. I'll have to look."

"I should be done showing the house by three, and then I'm coming over. We'll raid your closet, and if you can't find anything, we'll go shopping."

She chewed her bottom lip and tried to calm her sprinting heart. "Sounds good. I don't have any appointments today, so I could sure use the distraction while I wait for seven o'clock."

Logan called the restaurant to change his reservation from two to three; then he dialed his sister's number.

"Hey, Lisa. Are we still on for tonight? Seven-thirty?"

"Of course we are. You're not trying to back out on me, are you?"

"No." He switched the phone to his other ear. "I'm bringing someone with me."

"Who? Trent? Is he still in love with me?" He could hear the smile on Lisa's face as she joked.

"He was seventeen. Are you ever going to let him forget that?"

"Probably not."

He leaned back in his office chair and swiveled side to side. "I hate to disappoint you and your ego, but Trent's not coming."

Silence hung between them. "Are you bringing a woman?"

"Her name's Allison, and I want you to meet her. Do you mind?"

"Of course I don't mind, Baby Brother. I'd love to meet your girlfriend!" Excitement bubbled in her voice.

"Don't call her that. I haven't known her very long." He leaned his elbow on the desk. "And you better not embarrass me."

Lisa laughed. "Would I do that?"

"Not you, Lisa. Never."

"All right. I'll try to behave myself."

"Thanks. I'll see you tonight."

He put the phone in his pocket and strummed his fingers on the desk. It would be another five hours before he could pick up Allison, so he needed to keep himself busy. Nausea twisted in his stomach, and his leg bounced under his desk. He'd never taken a woman to meet his family before, and his sister's enthusiasm scared him.

Though he always said he didn't want to get involved, he secretly hoped he could have a family like hers one day. Meeting Allison only fanned the flames of that hope.

But he shouldn't get too excited. He still wasn't sure what to do about his damn vision. Hopefully, Allison could help him. Otherwise, he was setting them both up for a tragic ending.

CHAPTER TWELVE

By the time Tina got to the apartment, Allison had every dress she owned laying out in her bedroom. Nervous tension twisted in her stomach as she paced around, looking for the perfect outfit.

"Jesus, Allie. How many little black dresses do you own?" Tina eyed the clothes strewn about the room and laughed.

"A few, but most of them are at least five years old. I don't know if any of them will fit me." She held a dress up in front of the mirror and stretched it around her hips.

"Oh, please. If anything, you're thinner than you were five years ago."

"I'm also pushing thirty. I'm too old for miniskirts."

"You're never too old for miniskirts." Tina picked up a dress and held it out in front of her. "This one is a definite no, unless you want people to think he's paying you to be his date. Look at the neckline; it's cut down to your belly-button. I can't believe you own this."

Allison laughed. "That one's yours. You lent it to me a year ago, but I never wore it."

Tina pursed her lips and studied the dress again. "Oh. I guess I'll be taking this back then. I've got a date with a doctor Friday night."

"Really? Anyone I know?"

"Dr. Ortega."

Allison's eyes widened. "The gynecologist? *Your* gynecologist?"

"That's the one." Tina grinned.

"Oh, yuck. How can you? When he examines your… Eww!"

"Don't knock it till you've tried it. He knows his way around a woman's body."

"Can we not talk about that?" She crinkled her nose. "I think I'm going to have to find a new doctor."

"I'm not." Tina wiggled her eyebrows.

"Gross." Allison gave her body an overexaggerated shudder. "Anyway, what should I wear? What about this one?" She held up a long-sleeved dress.

"Sure." Tina shrugged. "If you're looking for another four years of celibacy. You have to find the right balance. You need to be sexy without being slutty."

"And you think *you* can help?"

"Very funny."

Allison hung the long-sleeved dress in the closet.

"I found it," Tina called from the bedroom. "I found the one." She held up a short black dress with spaghetti straps and a matching beaded shrug. "This is beautiful, and it still has the tags on it."

She took the dress from her friend. "I forgot I had this one. I bought it for a party last year, but I didn't end up going."

"I remember that. You were still recovering from your

Halloween incident. Oh, yeah. You said you talked to a ghost for someone? When?"

"Yesterday." She changed into the dress as she told Tina about Gage and contacting Nana's ghost.

"That's great. I know you always loved working with DAPS, and Gage is hot too. Is he still single?"

"As far as I know. I'll let him know you asked." She laughed as she put on the shrug.

"You look perfect. Sexy and sophisticated with a subtle promise that the dress will end up on the floor before the night is over."

Allison looked in the mirror. The dress was simple, solid black, and it hit her two inches above the knee. Fitted through the waist, it accentuated her curvy figure just right. She slipped on a pair of two-inch heels and did a spin for Tina.

"Logan's going to have a hard-on before he even gets you in the car. *If* you make it that far."

"Tina!"

"You know it's true."

She grinned. "Maybe." *Hopefully.*

Sure, she looked forward to going out to dinner and meeting his sister, but the anticipation of getting Logan back in her bedroom had her tingling all over.

"You're so lucky," Tina said wistfully.

"I know."

"Logan is hot, nice, and he's loaded. What a combination." Tina helped her hang up the rest of the rejected dresses.

"I don't care about his money."

"Not even a little?"

"Not at all." And she meant it. She had seen firsthand what money could do to people. To decent people. Mark had been a good man in the beginning, until his business took off and his entire demeanor changed. No, Allison definitely was not interested in Logan's money.

"That's probably why he likes you so much. I mean, in addition to your good looks and charming personality, of course."

"Of course."

"Hey! Has he mentioned anything about his ghost? Didn't you see one in his house at the party?"

"He hasn't mentioned it. He might not even know it's there, so I'm not going to bring it up. No need to freak him out if it's nothing."

"True. But what if he wants you to go back to his place? What are you going to do?"

"I hadn't thought about that. I guess I'll cross that bridge when I get to it. Now that I know she's a ghost, I think I can block her out." She changed back into her jeans and sweater and hung the dress on her closet door.

"Two more hours," Tina sang.

Allison sat on her bed and folded her hands in her lap. "Why am I so nervous?"

"Because you're going to meet your boyfriend's family. I'd be nervous too."

"He's not my boyfriend. We're just dating."

"Logan Mitchell doesn't date. From what I've heard, he's a one-and-done kind of guy, and this will be what? The third time you've gone out with him?"

"Technically, we didn't go anywhere last night."

"Even better. So this will be the third time you've *seen* him. He's your boyfriend."

Just the thought had Allison's heart racing, but a nauseated feeling sank deep in her stomach. Could a one-

and-done guy ever really settle down? "I'm not sure he even wants a girlfriend."

"Give him a reading. Then you can find out his real intentions."

She shook her head. "You know I won't do that without permission."

"So get permission." Tina shrugged. "At least it will put your mind at ease."

"I tried. He said something about every romance needing a little mystery."

"He's not wrong."

True, but she wasn't kidding when she said most people jumped at the chance for a reading. As soon as they found out what her abilities were, people she didn't even know would beg her for one. "Do you think he's hiding something?"

"If he is, it's probably the fact that he's falling in love with you."

Allison rolled her eyes. "Be serious."

"I am. The man's taking you to meet his family. He's your boyfriend."

"Well, until he says so himself, he's not. So don't say that around him, okay?"

"Uh-huh." Tina waved off her request. "You better get in the shower. You're running out of time."

Allison padded to her dresser. "You're right."

"Pick some sexy lingerie, and don't forget to shave your legs."

"Yes, ma'am. Are you going to stay?"

"I'll stick around a little longer."

Allison took her clothes into the bathroom and shut the door. The hot water from the shower worked wonders on her tense muscles, and she did a short meditation while she was in there. Feeling much calmer and grounded, she put on the dress and opened the door.

Tina leaned against the jamb. "What's Gage been up to? I haven't seen him in forever."

Allison combed her wet hair and plugged in her blow-dryer. "Why the sudden interest in Gage?"

"I don't know." Tina hopped on the bathroom counter. "I mean, you're obviously not going to go out with him now, so…"

"I never knew you liked him. Why didn't you say anything?"

"He was always asking you out, and I thought you might say 'yes' one day. You always talk about what a great guy he is."

"He *is* a great guy, but he's just my friend. I'm not attracted to him in that way, so if you want him, he's all yours." She dried her hair and turned to her makeup. "What do you think? Simple or dramatic?"

"Simple. Definitely. It's more you."

"Do you want me to talk to Gage for you?"

"I don't know. If you start working with DAPS again, I'll probably see him around more."

She swiped a light brown shadow across her lids and opened her mascara. "What about Dr. Ortega? I thought you were dating him."

Tina toyed with a tube of lipstick. "We're dating, but it's nothing serious. I don't think I could marry a man who looks at vaginas all day."

"Me neither."

Logan cringed as the sound of his dresser drawers opening and closing rattled through the bathroom. Why hadn't the ghost busters called him yet? This spirit was driving him nuts, and he needed her gone. Hopefully he could spend the night with Allison again, if she invited him. He sure as hell didn't want to stay here.

He put on a clean suit and tie and tousled his hair. "Here goes nothing." He picked up his cell phone from the floor—he *knew* he put it on the nightstand—and stuffed his keys in his pocket. If he could get out of the house without another incident, he could spend the evening in peace with the most intriguing woman he'd ever met.

But when he reached the top of the staircase, that same disembodied voice echoed through his mind.

"Why?"

"Because I want you out of my fucking house!"

He ran down the stairs and shot out the door, his determined gait carrying him straight to the garage. Fall leaves crunched under his feet as he cut across the yard, and he checked his watch, anxious for the evening to begin.

It was still too early to pick up Allison, so he took his Mercedes to a full-service car wash to have it detailed. After handing his keys to the attendant, he strode toward the lobby. The glass doors whooshed open, and the smell of soap and air fresheners filled his senses. Feelings of anxiousness, irritation, and lust—none of the emotions his own—bombarded him as soon as he stepped through the door. He tried his best to ignore the cacophony of negativity, but the moment he walked into the room, a vaguely familiar blonde cornered him.

"Hi, Logan! Remember me?" She ran her hands up his chest and locked them behind his neck.

"Hey, how are you?" He pried her hands apart and placed them at her sides.

"What are you doing tonight? Do you want to buy me dinner, and then maybe we can go back to your place?" She licked her lips and flipped her hair to the side.

He shook his head. A week ago, he might have taken her up on the offer, just so he wouldn't have to be alone. Not anymore. "No, thanks. I'm seeing someone."

"Don't be silly, Logan." The woman laughed and tried to take his hand, but he pulled it away. "You can at least buy me a drink."

"I'm serious. I have a girlfriend." He brushed past her and went outside to wait for his car alone. Sitting on a bench near the wall, he rolled his last words over in his head. Was Allison his girlfriend? He hadn't talked to her about being exclusive, but he couldn't imagine being with another woman. And the thought of her being with another man… *Shit.* He couldn't even think about that.

The woman from the lobby strutted past him with her nose in the air, and he could feel the sting of rejection and the burn of anger rolling off her. She got in her car and sped away without saying a word to him, and he sighed, disgusted with himself for creating such a persona.

Allison saw right through his party boy image. He was scared and lonely, and she knew it. She saw the real him, and damn it, she still liked him. He'd be a fool to let her go.

The car wash attendant waved a white towel in the air, signaling his car was ready. He tipped the man and tried to calm his nerves as he headed up East Jefferson Avenue toward Allison's apartment.

CHAPTER THIRTEEN

Logan climbed the stairs to the third floor and prayed to God his sister wouldn't embarrass him tonight. He could imagine her going into a story about how he used to wet the bed when he was a kid or something else equally humiliating. He loved Lisa, but she didn't know when to shut up sometimes. Of course, he'd never introduced her to a girlfriend before, so maybe she'd be on her best behavior.

He'd never had a girlfriend before.

He paced outside Allison's door, clenching and unclenching his fists. He wanted her to be his and his alone, but should he bring it up tonight? If he waited too long, she might get away, but if he asked her too soon, she might bolt. *Hell.* He didn't know how to play the relationship game; he'd never been in this situation before.

He took a deep breath and knocked. When she opened the door, his breath caught in his throat. A knot formed in his stomach, and heat pulsed through his veins. Her little black dress hugged her curves in all the right places, revealing just enough skin to be oh-so-sexy.

Damn.

"Hi." Her warm smile and soft voice only heightened his arousal, and his hands twitched with the urge to touch her.

"Wow. You look…Wow."

"Thank you. You look pretty wow yourself." She kissed him on the cheek and motioned for him to come inside, so he crossed the threshold, never taking his eyes off her slender figure in the tight black dress.

"Thank you for going with me tonight. Lisa's excited to meet you."

She smiled and took his hand. "I'm excited too. Should we go?"

"We have a minute or two." He slid his free hand up her arm and took a step toward her. She grinned and melted into his embrace, brushing her lips to his. She was so soft. So warm. Her tongue lapped at his, her taste making his head spin, and as she cradled his face in her hands and pressed her body to his, what little blood he had left in his upper regions rushed to his groin.

He groaned and took her hands in his. "Maybe we should get going. If we keep this up, we might never leave."

"I think that's a good idea." She picked up a small beaded purse and followed him out the door.

In the car, an overwhelming sense of dread sank in his stomach. The thought of losing her tore at his heart, and he tried to push it out of his mind. But the harder he tried to forget it, the more obsessive it became. What if she decided she didn't like him after he'd opened up his heart to her? Or what if his vision was literal, and he lost her to suicide? He couldn't live with himself if he had a hand in her death. Maybe he'd dive out the window after her.

Shit.

He could see where he was headed, and he sure as hell didn't want to have a meltdown in front of her. What would she think of him then? He'd surely lose her if she found out what a nutcase he was.

Fuck.

With both hands on the steering wheel, he tightened his grip and counted the stripes on the road. *One, two, three, four...* He could feel Allison's eyes boring into him as he worked to keep from slipping into his own personal hell. Her concern pricked at his skin as she placed her hand on his shoulder.

"What's wrong, Logan?"

Eighty-seven, eighty-eight, eighty-nine. Unable to tear his concentration away from the stripes in the road, he kept his mouth clamped shut. The counting soothed him, but the obsessive thoughts still pressed on him like a weight. If he didn't get it under control, he might drive off the road. Then he'd end up killing them both.

His car approached an overpass, and he cringed at the morbid thoughts racing through his mind. He imagined the car crashing through the guard rail, the impact when it hit the concrete below. The air bags wouldn't be enough to save them when the entire front end crumpled into their faces.

Fuck! Fuck! Fuck!

The thoughts kept coming, twisting and storming through his mind like a tornado, destroying every ounce of sanity he had.

"Logan?" Allison softly stroked the back of his neck and put her other hand on his shoulder. She could tell he was losing it; he felt her concern tip toward panic.

From the corner of his eye, he saw her take a deep

breath and close her eyes. Her energy shifted immediately, and he felt her focus it on him. Leaning across the console, she rested her hand gently on top of his head and put the other one on his heart. She continued to breathe deeply, rhythmically, swaying gently back and forth as she concentrated.

"Take a deep breath for me, Logan. Let me help you."

He was skating on the sharp edge of disaster, and one more step would push him over. He took a deep, shuddering breath and tried to let her in. "I don't know what to do." His voice was a mere whisper as he pushed it past the lump in his throat.

"You don't have to do anything, Logan. Just breathe for me."

Her voice was calm, reassuring. The way she said his name and her gentle touch let him know he would be okay. She *was* helping him. Bringing him down from the ledge. He took another deep breath, and the knot in his stomach loosened. His muscles began to relax, and the thoughts no longer bore down on him like a crushing weight. Another deep breath and the anxiety passed. His tension uncoiled, and the need for order to ease his mind no longer pressed against him.

Allison folded her hands in her lap and looked at him. "Better?"

He nodded, pulled up to the valet, and helped her out of the car. "How did you do that?"

She blushed, looking down at her hands while she fiddled with her purse. "I did a little healing on you. I'm sorry I did it without your consent, but you looked like you really needed it."

He took her hand. "Don't apologize. *I'm* sorry. Sometimes my brain…my thoughts get out of control, and I can't stop them. But you… You made it stop. Thank you."

"You're welcome." She placed a soft kiss on his cheek.

"God, this is so embarrassing. You probably think I'm a freak now." He raked his hand through his hair and searched her eyes for any sign of retreat.

She smiled, never taking her gaze off his. "Not at all. Nobody's perfect."

He stroked her cheek with the back of his hand. "You are an amazing woman, Allison. Are you ready to meet my sister?"

Inside the restaurant, Lisa was already seated at a table near a huge aquarium. The myriad of colorful Cichlids swam peacefully about the tank, creating a calming effect in the room, and Lisa stood when they approached the table.

"Hey, Lisa. This is Allison."

The two women shook hands. "It's so nice to meet you, Allison. Please, have a seat."

Logan pulled out a chair for her and sat between them.

"It's nice to meet you too, Lisa. Logan tells me you live in New York?"

"Yes, I do. I had to meet with a witness today, but I'll be going home first thing tomorrow morning. I hate traveling, since my daughter is so young."

"Caitlyn's in first grade, right?"

A look of approval flashed in his sister's eyes. He didn't talk about his personal life with many people. She raised an eyebrow at him, and he smiled.

"Allison's going to school to be a therapist." He held her hand on top of the table, openly displaying his affection for her. "And she's an energy worker."

"Really? How interesting," Lisa said. "What kind of energy work do you do?"

"Mostly clearing and healing. I'm a Reiki practitioner."

"That's fascinating. I'd love to hear more about it sometime."

"If you're in town again, you could stop by my office for a reading and a treatment if you want."

He couldn't fight the smile tugging his lips. He knew Lisa would adore Allison. Who wouldn't? But seeing them getting along so well, so quickly, felt like a weight he hadn't realized he carried lifted from his shoulders. They ordered their food, and Allison excused herself to the restroom.

Lisa put her hand on his forearm. "I like her. She's a keeper."

"I know." He grinned as he watched Allison walk across the restaurant, her hips swaying with each step.

"I can't believe my baby brother actually has a girlfriend. How did it happen?"

He chuckled. How *did* it happen? How did Allison slip behind his carefully constructed walls? "I started talking to her, and we clicked. The scary thing is she sees right through me, and she still likes me. She *knows* me, Lisa. She's seen my flaws firsthand, and she's still here."

"Wow. Mom's going to be thrilled. You have to call her."

"I will, but I haven't talked to Allison about being exclusive. It's only been a few days, and I don't want to scare her off."

"Oh, please," Lisa scoffed. "If she knows you as well as you say she does, and she's still around…"

He huffed. "I don't know. I don't know how to play this game."

"Then don't play. Just tell her how you feel. If it scares her off, then she wasn't worth your time, but I think you know how she feels about you. You know she's not going anywhere."

He did know how she felt. Every time she was near him, he could feel the warm, tender emotions swirling around her, seeping into his consciousness. As much as he tried to convince himself otherwise, Allison cared for him as much as he cared for her.

Allison checked her makeup in the bathroom mirror one more time. The tension in her muscles eased now that she'd gotten the hard part over with. Lisa seemed like a good person, just like Logan. She had his same dark hair and bright blue eyes.

Logan seemed more relaxed now too. What was up with his little episode in the car? The anxiety had rolled off him in waves as he'd clutched the steering wheel. What had he been thinking about? Curiosity gnawed at her mind, but more than anything, she was glad she could help him.

He smiled as she approached the table, and her heart did a back flip in her breast. Their food had already arrived, and they'd both waited for Allison to return before eating.

"Sorry about that. You guys didn't have to wait for me." She placed her napkin in her lap and picked up her fork. "It smells delicious." She took a bite of her chicken pesto pasta and savored the taste on her tongue.

Logan had ordered spaghetti with marinara sauce and grilled chicken on the side. He ate all of the chicken before moving on to the pasta. She watched as Lisa stirred her bowl of food, taking bites of chicken, vegetables, and linguini all mixed together. Logan's eating habits definitely weren't a family trait. Could it be related to the obsessive thoughts he mentioned in the car? It sounded like a classic case of OCD. She laughed at herself switching into therapist mode with her boyfriend.

God, now Tina had her calling him her boyfriend. She had to be careful so she didn't slip up and say that to his face.

"Lisa, do you have any pictures of Caitlyn?" she asked.

"I sure do." Lisa beamed like the proud mother she was as she pulled out her phone and flipped through the pictures. "Here's the most recent one. I took it yesterday before I left."

"She's so cute," Allison said. "She looks just like you. And look—there's that missing tooth she called you about." She gave the phone to Logan, and his face lit up when he looked at the picture of his niece.

"She's getting big." He handed the phone back to his sister.

"She's growing up, and she misses her Uncle Logan. You two should come out and visit. I know Mom would love to meet Allison."

He took Allison's hand. "Would you like to do that sometime?"

"Sounds like fun." Heat rose on her cheeks. She met his sister. Now he'd invited her to meet his mom, and the thought didn't terrify her in the slightest like she expected it would.

His phone buzzed in his pocket, and he checked the

caller ID, cursing under his breath. "I need to answer this. Will you excuse me for a minute?"

She nodded, and Logan left the table to take his call.

"So, Allison. Do you think you could do a little reading on me? I mean, I don't want to put you on the spot or anything. I've just never talked to a real psychic before."

Lisa's request didn't surprise her. "Sure. What do you want to know?"

"Oh, just whatever you pick up."

"Okay. Can I have your hand?"

"Do you read palms?" Lisa extended her hand to Allison.

"No, but the contact helps my vision. I'm an empath. My strongest gift is the ability to sense people's emotions."

Lisa cocked her head. "Do you do it all the time? Can you feel the emotions of everyone in this room?"

She laughed. "If I wanted to drive myself crazy, I could. Most of the time, I shut it all out. I normally don't read people unless they ask me to."

"Oh, okay."

Allison closed her eyes and took a few deep, grounding breaths. Then she opened herself up to Lisa's energy, feeling the life force within her. She pushed a little harder. Something wasn't quite normal. Lisa's aura was strong, but there was something else. Allison smiled as her vision showed her what it was. She opened her eyes and let go of Lisa's hand.

"Well?" Lisa asked.

"You love your brother very much. You feel protective of him, like you need to take care of him, and that's hard to do with him so far away. You worry about him."

"Amazing." Lisa leaned forward on her forearms.

"And you're thrilled that…" She folded her hands in her lap. "You're glad he met me."

"You have no idea. Logan's never had a girlfriend before, and I am so, so glad he picked you. He hasn't had the best luck with women, but you are exactly what he needs. And he's crazy about you. I've never seen him act like this, and I've known him for thirty-two years."

What should she say to that? She let out a nervous laugh and glanced around for Logan, but there was no sign of him.

Lisa looked at her seriously. "I have a favor to ask of you."

"Sure, what is it?"

"Will you help him? He's… Well, I think he's an empath, like you. He won't admit it, but he reads people's emotions. Only, he can't control it. He can't block it out, and I think it's what triggers all his other problems. Do you think you could teach him to control it?"

"How long has he had this ability?"

"Since he was a kid. He's always been a little different. Quirky. But he hid it well. He's a people person, and he's always hidden behind his popularity. Not many people know what he can really do."

She took a deep breath, her drive to help those in need pulsing through her veins. She knew Logan was an empath, and she knew he lacked control. But she had no idea he couldn't shut it out at all. How debilitating that must be. No wonder he was so scared and lonely. To know what everyone thought about him all the time…that would be torture.

"I would love to help him, but he has to be open to receiving it."

"He'll listen to you. I know he will."

"I hope so… And Lisa? Your baby will be born in early summer. Do you want to know what you're having?

Her eyes widened. "Yes! Wow, I'm only a few weeks along. No one but my husband knows."

"You're having a boy."

"Carl is going to be thrilled. I can't wait to tell him." She lowered her voice and leaned toward her. "But please don't tell Logan. I don't want anyone else to know until I make it to the three-month mark. I've had three miscarriages since Caitlyn was born, so I don't want to get anyone's hopes up."

She gave her a reassuring smile. "Your secret's safe with me, but I think this one's going to be fine. Congratulations."

"Thank you." She looked over Allison's shoulder. "Oh, he's coming back. Please don't say anything."

"Hey. Sorry about that." Logan looked from Allison to Lisa and back again. "Why do I get the feeling you two know something I don't?"

"No reason." Allison kissed him on the cheek.

Lisa grinned. "I was just telling Allison about the time you flushed Mom's diamond earrings down the toilet."

He narrowed his eyes. "I think that's enough of that, seeing as how you spray-painted the cat green."

"Hey! You know I didn't see her in the box. Honestly, Allison, I didn't know she was there."

Allison laughed. "Oh, that's just awful! Poor little thing!"

"I know," Lisa said. "I cried for hours after I did it, but the cat was fine. She was green for a few weeks, but she was fine."

"And what about those earrings, Logan? Why on earth

would you flush them down the toilet?" She took his hand under the table, and he gave her a sheepish smile.

"They were supposed to be sunken treasure."

"In the toilet?"

"I was four years old."

She gave his hand a squeeze. "I'm sure I did some pretty stupid stuff when I was a kid too."

"Oh yeah? Like what?" He arched an eyebrow, daring her to join in the banter of embarrassing stories.

"Well, when I was fourteen, Tina and I decided to take my Dad's brand-new BMW for a spin around the block."

"That's not so bad," Logan said.

"I drove it into a lake."

Logan and Lisa stared at her for a few moments as if waiting for her to tell them she was joking. But she wasn't. Before she had control of her gifts, she swerved to miss a woman standing in the middle of the road. The woman turned out to be a ghost, and the car went off a pier and into the lake.

He narrowed his eyes. "You're serious?"

"As a car wreck."

After a few more moments of stunned silence, Lisa finally spoke, "Sorry, Baby Brother. Allison wins this round."

He laughed. "I think you're right. Wow. You drove it into a lake? How'd you get out?"

"It was a convertible. I was grounded for a year after that."

"I bet."

CHAPTER FOURTEEN

"I had a good time tonight." Allison took Logan's hand as they stood in front of her apartment.

"Me too." He stroked her soft cheek with his fingertips and brought his mouth down to hers for a gentle kiss. God, he wanted her to invite him inside. He lingered by her lips, her sweet breath warming his skin. When she didn't pull away, he kissed her again, slipping his tongue out to taste her. A soft moan escaped her throat, and she leaned into him, snaking her arms around his neck.

"Do you want to come in?" Her voice was a whisper against his lips.

"Do you even have to ask?"

She slipped her key into the lock and opened the door. With a wicked grin, she pulled him inside and held him with a seductive gaze. Fire coursed through his veins, and he took a step toward her.

"Hi." He traced his fingers along her bare arms, raising a trail of goose bumps on her skin.

"Hey."

"Do you…" He let out a nervous laugh. What was it about this woman that had him so tongue-tied? "You know, you still make me nervous."

She slid her hands up his chest. "I think I know how to fix that."

"Do you?"

"Uh-huh." She took his face in her hands and ran her thumb across his lips. His heart pounded in anticipation as her dark brown eyes held his. The way she looked at him. The way she touched him. He'd never felt so wanted in his entire life.

She pressed her soft curves against his body and coaxed his mouth open with her tongue. He shuddered at the tenderness in her kiss and held her tighter. Trailing her lips across his cheek, she nuzzled into his neck, her teeth grazing the delicate skin, and he took in a shaky breath.

"Is that better?" She caught his earlobe between her teeth.

"Much."

"Good." She slipped his jacket off his shoulders and laid it on the couch. Then she untied his tie and dropped it on top.

"Allison."

"I want you, Logan. I want to make love to you."

"Yes, ma'am." He worked the beaded shrug down her arms and slipped the dress straps over her shoulders, kissing her bare skin, gliding his tongue up her neck. She shivered as he slid his hands behind her and unzipped her dress, letting it fall to the floor. Stepping back to admire her, he ran his hands along her sensuous curves and marveled at her beauty.

"Take me to bed, Logan."

He scooped her in his arms and kissed her as he

carried her to the bedroom. He'd make love to this woman every day for the rest of his life if she'd let him. After laying her in the middle of the bed, he climbed on top of her. But the mischievous look in her eyes told him she had different plans.

She pushed him onto his back and straddled him, grinding her pelvis against him as she gave him a slow, deep kiss. *Fuck*, he wanted her. He wanted to be inside her. To feel her wet warmth squeezing him as he pleasured her. But she was moving slowly. Torturing him with agonizing pleasure as he had done to her the night before.

She unbuttoned his shirt, kissing and nipping his skin with each opening, his insides tightening and twisting in anticipation. With his shirt untucked, she laid it open, rubbing her hands along the ridges of his muscles. He could tell she sensed his overwhelming need as she roamed her hands lower on his body. She moved just long enough to slip off his pants before she straddled him again, the thin strip of her satin panties the only thing separating them.

He watched her as she explored his body with her hands, her mouth, her tongue, finding her own pleasure in pleasing him. Her touch set fire to his soul, consuming the darkness inside him, leaving behind nothing but warm, loving light.

She took off her bra and guided his hands to her full, firm breasts. Her nipples hardened under his touch, and she moaned softly as he caressed her.

"Take me, Logan."

She rolled onto her back, and he slipped her panties down her legs before rolling on a condom. He wanted her in a way so basic and primal. Possessive. She belonged to him. He took her, sheathing himself in her warmth, drowning himself in her love.

He twisted his hands in her hair and breathed into her ear as he thrust his hips. "You're mine, Allison."

"I know."

She wanted to be his. To belong to him and no one else. God help her, but she was falling in love with Logan. She held on to him, her nails digging into his shoulders as he pushed her over the edge. She wrapped her legs around his waist, letting him in deeper until he found his own release.

With a deep, shuddering breath, he kissed her neck, her cheek, her mouth before rolling onto his side and pulling her into his arms.

She snuggled into the protective circle of his embrace and sighed. This was it. There was no turning back now. Her feelings for Logan ran deeper than she ever thought possible, and all she could do was pray he felt the same. Maybe she was asking for heartbreak, but Logan made her forget all her fears.

"I'm curious." His chest vibrated against her cheek as he spoke. "What were you and Lisa really talking about while I was on the phone?"

"Girl stuff. I could tell you, but then I'd have to kill you."

"Oh, I see how it's going to be." He chuckled.

"We were talking about you, Logan. What else?"

"What about me?"

She propped her head on her hand so she could see his eyes and ran her fingers along his cheek. "She worries about you. She asked me to help you learn to control your gift."

He raised his head to mirror her posture. "I don't have any gifts."

"What do you call it, then? The way you read people? You can feel their emotions, right?"

"I'm good at reading body language. That's all." He rolled onto his back and folded his hands on his chest.

"Okay." She reached for him, resting her hand on top of his. "So, tell me what it's like. What can you pick up from reading someone's body language?"

"Just…you know…their mood. If they're telling the truth. It's not like I can read their minds or anything."

"But you can sense their emotions."

"Yeah, I guess." He shrugged.

"Do you have to be looking at a person to pick up on their mood? Or can you sense it if, say…they're standing behind you?"

He scrunched his brows, a flicker of realization flashing in his eyes. "I guess it doesn't matter where they're standing. As long as they're in the same room, I can usually pick up on it."

"So it can't be body language, can it? If you don't have to be looking at them."

He took a deep breath and stared at the ceiling. "God, Allison, why do you do this? You just lay me open like a book."

"I'm not trying to make you uncomfortable." *Crap.* What had she done? She sat up, clutching the sheets to her chest. "I'm sorry."

"No. Don't be sorry." He moved to sit beside her and laced his fingers through hers. "You get me to talk about things I can't talk about with anyone else. You know me, and I can't begin to tell you how good it feels for someone to know me like you do. And you still stick around."

She gazed into his deep blue eyes, tight with worry. "Why wouldn't I stick around?"

"I feel other people's emotions. Something's wrong with me, with my brain."

"Nothing's wrong with you. You have a gift. You're an empath, like me."

His eyes widened. "You can feel other people's emotions too?"

She nodded.

"How do you keep it from driving you crazy?"

"I block it out. I don't read other people unless they ask me to."

He looked at her in disbelief, opening and closing his mouth a few times before speaking. "You block it out? Just like that? You can turn it on and off whenever you want?"

"Sure." She shrugged. "I couldn't always; it took a lot of practice. But now I'm so used to doing it, I don't even have to think about it anymore."

He was silent, staring at her with hope radiating around him. He held his eyes wide, as if he was trying to fight back tears. "Will you teach me? Help me learn to shut it out?"

"Of course I will. It's going to take time, though, and a lot of patience. There's not some magic switch you can throw to turn it off."

"I don't care. I'll do anything. Whatever you tell me to do, I'll do it. When can we start?"

She put her hand on his face and stroked his cheek with her thumb. "How about tomorrow? You could come over after work."

He smiled, flashing that adorable dimple on his left

cheek. "That sounds… Oh, shit. I can't. I have a…thing tomorrow night. For work."

Her heart sank at the thought of not spending another evening with him. Oh, yeah. She definitely had it bad for Logan Mitchell. "Can you come by on your lunch break? If not, we can do it another time."

"Yes. What if I pick us up some sandwiches and I come to your office? Would that be okay? Around noon?"

"Perfect." The excitement and relief on his face made her smile. She couldn't begin to imagine what it must be like for him, being constantly flooded with the emotions of others. Especially with the kind of people he dealt with every day.

"Thank you." He brushed her lips with his, teasing them with his tongue until she let him in with a slow, tender kiss.

Her body warmed with the affection. She hadn't realized what she was missing by shutting people out all these years. "You're welcome, but you should really thank Lisa. She asked me to talk to you."

"I'll have to do that."

"She loves you so much. You two have a great relationship. You're lucky."

"You don't have any siblings?"

"No, I'm an only child. I don't have any living relatives. Tina is the closest thing I have to family."

He stroked her hair. "She's a good friend."

"I know."

"Did you and Lisa talk about anything else?"

She bit her bottom lip. "Well, she also told me how happy she is that you have a girlfriend."

"Do I have a girlfriend?" He took her hand, lacing his fingers through hers and raising it to his lips.

Blood rushed to her cheeks. God, how she wanted to be his and his alone. She couldn't imagine being with anyone else, and the thought of him with another woman made her sick to her stomach. She couldn't deny her feelings anymore.

"Do you *want* to have a girlfriend?" She held her breath in anticipation of his answer.

The seconds seemed to stretch into forever as he held her gaze, a tiny smile playing on his lips. A knot formed in her stomach, and she swallowed down the lump in her throat. He stroked her cheek and let his fingers glide down her arm.

"Only if it's you, Allison. I only want you."

"And I only want you."

CHAPTER FIFTEEN

"No! Oh, God, Allison! No!" Logan shot up in bed, gasping for air. His vision of Allison— the two versions of Allison— felt so real, he panicked. His pulse pounded in his head as he reached out in the darkness. "Allison."

"I'm here."

Her sleepy voice eased his fears, but it wasn't until she wrapped herself in his arms that he convinced himself the vision wasn't real.

"It's okay, Logan. It was just a dream. I'm here." She nuzzled into his neck, stroking his bare chest with her hand. "I'm here."

His vision left him trembling, his skin slick with sweat. The idea of losing her became more and more frightening with each dream. He took her mouth in an urgent kiss as he laid her back on the bed. She was okay. She was there in his arms, and he would never let her go. He held on to her, his hands traveling the course of her body, reassuring him that she was very much alive and with him.

"That was some nightmare," she said.

"You have no idea." He held her tighter, trying to banish the vision from his thoughts. But the harder he tried not to think about it, the more insistent the thoughts became.

She stroked his hair then wrapped her arms around him, hugging him tight. "Do you want to talk about it?"

"I don't know where to begin."

"Was it your vision again?"

He nodded.

"Was it different this time?"

"No. Kind of. It felt so real." He squeezed his eyes shut. "I don't want to lose you."

"We'll figure it out. You said the women don't have faces, right? So maybe it's symbolic, and they aren't women at all."

He propped his head in his hand, keeping his legs entwined with hers. It was time to come clean. "I didn't tell you everything before. Since I met you, the vision has been getting clearer, and I can see their faces. They're both you."

She knit her brow. "I think it's safe to say it can't be literal, then. I'm only one person."

"I guess so." Her logic made sense, but he wasn't completely convinced.

"And I can promise you with one hundred percent certainty that I will never jump out a window." She put her hand on his cheek and looked into his eyes. "Never."

He held her hand to his face. "Allison…"

"You still have doubts, don't you?" She sighed. "My dad died of a heart attack when I was sixteen. I know what unexpected death does to the people who are left behind."

"I didn't know. I'm so sorry."

"It's okay." She shrugged. "I don't talk about it much."

"What happened? If you don't mind talking about it with me."

She smiled, but it didn't reach her eyes. "I guess it's only fair, since you've opened up so much with me." She propped her head on her hand and traced his chest with her finger.

"We'd been arguing. I can't even remember what it was about, but I'm sure it was something stupid. He left for work, and as he was getting into his car, I ran out into the driveway and shouted, 'I hate you.' It was the last thing I ever said to him."

She glanced at his eyes before focusing her gaze on his chest. "I could feel the pain my words caused him, but I turned on my heel and marched back inside. He died thinking I hated him. I can't even begin to explain the guilt I've carried since. Then my mom died of cancer, and I've been alone ever since."

He wiped a tear from her cheek and pulled her into his arms. "I'm so sorry, Allison."

She took a deep, shaky breath. "I haven't talked about it in so long."

"Hey. It's okay. You don't have to talk about it."

"No. I need to. It's just… Well, I'm a healer and an empath. I never should have said that to my dad, and my mom… She didn't tell me about the cancer until it was too late. She was trying to protect me, thought it would be better if I didn't know. I could have helped her. I could have helped them both."

He held her tight to his chest as she cried. He felt the pressure of her grief and the sharp, stabbing pain of the guilt she felt for not helping her parents. She clung to him, unloading all the built-up emotions she had locked away years ago.

"It's not your fault. People have to want to be helped. You did all you could."

"But I could have done so much more if they would have told me."

"But they didn't. For whatever reason, they didn't tell you what was going on. Whether it was for your protection or not, you didn't know. And you were just a kid when your dad died. It's not your fault."

She wiped her tears and looked into his eyes. "Thank you. Deep down I know it wasn't my fault, but sometimes I need to be reminded."

"Is that why you didn't want to get involved with me? Because of what happened with your parents?"

"It's part of it. I was also engaged to a man who got wealthy and then left me alone without a dime to my name. Money is evil." She drew her bottom lip between her teeth and searched his eyes.

"It can be. But I try to use my powers for good."

She laughed. "I know that now."

"I remind you of your ex-fiancé."

"At first you did, when all I knew was your image. But now that I know *you*… You're nothing like him, and I'm not scared anymore."

"Good, because I would never do anything to hurt you."

CHAPTER SIXTEEN

Allison lit a jasmine-scented candle and rearranged the pillows on her treatment table. It would be another hour before Logan got there, and her stomach twisted in knots as she waited for him. They shared so much the night before—their bodies and their feelings. She opened up to him in a way she never thought possible, and she felt lighter now that he knew about her past. Her *demons*, as Lucia had called them. She may have finally buried them, after all.

Her phone vibrated in her pocket, and she checked the caller ID. It was Tina. *Crap*, she'd forgotten to call her. "Hello?"

"Are you still with him?" Tina whispered like she was trying not to disturb them.

Allison lowered her voice to match her friend's. "No, I'm at work."

"Then why haven't you called me?" she shouted into the phone. "I've been on pins and needles all morning waiting to hear from you."

She laughed and curled up in her favorite chair. "I'm

sorry. I had a few clients this morning, and I was running late. And I've been a little preoccupied thinking about *my boyfriend.*"

"Tell me everything!" Excitement raised Tina's voice an octave, and Allison imagined her sitting on the edge of her seat, her knees bouncing up and down as she spoke.

"Well, I met his sister…"

"And?"

"I really liked her. We got along, and she and Logan have a great relationship. She invited us to visit her family in New York."

"Us? As in *you* and *Logan*?"

"Yeah. And after dinner, we went back to my apartment."

"And you screwed his brains out."

"Tina!"

"What? Tell me you didn't."

She giggled, pushed her office door shut, and lowered her voice. "Okay, I did. And he was *incredible*."

"And now you're exclusive? I mean, did you talk about it? You're not just assuming, are you?"

"No, we talked about it. He said he didn't want to see anyone else, and I said I didn't either, and…"

"Allie has a boyfriend," Tina sang. "I'm so happy for you! When are you going to see him again?"

"We're having lunch today."

"I'm so jealous. Does he have any friends you could hook me up with? What about that cute lawyer he's always hanging out with?"

"What happened to Dr. Ortega? Aren't you seeing him this weekend?"

"Sure I am, but I told you about him and the vagina thing."

"Right. And what about Gage? Last time we talked you were interested in him."

"I am interested in him. But *he's* interested in *you*."

She sighed. "You don't know that. It's been a long time since we've hung out. I'm sure he's over it by now. Besides, I'm with Logan. I still can't get used to that. I have a boyfriend."

"Yes, you do." Tina laughed. "Listen, I have to go, but I want you to keep me updated, okay? I want all the details."

"All right. I'll be sure to call you the moment something happens."

"You better."

"I'm going to grab some lunch. You want to come?" Trent held his keys in his hand as he stood in Logan's doorway.

Logan glanced at his watch and smiled. "No thanks. I'm going to meet Allison."

Trent sauntered into the office and sat on the arm of a chair. "How's that working out? You saw her last night?"

"Yeah. My sister was in town, and we met her for dinner."

Trent closed his eyes. "Mmm…Lisa."

Logan laughed. "You know, she still talks about how you were in love with her when you were seventeen. She's never going to let you forget that."

"How could I forget? I'm *still* in love with her." He grinned and raised his eyebrows. "Anyway, man… You took Allison to meet your sister? That's getting deep."

"I know. I'm already in it deep."

He lifted his chin and looked at his friend. "I see that. How'd it go? Did Lisa like her?"

"She did. A lot. So do I."

"All right. I guess I'm going to have to find a new wingman, huh?"

"Yeah. I think you are."

Trent stood and gave him a quick hug and a slap on the back. "Congratulations. I'm happy for you."

"Thanks, Trent. That means a lot."

He turned to leave but stopped before he reached the door. "What's going on with the ghost busters?"

"They're coming back again tonight, and they want me to be there. They said they're going to bring in some kind of medium who can communicate with ghosts and clear them out. I don't know what's going to happen."

"Does Allison know about it?"

"She hasn't been back to my place since the party. Hopefully I can get rid of it, and she won't have to know."

Just as Allison hung up the phone, a knock sounded on her office door. She glanced at the clock, and her pulse quickened. Logan wasn't supposed to be there for another half hour. She took a deep breath and opened the door.

"Gage! I didn't know you were coming." She smiled and gave her friend a hug. He wrapped his arms around her, holding on slightly longer than necessary. She pulled away and looked at the clock.

"Were you expecting someone else?" He flashed a crooked smile and strode across her small office in two steps. He sat on the treatment table and motioned for her to sit next to him.

"I was, but that's okay. It's good to see you again." She sat next to him, curling one leg underneath her as she turned to face him.

"You seem a lot happier than the last time I was here."

A smile tugged at her lips. "I am. Remember the guy I went out with, the one I didn't want to see again?"

He arched a brow. "Yeah."

"I changed my mind. We're dating now." Her smile grew wider.

"You're dating someone." He cast his gaze to the floor and slumped his shoulders. "Why, Allison? I thought you didn't want to get involved."

Well, that wasn't the reaction she expected. "I don't know. It just happened. I thought you'd be happy for me." She moved across the room to sit in her chair. "I thought you'd want me to be happy."

He sighed and shuffled toward her, taking her hands in his. "I am happy for you. I'm just surprised." He looked at their hands and rubbed his thumb across her palm. "And a little disappointed."

"Disappointed?"

He let out a nervous laugh. "I guess I was hoping that when you did decide to date someone, you might consider dating me."

"Oh, Gage. I…"

"I thought we had something, you know? Huh. I guess I was delusional." He shook his head, went back to the table and leaned against it, crossing his arms over his chest.

"I'm sorry. I don't know what else to say. I love you, just not in that way. I never have, and I'm sorry if I made you think otherwise."

"You never gave me a chance."

"Please don't do this." She leaned against the table next to him. "I'm sorry. I really am."

"You know what? Don't be sorry." He put his arm around her and pulled her to his side. "It's my fault. I'll deal with it. I'm happy that you're happy, so don't worry about me, okay? I don't want things to get awkward between us."

She let out a relieved breath. Hopefully he meant it. "Okay. No awkwardness."

He stared straight ahead like he didn't know what to say. Neither did she. She knew he'd had a crush on her when she worked for DAPS, but she'd been gone for so long… *So much for no awkwardness.*

Gage nodded once. "What's he like?"

"I think you'd like him. He's sweet and honest…"

"Do you love him?"

She sucked in a sharp breath and exhaled slowly. Did she love Logan? "Maybe. I mean… Yeah, I think I do."

He chuckled. "He's a lucky man."

She playfully jabbed him with her elbow. "I'm guessing you didn't come here just to say 'hi.' You need my help, don't you?"

He sighed and paced the small office. "Yeah. We do."

"And Richard sent you, because he thought you could convince me with your good looks and boyish charm?" She smiled at him, and he laughed.

"Actually, I volunteered to come. Richard would have put you on a guilt trip to convince you, even if you weren't ready. I'm giving you a choice. All you have to do is tell me no, and I'll drop it. I'm not going to push you."

She hopped onto the table and crossed her legs. "I'll do it."

He stopped pacing and arched an eyebrow. "Allison,

you don't have to. Really, just say you're not ready. It's okay."

She held out her hand to him, and he took it. "I *am* ready. I'll do it."

"Just like that?"

"Just like that. I thought about what you said before, and I think I'm ready to get back into it."

"Are you sure?"

She laughed. "Yes! Would you quit trying to talk me out of it and tell me when we're going in?"

He took a deep breath and stared at her for a moment as if waiting for her to change her mind. When she didn't waver, he nodded.

"Can you make it tonight? The client's going to be there. He's…"

Allison put up her hand to stop him. "Shh…don't tell me any more. I don't want to be influenced by the details, so I'll go in blindfolded. What time are you picking me up?"

Excitement flickered in Gage's eyes. "Nine-thirty, okay? I need to help them set up, but Richard and Lindsay are going to do a little work before you get there. Try to wear the ghost down, so you aren't overwhelmed."

"Sounds great. I'll be ready."

"Allison…" His concern pricked at her skin.

She gave him her most reassuring smile. "I'm ready, Gage, and I'm excited to work with you again. I've missed you."

He pulled her into his arms and hugged her tight. "I've missed you too." He inhaled deeply, and she could only hope he wasn't smelling her hair.

Clearing his throat, he let her go. "I'll see you tonight."

"I can't wait."

The antique store door chimed when Logan entered carrying a bag of deli sandwiches in one hand and balancing a tray of drinks in the other.

"Good afternoon, Lucia. How are you today?" He beamed with excitement as he set the drinks on the counter. It had only been six hours since he'd said goodbye to Allison at her apartment, but those six hours had seemed to drag on and on.

Lucia's smile was warm and knowing. "Hello, Logan. I'm well. How are you?"

"Never better. Here, I brought you some lunch. I hope you like turkey." He pulled a sandwich out of the bag and handed her a drink. "Is Allison in her office?"

"How very thoughtful. Yes, she's expecting you. Go right in."

He tapped lightly on the door and opened it slowly. His breath caught when he saw Allison sitting cross-legged on a large blue pillow in the middle of the floor. Her eyes were closed, and her hands rested on her knees. She wore faded jeans and a pale yellow sweater, and her silky hair fell loose around her shoulders. A slight smile tugged at her lips, and he stood in the doorway watching her breathe. How did he get so damn lucky?

She looked serene. Peaceful. He reached out to read her, and he felt nothing but contentment. She was in another world, away from all the stress and negativity of this one, and he longed to learn how to go there with her. He stepped inside the room, put their sandwiches on the table, and settled into a plush red chair.

He felt her when she came back. Felt her energy warming his skin, her pulse quickening in her chest. She knew he was there, and he felt her happiness bubble to the surface as her eyes fluttered open and she smiled.

"Hi." She relaxed her posture and unfolded her legs.

"Hey. I hope I didn't disturb you."

"Of course not." She put the pillow on the table and curled into his lap, wrapping her arms around his neck. "I've missed you."

"I've missed you too." He cradled her against his chest and kissed her, savoring the sweet taste of her.

"What did you bring us for lunch?"

"Sandwiches. I hope you like turkey. I forgot to ask."

"Turkey's great." She slipped off his lap and pulled the table closer. Perching on the arm of the chair, she nibbled her sandwich. "How is it you can eat a sandwich with all those vegetables mixed in it when you don't even like your food to be touching on your plate?"

Damn, she was perceptive. Nothing got past this woman, and he loved that about her. "I'm not sure. I guess because it's all wrapped up in a piece of bread. I never thought about it. Does it bother you? The way I eat?"

"Not at all. I was just curious."

"You're not psychoanalyzing me over there, are you?" He chuckled. "Because I've got more issues than you probably want to deal with."

"That's why you're here, isn't it? So I can help you deal with your issues? With your psychic ones, anyway."

He sighed. "I guess I am, but you know that's not the only reason, right?" He put his hand on her cheek and pulled her face to his. "I'm also here because I love spending time with you."

"Good. Because I love spending time with you too. And I think once you get your ability under control, your other issues won't seem quite so ominous."

"I hope so."

She picked up their trash and put it in the wastebasket. Then she moved the table back in place and put two big pillows on the floor. "I don't know how you've made it this long, honestly. With the people you have to associate with, I'd have gone crazy by now. I don't know if you remember or not, but I was at the party you threw at your new house."

He grinned. "Oh, I remember. That's the first time I noticed you. I haven't been able to get you off my mind since."

Her cheeks flushed with color as she sat on one of the pillows. "It seems like all those people think about is sex and money. I felt it pulsing through the room, even though I wasn't trying to read anyone. It was like background noise, but it was still annoying. I can only imagine what that must feel like for you, not being able to shut any of it out."

He looked at the floor. "It's bad. Hell, it's awful. Can you teach me to make it background noise?"

"That's what we're going to work on. Come sit with me." She folded her legs and turned to face him, taking both of his hands in hers. "I'm not perfect. Sometimes stuff gets through, even when I'm not trying."

"Really? Like what?"

She blushed again, and she looked at their entwined hands. Damn, she was cute when she acted shy.

"Like you. At your party, I knew you were different. It was like you were screaming for help, and no one could hear you but me."

"I got a different vibe from you. I could tell sex and money didn't interest you. I tried to talk to you that night, but you ran out so fast, I didn't get the chance."

"Sorry about that."

He shrugged. "I found you."

"Yes. You did."

He struggled with the urge to take her in his arms and make out with her right there in her office. She was so sensual. So feminine. The way she licked her lips before she spoke had his blood racing through his veins. Did she know she was driving him crazy?

He cleared his voice and shook himself. "We should get started. What do I do?"

"Let's start with a simple meditation."

"I don't know how to meditate."

"We'll do it together. Close your eyes and take some slow, deep breaths with me." She fluttered her lids shut and inhaled deeply, her chest rising and falling as she breathed. She took another breath and opened one eye a slit. "Close your eyes, Logan."

"Sorry." He grinned and shut his eyes, focusing on the soothing melody of her soft voice.

"Imagine a beam of light from the universe coming down into your body. It enters through your crown and goes all the way through to the floor, grounding you. Allow the light to grow inside you, filling you up."

He tried his best to focus. He saw the light, and he felt it inside him.

"Now, imagine yourself inside a bubble, and allow the light to fill it up. This is your protection. Nothing negative can get inside your bubble. Only things you invite in are allowed to enter. You feel calm, peaceful. Nothing from the outside world affects you when you're in your bubble. Let's stay here for a while and breathe."

He saw the bubble. He felt the peace and serenity inside it, but it wasn't long before his mind started wandering. The harder he tried *not* to think the thoughts swimming through his brain, the more they commanded his attention.

He blew out a hard breath and opened his eyes. "I'm sorry. I was feeling it. I really was, but my mind goes wherever it wants. What am I doing wrong?"

Her eyes fluttered open. "Nothing. Meditation takes a while to master. You put in a good three minutes, and that's great for your first time. The more you practice, the better you'll be."

"That's it? I just imagine I'm in a bubble, and it will all go away?"

"Well, it's not *that* simple, but it's a good start. Do that meditation a few times a day and whenever you're feeling overwhelmed by emotions. It will help."

"Thank you." He reached out his hand and stroked her cheek. "God, I wish I could see you tonight. I'm tempted to cancel that damn work thing."

"Me too, but I have plans with some friends. Tomorrow night?"

"Definitely."

She flashed a wicked grin and crawled onto her hands and knees. "But you don't have to rush back just yet, do you?" She slunk toward him like a cat sneaking up on its prey.

His heart pounded, and heat flushed through his veins. "Not just yet…"

"Good." Her mouth met his, and her hands slid up

his chest and behind his neck as she pulled herself into his lap. "Because I'm going to miss you tonight."

He stifled a groan and wrapped his arms around her. She had to be the sexiest woman alive.

"I don't know what it is, Logan, but I lose control when I'm with you. I'm not usually this forward."

"Don't hold back on my account."

"I won't." She pressed her body against his, and he indulged in the sweetness of her embrace. They held each other, touching and tasting until a knock on the door brought them down. Lucia peeked her head in the room.

"Ahem…your one-thirty is here, Allison. Do you want to reschedule?" Lucia didn't hide her grin.

"Oh, crap! Oh, no. No, just…tell them I'll be ready in a minute." She shot off his lap and looked in the mirror, adjusting her clothes and smoothing her disheveled hair. "I'm sorry, Logan. I completely lost track of time. Will you… Can we…"

He pulled her into his arms and kissed the top of her head. "I'll call you tomorrow."

"Okay. Thank you."

"Thank *you*, Allison. For everything."

CHAPTER SEVENTEEN

Allison finished with her last client at five o'clock and was locking up her office when Tina strolled through the front door. Her friend wore dark jeans with black leather mid-calf boots and a burgundy sweater. Not at all her normal work attire.

"Hey, Tina. Were you off today?"

"I stopped by my house to change on the way here. I'm taking you out for dinner tonight. We need some girl time before I lose you completely to your new man."

She slipped her purse on her shoulder. "And what if I already have dinner plans?"

Tina arched a brow. "Do you?"

"No." Even if she did, she would always make time for her best friend.

"Then let's go. It's ladies' night at Molly's Place, and happy hour just started."

Allison rolled her eyes and followed her out the door. Molly's Place, a combination restaurant and singles bar, was casual, which was nice, but the music was loud, the décor more like a sports bar, and they served mostly fatty, fried food.

"Molly's Place? Really?"

"Oh, quit whining. When *haven't* we had a good time there?"

She climbed into the passenger seat and put on her seatbelt. "You're right. We do always have fun, but that's usually because you end up dancing on the table while I laugh my ass off."

"See? All good times." Tina pulled the car onto West Fort Street and headed toward the restaurant.

"All right," Allison said. "But I need to be home by nine. Gage is picking me up at nine-thirty."

Tina stomped the brake at the light and jerked her head toward Allison. "Gage? Why is Gage picking you up at nine-thirty?"

"I'm working on an investigation with DAPS tonight."

Her eyes narrowed warily before she pulled into the parking lot at Molly's and turned off the engine. "How'd they convince you to do that?"

Allison unbuckled her seatbelt and clutched her purse to her chest. "I know what you're thinking, and they didn't have to convince me. I'm ready."

"Uh-huh." Tina got out of the car, and Allison followed her across the parking lot and into the restaurant.

The bar was already crowded with people just getting off work, an eclectic bunch with business men and women, college students, and even a few construction workers in the mix. Big-screen TVs displaying sports or the local news hung from the ceiling, and girls in shorts and tight t-shirts ran around with trays full of beer and other mixed drinks. A large mirror hung behind the bar, and a small stage sat off to the side for live music and karaoke. Tina grabbed Allison's hand and weaved through the crowd to find a table in the restaurant behind the bar.

"Did Richard send you on a guilt trip?" Tina handed her a menu as they settled into a booth beneath a picture of the 1987 University of Michigan football team.

"No, he didn't. You said yourself I should get back into it. Remember?"

"I remember. I just didn't think you'd be doing it so soon. Are you sure you're ready?"

"I really am. And, honestly? I'm excited. I've really missed DAPS. Especially Gage."

The waitress, a girl who didn't look a day over eighteen, arrived to take their order. As soon as she stepped up to the table, Allison felt a wave of anxiety rolling off her. Her disheveled hair hung in a loose ponytail with stray strands falling around her face. A smudge of mascara ran down her cheek, and her eyes were tight with worry.

"You look like you're having a rough day," Allison said.

"You have no idea," the waitress replied. "I'm new here, and this place is crazy. I'm totally in the weeds, and I'm running out of steam fast."

Normally, Allison wouldn't force her help on anyone, but a little extra push of energy wouldn't hurt the poor girl. She took a deep breath and imagined a light growing brighter in her core. Then she pushed that energy out toward the waitress and visualized the light filling her up.

She patted the girl on the arm. "It will get easier. Just have faith you can handle it."

"Thanks." The tension in her shoulders released, and she smiled. "I'll sure try. Are you ready to order?"

Tina asked for an avocado burger with onion rings, and Allison got the club sandwich with fruit salad. The waitress wrote it all down on a notepad and scurried back to the kitchen.

"What did you just do to her?" Tina grinned.

"I gave her a little extra shot of energy. No big deal." A twinge of guilt pinched in her chest for forcing her healing on the girl, but people didn't always have to verbally ask for help. The look on the waitress's face said enough.

"A club sandwich again?" Tina changed the subject before Allison could feel too guilty. "You always get the same thing when we come here. Why don't you go out on a limb and try something new? Be adventurous."

"It's the only thing they serve that isn't a heart attack on a bun." She shrugged and sipped her tea.

"Anyway, how is our friend Gage?" Tina smiled and raised her eyebrows.

"Oh, he's fine. You know. Same old Gage." She smoothed her napkin in her lap and picked at some imaginary lint on her sweater.

"You mean he's still in love with you."

She folded her arms and leaned back in her seat. "I wouldn't say he's in love with me, but he wasn't thrilled when I told him about Logan."

"Maybe he doesn't trust him. Logan's got a reputation."

"Actually, I don't think I ever told him *who* I was dating. Just that I *was* dating. But he'll get over it." She leaned her forearms on the table. "Maybe you can take his mind off it."

Tina tapped her finger against her cheek, feigning thought, but then shook her head. "I don't think so. He's too close to home. If you're going to be working with DAPS again, I'll probably be seeing him all the time. I don't want to be his fling or his rebound or anything like that. It would be too weird."

"How very mature of you."

She stuck out her tongue.

"Okay. I take that back."

"I don't know. We're getting older, and maybe it's time for me to settle down. You know? Start dating guys I would actually want to keep around."

Allison laughed. "You mean your slut days are over?"

"Far from it. I just might be a little more selective about who I sleep with. That's all."

"Oh, if that's all."

She understood exactly how her friend felt, and not because she was psychic. They were both pushing thirty, and as all their friends married off, their selection of decent men got smaller and smaller. She'd all but given up hope of ever settling down herself. Until she met Logan.

"Wow! That was fast," Allison said as the waitress set their plates in front of them and refilled their drinks. The girl was smiling, and Allison didn't feel the rush of anxiety she picked up from her last time. "Is your day getting any better?"

"Actually, it is," the waitress said. "I'm catching up with my tables. Can I get you anything else?"

"I think we're good. Thanks."

Tina slid out of her seat. "I have to go use the potty. Don't eat all my onion rings while I'm gone."

"Don't worry."

Allison took a bite of her club sandwich and looked at the fruit salad on her plate. Grapes, apples, strawberries, and cantaloupe, all mixed together in a colorful medley of sweetness, reminded her of Logan and his peculiar eating habits. What was with his need for everything to be separated? In order?

She picked up her fork and organized the pieces into neat little piles, grinning as the rainbow of fruit started taking shape: purple grapes in one pile, red strawberries in another. Then the green apples and orange cantaloupe.

It had only been four hours since she'd last seen Logan, but she missed him like crazy. Sleeping in her big bed all by herself didn't sound the least bit appealing. Of course, she'd probably get a lot more sleeping done.

As she popped a grape into her mouth, an obnoxious guy in a cheap suit slid onto the seat next to her, interrupting her thoughts.

"Hey, baby. You look like you could use a little company." His eyelids were heavy, and his breath smelled like beer. It was only five-thirty, and he was already trashed. He put his arm around her and tried to pull her closer to him.

Allison ducked from his grip and scooted to the far side of the seat. "I don't need any company. I'm here with a friend."

"You look like you're all alone to me. Can I buy you a drink?" His slurred speech and exaggerated movements told her he was beyond buzzed. She looked around the room for Tina, but all she found was a table full of guys staring at them and laughing. Obviously his buddies.

Crap.

He slid closer to her and tried to put his arm around her again. She ran through her self-defense moves in her mind and was just about to use them when a vaguely familiar voice rescued her.

"Hey, man. You're in my seat."

Allison glanced up to find Trent with his fists clenched and his arms folded across his chest.

"Huh? Oh, this is your girl?" The drunk swung around to face Trent and swayed as he tried to stand.

Trent caught him by the arm. "Whoa, buddy. Those your friends over there?"

"Yeah."

"How about you go join them and leave this young lady alone?" He slapped the drunk on the back and gave him a push toward his friends. The guy stumbled back to his table, and Trent slipped into the booth across from Allison.

"Are you okay?"

"Yeah. Thanks for getting rid of him."

"You're Allison, right? I'm Trent. We met at the benefit the other night."

She wrapped her arms around herself, the heat of embarrassment flushing her cheeks. "I remember." She let out a nervous laugh. "It's nice to meet you…again."

"It's nice to meet you too. Who ordered this?" Trent looked at the burger and onion rings in front of him.

"That's Tina's. She went to the restroom."

"It looks good." He eyed the rainbow on Allison's plate and chuckled. "How colorful."

She circled her fork through the fruit to break up the pattern. "How long have you and Logan been friends?"

"Since high school. We played football together."

"Logan played football?" She tried to imagine him running a ball down the field. Why did that surprise her? He was built like an athlete, so it shouldn't have.

"Just in high school. He could have played in college, but he lost interest."

"What about you? Did you play in college?"

"Nah." Trent dismissed the idea with a wave of his hand. "It was fun in high school, but in college, it's too serious. I wasn't interested in going pro, not that I was good enough."

"I see. Do you work with Logan?"

"I'm his lawyer."

"That's nice you get to work so closely together."

"Logan's a great guy." He held her gaze, studying her.

She grinned. "I know."

Trent leaned back and crossed his arms over his chest. "And what a catch. He's good-looking, rich…" How cute. He was concerned about his friend. Perhaps she should put his fears at ease.

"I don't care about his money, and I don't have any ulterior motives. I'm not going to hurt him."

"Good." He nodded, uncrossing his arms. "I have to look out for my boy. He's been through a lot."

"I understand. He's important to me too, but don't you think if I were after his money, Logan would kind of…know?" Being friends for as long as they had, he must have been at least somewhat aware of Logan's ability.

"I suppose he would, but you know what they say… Sometimes love is blind."

Her pulse quickened, and a smile tugged at the corners of her mouth. "What do you think, Trent? Am I good enough for him?"

"Honestly? I think you're perfect for him. Listen, I'm here with some co-workers, and I need to get back. I'm sure I'll be seeing you around though."

"Thanks again for your help."

"Anytime. Take care."

Allison popped a strawberry into her mouth and contemplated what Trent said. "Love is blind." Butterflies flitted in her stomach at the thought that Logan might be falling in love with her.

Tina slid into the booth and took a bite of an onion ring.

"It's about time you got back," Allison said. "Your food's probably cold now."

"Nope. Still warm." She took another bite.

"What took you so long?"

"I was distracted by a hot body with a gorgeous set of eyes. Then I found out he was 'between jobs.'" She made air quotes with her fingers. "What did Logan's cute lawyer friend have to say? I saw you talking to him."

She laughed. "He has a name, you know. It's Trent."

"I know, but 'Cute Lawyer Friend' is so much more fun to say."

"Well, first he rescued me from a drunk. Then, he asked me what my intentions were with his friend."

Tina gaped. "Did he really? He asked you what your intentions were?"

"Not in those terms, but he was feeling me out, making sure I wasn't a gold digger or anything."

"Aww…" Tina pressed her hands to her heart. "What a sweet guy, looking out for his friend like that."

"He's still here, you know. You could go talk to him." She gestured to Trent's table, and Tina bit her bottom lip, looking thoughtful.

She shook her head. "Nah. Not tonight. I came here to spend time with my BFF."

Allison shook her head. "You're scared, aren't you?"

"Maybe a little."

CHAPTER EIGHTEEN

Logan watched as Gage taped down the last of the wires and checked the angles on the cameras. This would be DAPS' third, and hopefully final, night in the mansion. Their medium would be able to clear the spirit out, and then he could get on with his life. Maybe Allison could spend the night with him for a change.

"All right. I think that will do it." Gage packed up the tape. "Lindsay, did you tell him what you found out about the place?"

"Not yet." Lindsay handed him a newspaper clipping. "I did a little research on the location, and I think I've identified your ghost. Back in the eighties, the original owner of this house was Alexander McAdam. He had a wife named Lily. It seems Mr. McAdam loved throwing parties, and he loved the women who attended. He had quite a few mistresses, and poor Lily couldn't take it anymore. She committed suicide in this house when he told her he didn't love her anymore."

"Jesus." The newspaper article said Lily jumped out of

a second-story window. "I wouldn't think it'd be high enough to kill her, though."

"It is if you go head first into the concrete." Richard nodded at Gage and picked up a hand-held camera.

"Logan, you're going to wait in the van with me for a while. Richard and Lindsay are going to try provoking the ghost to get her to expend most of her energy so she doesn't overwhelm our medium…or you."

"You're the experts." Logan didn't know the first thing about ghost hunting, and he wasn't afraid to admit it. He followed Gage to the van, leaves crunching under their feet as they crossed the front yard. He could feel Gage's excitement, his love of the hunt. It was refreshing to find someone who truly loved what he did. Most people just worked for the money.

Gage opened the sliding door, and Logan's eyes widened as he took in the technological backstage of DAPS. A series of flat panel monitors lined one wall, and multiple computers and keyboards occupied a table beneath. Gage sat in a swiveling chair and invited Logan to sit in another one.

"Impressive." The monitors displayed different views of his house: the kitchen, upstairs where he heard the voices, his bedroom. "I never realized what all goes into this. It's incredible."

Gage chuckled. "It's all right. Wait till our medium gets here. *She's* incredible."

He smiled at Gage's admiration of the medium, and he sensed there might be something more than respect between the two.

"Are you close?" It wasn't any of his business, and as soon as the words escaped his mouth, he was sorry he'd asked. Allison's inquisitive nature was already rubbing off on him.

"I guess. She has a new boyfriend now, so who knows, right?" He opened a drawer under the table and pulled out a pack of Twizzlers. "You want some?"

"Mmm…sugar-coated plastic. My favorite." He took a piece of the candy and chewed on the end. "What's this medium going to do? How's she going to send the ghost packing?"

Gage's fingers flew across the keyboard as he typed in some codes, then he swiveled around to face him. "I don't know how she does it, honestly. Ghosts talk to her, and she can hear them. Hell, she can *see* them, and I'm looking at the same place she is, but I see nothing. It's some crazy shit. She tells them to go to the light, but there's got to be more to it than that. She's doing *something*, but I have no idea what it is."

"Is she a psychic? I mean, what's the difference?"

"Yeah. Psychic. Medium. She does it all."

Logan chewed on his Twizzler and thought about Allison. She'd never mentioned communicating with spirits. Was that something she ever practiced? He probably should've told her what he was doing tonight. He didn't even consider she might be interested in his problem. He was too worried she'd think he was crazy.

Well, shit. It was too late now. She said she had plans with friends anyway. She was probably out with Tina at a bar somewhere getting hit on by all kinds of losers. A twinge of jealousy stabbed in his gut. He had to stop thinking about it right then and there before he spiraled into a meltdown. "What are they doing in there?"

"They're provoking. Trying to make the spirit mad so it'll use up some of its energy. Your ghost is strong. I mean, it scratched Lindsay, for Christ's sake. That doesn't happen very often."

"She's not scared to be in there again after that happened?"

Gage laughed. "She's probably scared shitless, but it's part of the job. You have to get over your fears and do what you came to do."

Gage's walkie-talkie buzzed with Richard's muffled voice. "You can send him in now."

"They're ready for you, man. I'm going to pick up the reinforcements. See you in a bit."

In the silence of Allison's apartment, the memories of her last escapade with DAPS rushed through her mind. Memories she'd worked hard to suppress. All those spirits, all those twisted emotions flooding her senses. She shivered as she slipped out of her clothes and turned on the shower.

This time would be different. Gage said it was only one ghost. Surely she could handle that. Even a really strong spirit shouldn't be a problem for an experienced professional. Not if there was only one.

The hot stream of the shower relaxed the tension in her muscles and cleared her mind. She breathed deeply, transcending into a shallow meditative state as the water cascaded down her body, washing away her anxiety. Shutting off the faucet, she slipped into a fuzzy blue robe and dried her hair. She had just finished her makeup when someone knocked on her door. She tightened the belt around her waist and padded through the living room to find Gage standing outside with his hands in his pockets and his eyes cast downward.

"Hi, Gage. You're early."

His cheeks flushed as his gaze traveled up and down her body. He swallowed hard. "I, uh…I'm sorry. I wanted to talk to you."

She clutched the top of her robe and stepped aside so he could enter. "Let me get dressed, and I'll be right out."

"Okay."

She hurried to her bedroom and threw on a pair of jeans and a burgundy sweater. When she returned, Gage was perched on the edge of the couch, wringing his hands. He stood up as soon as she entered the room.

"Allison, I'm sorry."

"Don't worry about it. I'm ready now." She dismissed his apology with a wave of her hand and dug in her purse for her keys. When she turned back to Gage, he had a pleading look in his eyes.

He crossed the room to stand in front of her. "Not for that. I mean…I am sorry I got here so early, but…" He sighed and took her hand. "I wanted to apologize for the way I acted this morning. I was out of line."

"It's okay."

"No. No, it's not. You were right. I should've been happy for you. I *am* happy for you, and I'm sorry for making things uncomfortable between us. Can you forgive me?"

She put her hand on his cheek. "There's nothing to forgive. I'm the one who should apologize for leading you on."

"No. You were just being you. You're kind, caring, and sweet, and you're like that with everyone. I was hoping we could forget I ever said anything and go back to being buddies."

"Of course we can."

He exhaled sharply and nodded. "Are you ready for this?"

"I am."

"Then, let's do it… Oh, do you have a blindfold?"

"Right here." She pulled a black velvet sleep mask out of her purse. "But I think I'll wait to put it on until we get in the car."

He chuckled. "Good idea."

They walked side by side through the parking lot, and she shivered in the crisp autumn air.

"Are you cold?" Normally Gage wouldn't have hesitated to wrap his arms around her and warm her up, but now he just looked at her with his hands in his pockets.

"I'm okay. Just had a little chill." She rubbed her hands on her arms and climbed in the car. As she slipped her blindfold over her eyes, all of her other senses sharpened with the loss of her vision, especially her sixth sense. She felt Gage's conflicted emotions and quickly put up a wall between them. She'd already rejected him; she didn't need to be nosing around in his psyche.

As he started the engine and pulled out of the parking lot, she tried to ignore the turns he took. She already knew too much as it was: the owner was male, the ghost was female, and she was hostile toward other women. Allison would have to push those thoughts out of her mind so they didn't sway her perception.

Being a psychic wasn't an exact science, and sometimes outside influences or preconceived notions could affect what she saw in her mind's eye. It had taken years of practice to eliminate her personal feelings from the mix and rely purely on her senses. She breathed deeply and cleared her mind for the job ahead.

"We're here. I'll come around and help you out." Gage slid out of the car and opened Allison's door. This was his favorite part of the hunt, she remembered. He loved watching her work, being her anchor. Of course, now she knew it was more than that for him. She sighed and took his hand.

They walked across the yard, and leaves crunched beneath her feet with each careful step. Gage stopped and put his arm around her shoulders.

"We're going up some stairs now. Five steps, okay?"

She nodded and began the climb, trusting Gage to guide her. When they reached the top, familiarity swirled through her senses, and she put her hand on his chest to steady herself. "I've been here before."

"Do you know where you are?"

"No, but I know I've been here."

"Well, try to push it out of your mind and put up your shields because we're going in."

Richard mumbled something into his walkie and turned to Logan. "Our psychic's here. She'll be blindfolded when she comes in, and it's important that you don't speak until she takes it off."

"Why is she blindfolded?"

"So she's not affected by any outside influences. Your ghost is strong, and if she's going to clear it out, she needs to be able to connect with it. She has no idea where she is or who you are, and we need to keep it that way."

"All right." He shrugged. "Just tell me what you need me to do."

"For now, we just need you to be here. We wore the ghost out provoking it, so it's weak. It used up its energy banging around and throwing stuff at Lindsay, but it's attracted to you, so we need you to be in the room." Richard spoke into his walkie again. "Bring her in, Gage."

The front door opened, and Allison stepped in, wrapped in Gage's arms. Logan's heart stood still for a beat or two before slamming into his chest. *She* was their medium. *Shit.* How could he be so stupid? He should have known. He started to call out to her, but a sharp look from Richard stopped him short.

They walked into the living room, and Logan felt Gage's affinity for Allison. *She* was the one he went on about in the van. She was the one who had won his admiration and maybe a little more. Allison was the one Gage wanted.

Fuck.

Jealousy twisted in his gut as he watched Gage lead Allison around the house. The way she held on to him. The way she trusted him. She never flinched as they explored Logan's living room, like this was something they did all the time. He took a deep breath to steady himself. This probably *was* something they did all the time. They worked together.

Gage mentioned he knew Allison was spoken for. Did she not tell him whom she was dating?

"I can't shake this feeling that I've been here before," Allison said. "It's stronger now that we're inside."

Gage glanced at Logan for confirmation, but he stared back blankly. Could Allison sense him? Could she figure out where she was on her own?

"What do you want to do?" Gage asked. "Do you want to know where you are, or do you want to talk to the ghost first?"

"I'll try talking to the ghost first." She took a step away from Gage and reached out for his hand. Gripping him tightly, she inhaled a deep breath and let it out slowly.

"Whoa. It's definitely female. She's strong too. She doesn't want me to be here. 'Alex…Alex is mine…' Oh, God." She covered her mouth as she began to sway.

Gage pulled her close. "What is it? What do you see?"

"She killed herself. Okay, I need to stop for a minute." She pressed her fingers to her temples as she leaned into Gage, and he rubbed her back, making the jealousy wring Logan's insides even tighter.

"It's okay, sweetheart. Just take your time." Gage's voice was soft and full of concern.

Allison pulled away from him with a laugh, and Logan reached out to read her. He had to know if she had feelings for this guy. All he sensed from her was a nervous awkwardness.

"I'm okay. Did her husband cheat on her?" She didn't wait for an answer. "He did. Many times, and she killed herself. He didn't love her."

"That's exactly right," Richard said.

"And she thinks the owner is her Alex. She hasn't been aggressive to the owner, has she? No. She still loves him. She still loves Alex."

Well, shit. The ghost thought he was Alex.

Wait… Alex. The woman in white diving out the window. Could that be what his vision was about? *No. Hell no.* That was crazy. He'd had the dreams long before he moved into the place.

"What's over here?" Allison moved toward the stairs, and Gage grabbed her elbow to guide her.

"It's a staircase." He put her hand on the rail and let her go.

As soon as she touched the wooden railing, she stiffened. "Oh my God...Logan?" She pulled the blindfold off and turned around, blinking as her eyes adjusted to the light. "Logan…"

"Allison." He hesitated but then walked toward her and took her hand.

"Why didn't you tell me? I would have helped sooner if I'd known it was you." She leaned into him, resting her head against his chest.

He took a deep breath and exhaled sharply. "I'm sorry. I should have told you. God knows I've told you everything else, but I was embarrassed."

She cradled his face in her hands. "It's nothing to be ashamed of. The ghost was already here when you bought the house. I saw her at your party."

"You saw her? The ghost?"

"Yes. I thought she was a person. She was sitting on the stairs, right here, and she was crying, devastated. I tried to console her, but she disappeared. That's when I left. Her emotions overwhelmed me, and I had to get out."

"That's why you were so upset that night? Why didn't you tell me about the ghost?"

"You never mentioned it, so I didn't think it bothered you. There are spirits everywhere. I block them out most of the time, and they usually don't mess with anyone. I didn't want to freak you out if she hadn't made her presence known."

Gage looked back and forth between Allison and

Logan. "Wait a minute. *Logan* is your new boyfriend? The one you said you—"

"Yep. This is him." She flashed Gage a sharp look.

"Aw, hell." Gage shook his head and walked away.

"You didn't tell me you were a ghost buster." Logan tucked a piece of hair behind Allison's ear.

"A ghost buster?" She laughed. "I haven't done it in a long time, but I think it's something we're going to have to talk about later. Richard is getting impatient."

The leader of DAPS stared at them with his arms crossed over his chest. "Are you two lovebirds ready to get rid of this ghost or what?"

Allison smirked. "Excuse me, Richard, for having a personal life. I'm ready now." She walked into the living room and sat on the sofa. "Gage, are you ready?"

He took a deep breath, sighed, and shook his head. "Yeah. I'm ready." He sat on the couch next to Allison and took her hand. Richard and Lindsay stood across from them with video and audio recorders ready, while Logan sat in a chair adjacent to the sofa.

He wrung his hands and stared at his girlfriend holding another man's hand. Why hadn't she shared this part of herself with him? She was nervous; he was sure of that, and maybe a little scared to call on the ghost again. But why? He wanted to comfort her, to be the one holding her hand and helping her with her gift.

He tried to read her again. He wanted so badly to know how she was feeling, but the tension in the room was high, and he couldn't single her out. Everyone was nervous. Had something gone wrong before? Was that why she hadn't done this in a long time? With all the electric stabs of anxiety pricking at his skin and the heavy feeling of worry weighing down the room, that was all it could be.

"Is there anything you need me to do, Allison?" Logan asked.

"Just be here. Lily is attracted to you. Actually, she's standing right next to you."

He jerked his head to one side and then the other, but he didn't see anything. "What the hell? Where?"

Gage laughed. "I told you, man."

He settled back into his chair as Allison closed her eyes and took a few deep breaths.

"Lily, why are you still here? This isn't your home anymore." Allison went deathly still as she communicated with the spirit that no one else could see or hear. Logan watched her face as a myriad of emotions flashed across her features. She was in another place, on another plane, and all he felt in her place was emptiness. The tension in the room built as Allison sat in utter stillness and silence, and Logan's heart dropped as he tried again to reach out to her and found nothing but a void.

Gage squeezed her hand. "What are you getting, Allison? Is she talking to you?"

Allison took a shaky breath and wiped a single tear from her cheek. "She loved him so much. She blames herself. If only she had been more supportive. Oh, Lily. It's not your fault."

Tears streamed from Allison's closed eyes, and Logan rose to comfort her.

Gage put up his hand to stop him. "She'll be okay. Let her work through it."

He cursed under his breath. Gage was the expert, but Allison belonged to *him*. He sat on the edge of his chair and clenched his fists as she cried.

"She couldn't take it anymore. He was so callous. He took them. He took the women in her own bedroom while she was in the house. Oh, God. She jumped out of the window at the top of the stairs." Allison trembled as she relayed Lily's emotions, and no one seemed to notice her pain. No one said a word as she sobbed into her hands. Gage rubbed her back, and Richard and Lindsay just stood there recording it all. Logan couldn't stand it anymore.

"That's enough." He knelt in front of her, resting his hands on her thighs, squeezing them gently. "Allison? Allison, it's Logan. Come back to me."

She opened her eyes and gazed at him with a feral look he'd never seen before. He sat back on his heels and reached out to read her again, but he still felt emptiness.

"Alex." She took his face in her hands. "I love you."

I love you too. He bit back the words. No matter how badly he wanted to believe she meant it, he knew it wasn't her. The look in her eyes… They weren't Allison's kind, soft eyes; they were wild and pained.

"What?" He pulled her hands away from his face and held them tight.

"She's channeling, man. It's not Allison." Gage put his hand on her shoulder.

"I love you. Doesn't that mean anything to you? Damn it, I'm your wife, Alex. Don't you love me?"

His breath caught, and he stared at her wide-eyed. It suddenly all made sense. The vision. The two versions of Allison. She was channeling the spirit of Lily. The spirit who took her own life by diving out of a window, just like in his dream.

"No." He stood and shook his head, wiping his hands on his pants. "No. I don't love you, Lily. You have to leave me alone. I'm not Alex." It couldn't be happening. All those years, all the steps he'd taken, all the joy he denied himself to avoid this moment was for nothing. He looked into Lily's untamed eyes and searched for Allison. She had to be in there somewhere. "Allison. I'm with you, Allison. Come back to me."

"Oh, God!" She covered her mouth as she leaped to her feet and ran toward the stairs.

"Allison! No! She's going for the window!" Logan flew over the back of the couch and raced toward her, catching her by the arm when she was halfway up the staircase. "Come back, Allison." He pulled her to his chest and stroked her hair. "Allison. Please."

She inhaled a deep, shuddering breath and blinked at him. "Logan? I…"

"You were about to jump out the window. You…" He closed his eyes. This was his fault. It was selfish of him to get close to her when he knew the consequences it would bring. He'd put her life in danger, and he would never forgive himself for that. "You have to leave. Gage, get her out of here."

His heart shattered as he said the words, but he couldn't think of any other way. His vision was literal. Allison was going to jump out the window, and the only way he knew to stop her was to send her away. As long as the ghost existed, she'd never be safe.

"This is why we can't be together. I won't risk your life to make myself happy." She had to go before Lily got inside her head again and she could never come back.

"Logan, we can work it out. We'll send her away." Fresh tears streamed down her face as she pleaded with him. They were Allison's tears this time, and it tore him apart.

He held her by the shoulders and looked into her eyes. "It's not worth it. I won't have you dying over me."

"I'm not going to die."

"Don't you see? My vision…the two versions of you? It's Lily. I saw you jump out the window in my dreams. It's *going* to happen if you stay with me."

"No."

"It will. It's already started. I'm sorry, Allison. It's better if you never see me again."

"Please don't do this."

She loved him. He knew without a doubt she did, and he was sending her out the door. But what else could he do? The ghost would follow him wherever he went. This was his curse to bear, and she wasn't safe with him. "Please, Allison. Just go."

She swayed on the steps, and Gage grabbed her arm to steady her. All her pain slipped into the void as Lily returned.

"Alex, I love you."

"Get out of my house."

She burst into tears and clutched Gage's chest. "He doesn't love me." Was she Allison again? Or was she still Lily? Allison's energy battled with the spirit's for control, the light and the nothingness spiraling inside her.

She blinked up at Gage and shook her head. "Gage?"

"Come on, Allison. There are plenty of us who do love you. Let's get you home." He held her close to his chest and glared at Logan as he led her down the stairs. Allison swayed again and tried to tear away from Gage's embrace.

"Alex! Don't do this!"

"Shit. She's still channeling." Gage patted her face as he led her out the door. "Come on, Allison. Leave Lily here where she belongs."

CHAPTER NINETEEN

The second she left the house, Allison sucked in a sharp breath and came back to herself. Drained, both emotionally and physically, she nearly collapsed in Gage's arms as she stumbled down the front steps. He swept her up and carried her the rest of the way to the car.

"Are you okay?" He slid her into the passenger seat and buckled the seatbelt around her.

"Not really. I just got dumped." She choked back a sob.

He let out a cynical laugh and shut her door before slipping into the driver's seat and starting the engine. "What about the spirit? You're not bringing her with you, are you?"

She wrapped her arms around herself and pulled her knees to her chest. "No, she's attached to the house. God, Gage. What happened? I shouldn't have lost control like that."

"Come on. You and I both know what happened. You're in love with the guy. You were too close to the situation, and your own feelings mixed in with the crazy ghost's. What did you expect to happen?"

"I didn't expect I'd try to jump out the window. And I didn't expect him to dump me." She fought back the tears that welled in her eyes.

Gage rubbed her arm. "I'm sorry, but you know what? You're better off without him. You don't need a coward who's going to run as soon as the water gets a little too hot. What an asshole. I'm surprised you went for him at all."

Just a week ago, she thought the same thing about Logan, but that was before she knew him. He certainly wasn't an asshole. A coward, maybe, but deep down, who wasn't? She had been running from her fears for years, so who was she to judge? But if it was just the ghost issue, they could work it out. She could get rid of Lily if she prepared for it, and now she knew what to expect.

Then again, maybe it was more than that. Maybe Logan was using the ghost as an excuse. An easy way out because things were getting too serious between them. Maybe he decided he preferred the one-and-done lifestyle. So many tangled emotions twisted through her heart, she didn't know what to believe anymore.

"I'm so tired. Lily drained me."

Gage rested a hand on her thigh, then jerked it away. "Sorry." He gripped the steering wheel. "How are you holding up emotionally? Lily had some intense feelings. Are you okay?"

"That part of me is fine. It's my own broken heart I have to deal with now."

The muscles in his jaw flexed as he ground his teeth.

"Really, Gage. It's not going to be like last time. I'll be

fine. Will you do me a favor and call Tina for me? I don't want to be alone tonight."

"I could…" He let out a sharp breath. "Yeah. I'll call her."

She fought to keep her heavy lids open. There had to be a way she could convince Logan of her safety. She'd gone far too deep with him to give up so easily. Resting her head on her arms, she let the rhythmic hum of the tires on the road lull her to sleep.

When she came to, she rubbed her eyes and sat up in bed. Gage must have carried her in.

"Good morning, sunshine." Tina padded into the room and handed her a cup of tea.

"Is it morning already?" She sipped the warm liquid. Chamomile with honey. Her favorite.

Tina sat on the edge of the bed. "Well, it's after midnight, so technically, yes. And I just really like saying that."

"Where's Gage?"

"He's still here, worrying about you. I told him I had it under control, but he insisted on staying until you woke up."

"Logan?"

She patted her hand. "Haven't heard from him. Gage told me what happened. I'm so sorry, Allie."

Allison sniffled, and fresh tears spilled from her eyes as she set the mug on the nightstand. Doubling over, she wrapped her arms around herself and curled onto her side. "Why did I let myself fall in love with him? I should have known." She sobbed into her pillow, her heart wrenching in pain.

"How could you have known?"

"I'm psychic, remember?"

Tina laughed. "You know it doesn't work that way; don't be so hard on yourself. He seemed like a great guy. I probably would have fallen for him too, the way you described him. He got scared. Who knows? Maybe he'll come around."

"Allison?" Gage stood tentatively in the doorway.

"Not now, Gage," Allison said between sobs.

"Give her a few minutes," Tina said. "This is personal. Girl stuff."

"All right. I'll be in the living room if you need me." Gage shuffled out the door and closed it behind him.

"What am I going to do? I love him, and if the ghost is the only issue, I know we can work it out. I just…God, Tina. I love Logan." She squeezed her eyes tight and choked on another round of sobs.

"I'll tell you what you're going to do. Right now, you're going to sleep. That little adventure drained you, and you're white as a sheet. So you're going to go to sleep, and then tomorrow you're going to march your happy butt over to his house, and you're going to tell him how you feel."

"I can't do that."

"Why not? What have you got to lose? Go tell him you love him, and see what he says. If he doesn't love you, then you'll get on with your life and forget about him. But you'll never know unless you try."

She sighed and pulled the covers up to her chin. "I'll think about it."

"Sleep on it."

Tina was right. She had nothing to lose by telling Logan how she felt. Her heart had already been ripped out of her chest. All he could do was stomp on it.

"That's the last of our gear, so we'll be getting out of your hair." Richard picked up a camera case and shook Logan's hand.

He handed him a ten thousand dollar check and opened the door.

Richard's eyes widened. "This is double what we talked about before."

"I didn't realize how much work went into it. You guys earned it. Thanks for your help." He opened the door wider, hoping he'd take the hint and leave. The curiosity and pity emanating from Richard compounded the nauseating effect of his own emotions whirling around in his head.

"Well, if there's anything else we can do for you." Richard started to walk out the door.

"Is Allison the only psychic you work with?" Whether she was going to be in his life or not, he still wanted the ghost out of his house.

Richard gave him a sympathetic look. "Honestly? We've worked with others, but Allison is the only one who can clear out an energy this strong. She's special." Richard slapped him on the shoulder and gave him a squeeze for emphasis. "Take care, Logan."

Shit.

He closed the door and turned to face his empty house. What did he just do? He broke up with the only woman who had ever taken the time to get to know him, possibly the only woman who ever loved him. What the hell was his problem?

He stormed through the living room toward the kitchen, needing something to get his mind off the way he just fucked up the only relationship he'd ever had. He opened his neatly organized fridge and scanned the labels of the Tupperware containers, but food was the last thing on his mind. He cursed and slammed the door shut.

He was letting that fucking vision ruin his life. It had been ruining his life for the past seven years. He stomped back to the living room, intent on reorganizing his paperback collection yet again, but he stopped with his hand on the cabinet. Maybe Allison's meditation would help him. Maybe he could stop the thoughts before they spun too far out of control.

He sat on the couch and closed his eyes, breathing deeply and imagining the light like Allison taught him. He relaxed, and for a moment, his mind focused, his thoughts becoming clear.

Breaking up with Allison was a mistake. Everyone else had faith that she could take care of his ghost, so why didn't he?

Because he was a fucking idiot.

He wouldn't let her jump out that window, no matter what happened. He'd nail it shut. Hell, he'd sell the house. Maybe the ghost was attached to the structure and not to him, so he could still be with her. He'd do whatever it took to get Allison back. He shot to his feet and headed for the door. He'd apologize and beg for her forgiveness.

But it was one o'clock in the morning. He couldn't show up at her apartment this late. Gage had taken her home, and she was probably asleep. He might even still be there, comforting her. If he put his hands on her... But what if she initiated it? What if she was so shaken up, and she knew how he felt about her… What if she wanted his comfort?

Shit!

What would he do if Allison turned to Gage because he'd broken her heart? With a groan, he threw open the doors to his paperback collection and swiped all the books off the shelves and onto the floor. He looked at the mess on the rug, and his fingers twitched with the need to organize it. To bring order back to the chaos. He fell to his knees and picked up a title.

"You know what? Fuck it."

He hurled the book against the wall and high-tailed it out the door before he could change his mind. He knew where he was going, though he didn't know what he was going to do when he got there. Driving almost on autopilot, he paid attention to nothing but the inward battle in his mind. He wanted Allison. He *needed* her, and he had to have faith they could make it despite his visions.

Gage's Jeep still sat in the parking lot, and Logan exhaled a curse. He didn't think twice when he got out of the car and sprinted up the steps to Allison's door. He raised his hand to knock, but a sickening feeling twisted in his gut. What if she were in his arms right now? He couldn't bear to see that.

Hell. He turned to leave, but he hesitated when he heard laughter coming from inside the apartment. He stepped closer to the door, listening to the muffled voices on the other side. It was a man and a woman, but the woman didn't sound at all upset. And she didn't sound at all like Allison.

He tapped lightly on the door, and the laughter stopped as someone turned the knob to answer it.

Gage opened the door a crack, and his cold stare landed on Logan. "What do you want?"

"I need to see Allison."

"She's asleep. Why don't you go home and let the

people who love her take care of her?" Gage pushed the door shut, but Logan put up his hand to stop it.

He took a deep breath and exhaled sharply. "God damn it. I do love her." A smile tugged at his lips as a heavy weight seemed to lift from his shoulders. "I'm in love with her."

Gage cocked an eyebrow and opened the door halfway.

"Would you let the man inside?" Tina grabbed the knob and swung it open, pulling Logan in. "I knew you'd come back. She's in her bedroom. Don't wake her up, though. She's drained."

He carefully opened the bedroom door and stood in the threshold. Allison's hair was matted to her forehead, and her tear-stained cheeks were paler than he'd ever seen.

"I did this to her." Tears welled in his eyes, and he didn't try to hide them. He blinked at Tina. "Is she okay? The ghost…?"

Tina put her arm around his shoulders. "She'll be fine. Believe me, she's been through a lot worse with ghosts. A good night's sleep is all she needs to get over *that*. Getting over you is a different matter."

"Hopefully she won't have to get over me. If she'll have me."

He stepped into the bedroom, and Tina pulled the door shut behind him. A single lamp burning in the corner provided the only light in the room, and he knelt beside the bed as his eyes adjusted to the darkness.

He brushed her hair out of her face and leaned down to place a kiss on her cheek. She stirred with his touch and pulled his hand to her chest, a small smile curving her lips.

"I'm so sorry." His voice was a whisper as he watched

the peaceful rise and fall of her chest. She was so precious. So beautiful and kind. He would never hurt her again. Ever. "I was afraid the ghost would harm you if I didn't push you away, but I didn't mean it. I didn't want to… I'm sorry. I love you, Allison."

Her lids fluttered open, and she gazed at him with a sleepy smile. "I love you too. I know we can make this work. I can get rid of her for you. I…"

"Shh…" He put a finger to her lips. "We'll figure it out. Can you forgive me?"

"Yes. Of course I can."

"God, I love you."

She tightened her grip on his hand. "Stay the night with me. I want you to hold me."

"I would love to hold you all night. I'll tell Tina and Gage they can go."

"Gage is still here?"

"He's worried about you. You know he has feelings for you, right?"

She sighed and ran her fingers through his hair, resting her hand on the back of his neck. "Yes, I do, and he knows I am in love with you."

He kissed her on the cheek. "Give me a sec, and then I'll hold you."

He opened the bedroom door to the inquisitive stares of Tina and Gage. "Allison asked me to stay the night, so you guys can go home."

Tina smiled and took Gage by the hand. "Come on. Let's go say our goodbyes."

She pulled Gage into the bedroom and gave Allison a hug. "I told you he'd come around."

"Yes, you did."

"Are you sure you're okay?" Gage squeezed her hand.

"I'm fine. Go home and get some sleep. And thank you. Both of you."

Tina hugged Logan and whispered in his ear, "No hanky panky tonight. She needs to rest."

He chuckled. "Yes, ma'am."

Gage approached and shook his hand. "Take good care of her. She's a special girl."

"I know. I won't hurt her again."

With Tina and Gage out of the apartment, Logan locked the front door and returned to the bedroom. He stripped down to his boxer-briefs, folded his clothes, and stacked them on the dresser. Sliding under the covers, he wrapped his arms around Allison and pulled her to his chest.

His heart raced as he lay there with her. He was in love with Allison, and nothing in the world would change that. Love was more powerful than fear. He knew that now, and they would work through conquering his vision together.

CHAPTER TWENTY

*L*ogan woke at nine a.m. and lay in bed watching Allison sleep. She looked so peaceful; the pink flush had returned to her cheeks, and her breathing was slow and rhythmic. He could have stayed in bed with her all day, but his mind drifted back to the nagging mess of books he left on his living room floor the night before. He couldn't leave it like that. He'd have to go home and clean it up to put his mind at ease.

Besides, he didn't have a change of clothes here, and God knew he couldn't wear his dirty ones all day. He could handle putting them back on to get home now, as long as he could take a hot shower as soon as he walked in his front door. He propped his head on his hand and chewed his bottom lip. What should he do?

He could run home and come right back. Spend the day with Allison. But he didn't want to leave while she was asleep. He'd have to wait until she woke up so he could tell her his plans. She didn't need to feel abandoned again, but how long would she sleep? She was so drained from that damn ghost last night. This was his fault, and he was going to take care of her.

He slipped out of bed, careful not to wake her, and shrugged into his clothes. His skin crawled at the dirty feeling of the soiled cotton, but he put it out of his mind and slipped into the living room to call Trent.

"I'm not coming in today. Can you hold down the fort for me?" he whispered into his phone.

"Sure. No problem. Everything okay?"

"It is now." He told Trent about last night, the ghost, and Allison. He even told him about the vision and how it played a part in it all.

"Shit, Logan. I don't know what to say. You got it all worked out now, though?"

"I hope so. I'm going to sell the house. She says she can get rid of the ghost, but I don't want to put her through that again. With any luck, the spirit will stay put, and we can move on."

"I hear you. Do what you have to do. I'm glad she's okay."

"Me too."

He hung up and called the antique shop. Allison usually went to work at eight, so Lucia would be wondering where she was. He told her what happened and about his plans to keep Allison home and take care of her.

"I think that's a marvelous idea," she said. "She has a couple of appointments today, but I will call them and reschedule for her."

"Lucia, you're the best."

"Thank you for taking such good care of her. She needs someone like you."

He shook his head. He was the reason she was in this situation.

With work taken care of, he crept back to the bedroom and found Allison sitting up in bed.

"Are you leaving?" She looked at him with worry in her eyes as she fidgeted with the sheets. He sat on the bed next to her and took her in his arms.

"I am, but I'm coming right back. I need to go home and change and take care of a few things. Then I'm going to spend the day with you. I already called Lucia, and she's rescheduling your appointments. I took the day off too."

Allison took a deep breath and gazed into his eyes. "Thank you. Last night seemed so surreal, I wasn't sure it actually happened. And I wondered if you really meant…"

"I love you. Is that what you were wondering?"

"Yes. It was."

"Well, I do. I love you with all my heart. I just need to run home, because I have this thing about wearing dirty clothes, and I can't…"

"It's okay." She stroked his cheek. "Next time, maybe you should pack a bag."

"I should. Are you going to be okay if I leave? Are you feeling better?"

"Much better."

"I'll be back in an hour. Call me if you need me."

"I will."

He slipped out the door and headed to his house, scratching at his chest the entire drive. He was going to break out in a rash if he didn't get these dirty clothes off fast. Pulling the car into the garage, he cut the engine. It was irrational. He knew that, but he couldn't stop his mind from making his body itch like he was covered in ant bites.

He swung open the front door and stopped in the foyer, his mind reeling with indecision. Which was a more pressing issue: the shower or cleaning up the mess on the living room floor? It could take him hours to organize that mess, and he told Allison he'd be right back. If he went for straight alphabetical again, he could probably get it done in thirty minutes. Especially since he wasn't having an episode. He'd go for the shower first. If he was clean and didn't have any distractions, he could be in and out of his house in forty-five minutes.

He darted up the stairs and went through his cleansing rituals in record speed with no sign from Lily. Hopefully she was still drained of energy from her little show the night before and he wouldn't have to mess with the spirit this morning. He got dressed and headed back downstairs to clean up his mess.

The central heat kicked on as he entered the living room, filling the house with that musty, first-time-of-the-season heater smell as he stacked the books on the shelves and lost himself to the routine. It was so familiar and comforting that his mind instantly cleared and the rest of the world slipped away. Even at his quick pace, he was focused, and the methodology of cleaning and organizing soothed his mind into an almost hypnotic state. A beeping sounded from somewhere far away, but he ignored it as he hurried through the routine.

At the halfway point, he lost his focus. His body felt sluggish, his movements becoming lethargic as the books grew heavier. It pained him to lift them, and it felt like he was moving in slow motion. He was tired…so tired…he couldn't sit up anymore.

He needed to move. To get out of the house. If he could make it to the front door—it was already open. Hadn't he closed it? He tried to stand, pushing off the carpet, but his arms gave out underneath him. He crumpled to the floor, his weakened muscles useless, his breathing labored.

He reached for his cell phone, pulling it from his pocket, but it slipped out of his grasp as darkness enveloped him. He couldn't move. He couldn't see. All he wanted to do was sleep.

Adrenaline raced through Allison's veins as she showered and got ready for Logan's return. She couldn't remember a time when she'd ever been happier. Her body felt rejuvenated; no effects from her energy-draining experience last night lingered, and she knew Logan was the reason. She danced around her bedroom, getting dressed, and her phone rang just as she finished her hair and makeup.

"Is he still there?" Tina's hushed voice held a tinge of excitement.

"No, but he's coming back. And guess what? He loves me!"

"I know!"

They squealed in unison like a couple of teenagers. Not the most mature way for almost-thirty-year-old women to act, sure, but she didn't care.

"He's skipping work today because he thinks he needs to take care of me."

"Well, you better let him."

"Oh, I am."

After a few more words of sisterly advice from her

friend, Allison hung up the phone and changed the sheets on her bed. Mascara streaks stained her pillowcase from the crying she'd done last night, and it was time to put their misunderstanding behind them. She busied herself cleaning up for another thirty minutes, waiting for him to arrive, and a sinking sensation formed in her stomach as she glanced at the clock. He said he'd only be gone an hour, but it had been an hour and a half.

She would give him another fifteen minutes before she called. Whatever he had to do probably took longer than he expected. Flipping on the television, she settled on the sofa and watched the local news. Fires, murder, robberies. It was enough to turn a sane person into a recluse.

She turned it off and looked at the clock. Where could he be? Almost two hours had passed, and the sinking sensation in her stomach turned into a hollow pit. Something was wrong. She tried to dismiss it as paranoia, but the feeling grew more and more intense as time passed. She called his cell phone but only got his voicemail. She left a message and drummed her nails on the coffee table.

Allison knew better than to ignore her instincts now, so she picked up her purse and keys and headed out the door. Maybe he lost track of time. Maybe she'd find him working in his office or cleaning up. *I hope.*

She climbed into her Toyota and took a few deep breaths to clear her mind. Something was definitely wrong. The hollow feeling bore deeper into her core, and she threw the car into drive, heading straight for Logan's house.

Everything looked normal when she pulled into his driveway. The garage was open, his car inside. She parked behind it and walked around to the front door. Her heart dropped when she found it ajar. She hurried up the steps, and the squealing sound of an alarm grew louder as she approached. Throwing the door fully open, she raced inside.

Allison gasped when she found Logan lying on the floor in a pile of books, and she ran to him, kneeling by his side. "Logan!" She put her hand on his chest, focusing on the shallow rise and fall of his ribs. He was breathing, but barely.

The alarm continued to squeal from the kitchen, and she ran to see what it was. "Carbon monoxide. Oh my God. Logan!"

She raced back to the living room. "We have to get you outside." She tried to get him to move, but he lay unconscious on the floor. "Oh, Logan. Come on. You have to get up." He was one-hundred-eighty pounds of solid muscle; there was no way she could carry him out. "Logan!" She shook him. She patted his face. Nothing. "Oh my God."

She slid her arms beneath his and clasped them on his chest, pulling with all her might. Somehow, she was able to move him. It would only be a matter of minutes before the invisible gas got to her, and they'd both be as good as dead, but she found the strength to drag him to the porch. Safely outside, she collapsed on his chest and kicked the front door shut.

She pressed her fingers to his neck and hovered her ear above his mouth. Weak pulse, shallow breathing, but he was still alive. He had a chance. She called 911 and did her best to help him while she waited for an ambulance to arrive.

Even in her frantic state, she centered herself enough to send healing light into him. He needed oxygen, but all she could give him was Reiki. She focused on Logan, acting as a conduit to fill him up with loving, healing energy. Hot tears streamed down her cheeks as she gave him everything she had.

Within minutes, the paramedics arrived. They hooked him up to an oxygen tank and loaded him into the ambulance. The EMT offered Allison a hand, and she took it, climbing into the back of the vehicle with Logan.

"How long has he been in there?" the EMT asked.

"I don't know. About two hours, maybe. The front door was open when I got here, and I found him on the living room floor."

He arched an eyebrow. "And you dragged him out? All by yourself?"

"I don't know how, but yes." She focused on Logan as she spoke.

The EMT patted her hand. "Adrenaline's an amazing thing. You saved his life."

She covered her mouth as fresh tears streamed down her face. "You mean he's going to be okay?"

"Yeah. See this meter?" The EMT pointed to a number on a screen. "That's his blood oxygen level. I'm surprised it's as high as it is, being exposed for as long as he was, but it's steadily climbing. He's going to be fine."

"Thank you." Allison took Logan's hand and stroked his face. When she leaned down to kiss his cheek, his eyes fluttered open.

"Logan?"

He looked at her, then looked around at the ambulance before he closed them again. He squeezed her hand, and she sobbed. "I love you, Logan."

The EMT gave Allison a sympathetic look. "Are you his wife?"

"No, I'm his girlfriend."

"Does he have any family you could call? A next of kin?"

She looked at Logan as she answered, "They all live in New York. I don't know how to reach them. Oh, wait. I can call his friend. He'll know how to contact them."

Allison dialed Logan's office and asked for Trent. Thankfully, he was there, and she told him what happened. He promised to call Lisa.

When they reached the hospital, the EMT wheeled Logan into the emergency room, and Allison waited in the lobby. She looked around at the people in varying degrees of hurt and illness and shuddered to think that she almost lost him. If she'd trusted her gut to begin with, she would've been there so much sooner. Maybe he would have still been conscious.

The hour in the waiting room felt like an eternity as she waited for news. She couldn't watch TV; she couldn't focus on a magazine. She couldn't even clear her head enough to meditate the time away. Just as she was beginning to go out of her mind, a doctor appeared from behind the doors.

"Are you Ms. Gray?"

"Yes. Is Logan okay?"

"I'm Dr. Williams." He held out his hand, and Allison took it. "Logan is going to be just fine. He's lucky you found him when you did."

Tears filled her eyes, spilling down her cheeks.

"He's awake now. You can go in, but he needs to stay overnight for observation. As long as he keeps improving at the rate he is, he can go home tomorrow morning."

"Thank you." She followed Dr. Williams down a long, twisting hallway to the place where they kept the overnight patients. Logan had a private room, and Allison tapped on the door before she went in.

He lay in bed with a plastic tube draped across his face. It had two openings at his nose, where it supplied him with a constant stream of oxygen. He had an IV in one arm, and a big bag of fluids dripped steadily through. On his other hand, a black plastic claw-like device clamped to his finger to monitor his heart rate and blood oxygen level.

He turned his head when she entered the room, and he gave her a small smile.

"How are you feeling?" she asked.

"Like I've been run over by a train."

"I'm so sorry this happened to you." She sat on the bed and laid her head on his chest. "I thought I lost you. When I found you on the floor, I thought you were dead."

"So did I." He put his arms around her and stroked her hair. "How did you get in the house?"

"The front door was open."

He tilted his head. "That's weird. I'm sure I closed it."

"Maybe Lily opened it."

"Is that possible?"

"She's certainly strong enough."

He hugged her tighter. "I don't want to think about that right now. Thank you for saving me."

"Thank you for not dying." She pulled a tissue out of a box on the table and blotted at her eyes. "I talked to Trent. He's going to call your family."

"I spoke to him right before you came in. He'll take care of the leak too."

"The doctor said you can probably go home tomorrow morning. If the leak isn't fixed by then, you can stay the night with me."

He grinned and rubbed her arm. "Can I stay the night with you even if it is?"

"Of course you can." She laughed. "You were supposed to spend the day taking care of me, and now I'm taking care of you."

"Sorry about that."

"Don't be. I don't mind at all, and I plan on being here until they kick me out. Or until you get sick of me."

"I'll never get sick of you."

"Good, because I don't have anything else to do today. Somebody canceled all my appointments for me." She smiled and patted his cheek.

He took her hand in his and kissed her palm. "Come lie down with me."

"I don't think there's enough room. These beds aren't made for two."

"We'll make room." He slid over, and she climbed onto the mattress. She had to lie on her side, but they both fit. Barely. "There now. Isn't this cozy?" he asked.

"Actually, it is." She laid her head on his shoulder and draped her leg across his. "What does carbon monoxide poisoning feel like?"

"Everything hurts. Like the flu, but a hundred times worse. My head is pounding. I'm exhausted."

"I'm so sorry. Go to sleep. You don't need to stay awake for me. I'm not going anywhere."

He yawned. "Maybe a little nap wouldn't hurt."

She stroked his chest, and he fell asleep within minutes. Closing her eyes, she snuggled into his side. How close she had come to losing him. Her core tightened at the thought, but he was here, alive, and she was with him, feeling the deep rise and fall of his chest as he breathed normally. She let the rhythmic sound of his breaths and the humming of the machinery lull her to sleep by his side.

When she opened her eyes and looked at the clock, three hours had passed. Logan was still sound asleep, so she did some more Reiki healing on him. Hopefully she could ease some of his pain.

She worked on him for a good twenty minutes before she heard the door creak open. Ignoring it, she finished her healing session before turning to acknowledge their guest. "Hi, Trent. He's still asleep."

Trent stepped through the threshold and clicked the door shut. "I see that. I came in about an hour ago, and you were both asleep. How are you holding up?"

"I'm good now. It's been a rough couple of days."

"It'll get better, especially once he sells the house. You won't have to worry about that ghost anymore."

She leaned on the edge of the bed and crossed her arms. "He's going to sell his house? Oh, he can't do that. I can clear out the ghost. I have to. It's personal now."

"You'll have to talk to Logan about that. He wants you to be safe." He sank into a chair in the corner. "Have you eaten anything today? Maybe you should take a break."

She looked at Logan before she met Trent's gaze. "I don't want to leave him alone."

"I'll stay with him. Go ahead. He'll be fine."

"All right. I guess I am a little hungry. I won't be gone long, though."

Trent nodded. "Take your time."

CHAPTER TWENTY-ONE

Logan woke with a start, alone in his hospital bed. He lay still for a moment, waiting for the pounding headache to slam against his skull, but it never came. He tentatively stretched his legs. The achiness was gone. Taking a deep breath, he pushed the button on his bed to make him sit up.

"Allison?" He rubbed his eyes and tried to focus on the person in the room with him.

"She's taking a break. She hasn't left your side all day." Trent lounged in a chair in the corner of the room. He flipped through an issue of *Cosmopolitan* and laughed. "And women gripe about *our* reading material being trashy." He dropped the magazine on a table and stood.

"How are you doing? That was one close call."

"Tell me about it." Logan glanced at the clock. "How long have I been out?"

"A few hours. How do you feel?"

"Better. A lot better, actually." He straightened his spine and rearranged the sheets to cover his lap. The thin hospital gown barely reached his knees. "How'd I get this thing on?"

"You know nurses. They're always trying to get us naked." Trent chuckled and sat on the edge of the bed. "What was Allison doing to you? When I came in, she had her hands on your chest, and she didn't even notice me. She moved around your body, touching you and taking deep breaths. It was kinda creepy to watch."

"That's how she heals; she does something with energy and passes it into you." He smiled, his heart warming at the thought of her caring for him. "That must be why I feel so much better."

Trent looked at his hands for a moment and licked his lips. Logan felt his friend's confusion, and he saw it in his eyes when Trent looked at him. "And it works? She lays her hands on you, and you're healed? Like magic?"

"Not exactly. She can't cure diseases; she just helps get your energy flowing right so your body can heal itself. I don't know how it works, but it does. She helped me get through one of my episodes the other day."

"Really?" Trent raised an eyebrow.

"Yeah, man. I was losing it fast, and she put her hands on me and told me to breathe. A few minutes later, I was fine."

"You're a lucky man."

"I know."

"Your mom's trying to get out here, but she couldn't get a flight till this evening."

He rubbed his hand across his forehead. "She doesn't need to come all the way out here. You told her I was fine, didn't you?"

"Yeah, but you know how your mom is. She's worried

about her baby boy." Trent smiled and pinched Logan on the cheek.

"Bite me."

"Hey, how about a little appreciation? I've got a contractor taking care of your leak. It should be done by tomorrow afternoon, and I brought you some clothes and your cell." Trent handed Logan the phone.

"Thanks. I appreciate it."

"That's more like it. Now, you better call your mom before she gets on that plane."

"You're right." He dialed his mom's number and prayed she would answer. "Hey, Mom."

"Logan! I'm so sorry I'm not there yet. I couldn't book a flight until this evening, but I'll be there as soon as I can. How are you, sweetheart? Trent told me all about it."

"I'm fine, Mom. Listen, you really don't need to come all the way out here. I'm going home in the morning, so there's no sense in you making the trip for nothing. The doctor says I'm fine."

"Nonsense, honey! You're going to need someone to take care of you. You'll have to take it easy for a few days."

"Mom, it's okay. I have someone to take care of me."

"Who? Trent? Honey, I know he's your best friend, but you're going to need some TLC."

He sighed and rolled his eyes. "No, not Trent. I have a girlfriend. Her name's Allison."

Silence hung on the other end of the line as Logan's mother processed what she heard. "You…have a girlfriend? Since when? And why didn't you tell me?"

"It's new; we haven't been together for very long, but she's amazing. You'll love her. Lisa does."

"What? Lisa knew about her before your own mother?

Well, you'll have to bring her to New York, so I can meet her."

"I will, Mom. Soon."

"Before Thanksgiving. We don't want to overwhelm her with the whole family the first time she meets us. You know how your Uncle Jim can be."

He chuckled. "Okay. Before Thanksgiving. I promise."

They exchanged a few more *I love yous* before Logan hung up the phone and glared at Trent's smirk. "I don't want to hear it."

Trent raised his hands in a show of innocence. "What? I wasn't going to say a word. In fact, I'm jealous. I wish I had that many women looking out for me."

"That many women?"

"Well, yeah. You've always had your mom and Lisa, and now you have Allison too. You've got it made."

He'd never thought of it that way. With so many people who wanted to use him, sometimes it was easy to forget about the people who actually cared about him. He was lucky.

"Hey, boys. I hope I'm not interrupting." Allison slipped through the door, balancing three paper cups in her hands. "The nurse said it was okay if you had some coffee." She handed a cup to Trent and one to Logan before she sat on the bed.

Yeah, he was damn lucky. He took a sip of the warm, bitter liquid and pulled Allison into his arms. "I missed you."

"I missed you too. How are you feeling?"

"Much better now. Thanks to you, I hear."

Endearing color flushed her cheeks, a shy smile curving her lips as she glanced at Trent and turned her gaze toward Logan. "I did what I could. I'm glad you're feeling better."

She leaned down to kiss him, and her mouth lingered over his. Her breath warmed his lips, and even with the oxygen blowing up his nose and the beeping monitors in the background, she still managed to get him worked up.

Trent cleared his throat. "It looks like you two have things under control here, so I'll head out."

Allison smiled and turned her head. "Bye, Trent."

When the door clicked shut, she got off the bed and closed the mini blinds that separated his private room from the nurses' station. "Now, where were we?" She rested her hands on his stomach. "Oh, yeah. Now I remember."

She kissed him again, sending blood rushing to his groin. If he wasn't hooked up to so many damn contraptions, he'd have taken her right there in the hospital bed.

She slid her hand down his leg and grinned as she glided it up to his hip. "You're not wearing anything under this gown, are you?"

He chuckled. "I think the nurse just wanted to see me naked."

"I can't say I blame her."

"Yeah, but now look what you've done. How am I going to hide *that* when they come in to check on me?" He nodded to the rise in the sheets.

She bit her bottom lip and arched a brow. "I would love to help you out with that problem, but, considering they're constantly monitoring your vitals, I better not. It would be easier to explain the tent you've made than a sudden spike in your heart rate."

He chuckled. "True. What a shame."

"I know. I hate to waste a good tent."

"You and me both." He let out a contented sigh and closed his eyes, unable to remember a time in his life when he'd ever been happier. He was in love with the most wonderful woman, and she loved him back. He was finally happy with his life. Nothing could spoil his mood. It took a few minutes, but the blood filling his groin finally dissipated, and he relaxed with Allison by his side.

A sharp rap sounded on the door, and he reluctantly opened his eyes. "Come in."

His father's commanding energy washed into the room before the man stepped through the door. "Hi, Logan."

"What are you doing here, Dad?" His tone was sharp, unwelcoming, and he tightened his arm around Allison.

His father stood there wringing his hands as he looked at the floor and then at Logan. "Lisa called me. I already had the jet chartered, so I dropped by to check on you before I head to California."

The muscles in Logan's jaw tensed as he spoke through clenched teeth. "Didn't she also tell you I'm fine, and I'm going home in the morning?"

"Yes, she did, but I wanted to talk to you. I wanted to apologize."

"Maybe I should leave you two alone." Allison started to get up, but he held on to her. He needed her grounding energy. Her support.

"Anything he has to say to me, he can say in front of you."

"I really don't mind waiting outside."

"Please stay." He gave her a pleading look. He didn't want to be alone with his father. No amount of apologies could make up for the way he'd treated Logan and especially the way he'd treated his mother. It was inexcusable; he couldn't stand to face the man alone.

"Okay, I'll stay." She settled back on the edge of the bed and rested a hand on his chest.

"Aren't you going to introduce me to your friend?" his father asked.

"Dad, this is my girlfriend, Allison Gray."

"It's nice to meet you, Mr. Mitchell."

"Please, call me Roger." He started to offer her his hand but let it drop by his side. "I didn't know you had a girlfriend." And why would he? Logan didn't owe the man an explanation.

"You told me you didn't care what the hell I did when I left New York, because once I was gone, I wasn't your son anymore."

His hands clenched into fists. "I made a mistake, and I'm sorry. That's why I came. I wanted to apologize, to mend my ways."

"It's too late for that. Lisa might be able to forgive you for what you've done, but I can't. I won't. You used me, and when I'd had enough of it, you disowned me." He was happy now, damn it, and there was nothing this man could do to take that away from him.

Tears flooded his eyes, and he didn't fight them. Crying in front of his father was surely a sign of weakness to him, but fuck it. He didn't care what the man thought anymore. "I want you to leave. Visiting hours are almost over, and I want to say goodbye to Allison…alone."

He looked at the floor. "All right. I'll go, but think about what I said. I really am sorry…for everything." He stood there and looked at Logan for a moment, but if he was waiting for a response, he wasn't getting one. Logan was finished with the man. His father shuffled out the door and closed it behind him.

Allison held his gaze but said nothing.

"I don't want to talk about it." He sighed and wiped the tears from his face.

"I'm here when you're ready to."

He huffed. "He thinks he can waltz in here, say he's sorry, and everything will be okay. It's not that easy."

She rubbed his shoulder. "I know. It's hard to let go of that much hurt. It takes time."

"Thank you for understanding. Most people don't."

CHAPTER TWENTY-TWO

"Mr. Mitchell." A nurse peeked her head through the door. "Visiting hours are over. Your guest will have to leave now."

Allison squeezed Logan's hand. "Are you okay?"

"I'm fine." The emotions rolling off him clearly said he wasn't, but the stubborn set of his jaw indicated he was done talking about it.

Her heart ached at having to leave him alone when he was feeling so bad. "I'll come get you in the morning. Call me if you need to talk."

"I will."

She blew him a kiss and slipped out the door. Some time alone would do her good. She had to figure out how to get rid of Logan's ghost. She *needed* to get rid of the ghost. Not just for Logan, but for herself too. So she could prove to herself she was over her fears. That she had regained control, and spirits could not ruin her life again.

She made a hard left to head back to the lobby and nearly ran right into Logan's father. "Oh, Mr. Mitchell… umm…Roger. I'm sorry, I didn't see you there."

"That's okay, Allison. Do you need a ride home?" He had a pleading look in his eyes, and she could feel pain and sadness rolling off his skin. She sighed. Why couldn't these Mitchell men keep their emotions to themselves?

While she preferred the company of her BFF to the man her boyfriend despised, Roger's anguish called to her. Hopefully she wouldn't regret this. "I was going to call my friend, but if you don't mind…"

"It's no trouble at all." Roger's face lit up at the chance to help, and she knew what he said to Logan was true. He really was sorry for everything. She could feel it, and she wasn't even trying to read him.

She followed him to his rental car, a gas-guzzling Hummer. Big surprise. He opened the passenger door for her, and she climbed inside, chiding herself for being judgmental. She'd had a low opinion of Logan in the beginning, and he turned out to be a wonderful man. She should at least give his father a chance.

"So, Roger. How does one charter a jet? Logan's mom couldn't get a flight until this evening."

He started the engine and backed out of the parking space before he answered, "I own it."

"Oh, well, that's convenient."

He rolled the car to a stop in the middle of the aisle. "Yes, it is. Allison, have you eaten dinner?"

"No, I've been with Logan all day." She clamped her mouth shut. That sounded like the beginning of an invitation she was loath to accept. A ride home was one thing, but to have dinner with the man?

He gripped the steering wheel and stared straight ahead. "Are you the one who found him? Did you save his life?"

"Yes, I did." Though it seemed Lily had helped by

opening the front door before Allison arrived. Without that stream of fresh air blowing in, he might not have made it.

Roger closed his eyes and dropped his head back on the seat. Then he let out a heavy, burdened sigh. "Can I take you out to dinner? To show my appreciation for saving my son's life?"

She stared at her hands clasped in her lap. Spending the evening with Logan's father was the last thing she wanted to do. "That's really not necessary, Mr. Mitchell."

"Please? I'll be leaving first thing in the morning, and I'd like to get to know my son's girlfriend. God knows it's probably the only chance I'll get."

The pain he carried weighed heavy in the car, like an iron blanket draped over their heads. There was more to it than he was letting on, and she could tell he wanted her to know. He needed her help, and she couldn't pass up the opportunity.

"There's a great little Italian place just up the road," she said.

"Thank you." He nodded and began to drive.

She directed him to the restaurant, and they were seated right away. The place was small, a hole in the wall, really, but the food was exceptional. It probably wasn't the kind of place Roger frequented, but then again, Logan was so down to earth, maybe his dad was too. She really had to stop judging him.

They ordered their food and sat in awkward silence. Where should she begin with the man she had only heard negative things about? What could she say? She swirled the water around in her glass and waited for him to speak.

"How long have you and Logan been together?"

"Not long." She set down her glass and folded her arms on the table.

"You're not serious, then."

"We're exclusive, if that's what you mean." She held his distrustful gaze and let down her wall to absorb his emotions. She shouldn't have. It was intrusive, something she rarely did without permission, but she had to know if there was an ounce of good in this man.

He emanated doubt and cynicism, certain she was only after Logan's money. His entire aura reeked of self-importance and distrust. How could anyone live like that? She put her psychic wall back in place and straightened her spine. "I believe in fate, and Logan and I are meant to be together. We're in love."

He tilted his head, looking down his nose at her. "I can appreciate that. I want my son to be happy."

"Do you, Mr. Mitchell? Because Logan doesn't think so."

He sighed and put his hands on the table. "What has he told you?"

"Enough for me to know how deep his scars run. It's going to take more than a half-hearted apology to make things right with him. You know that, don't you? Underneath that happy, outgoing exterior, Logan is very sensitive. He's not going to forgive you that easily."

Roger laughed cynically. "How is it you know so much about my son in such a short amount of time?"

"I told you. I'm in love with him."

He leaned back in his chair. "Maybe you are, Allison. Please accept my apology for assuming otherwise."

"Apology accepted. Now, what is it you want to tell me?"

He crossed his arms. "What makes you think I want to tell you something?"

She leaned forward and lowered her voice. "Let's just say that Logan and I share similar gifts. I don't normally tune in to the emotions of others, but you and Logan seem to scream at me silently. You need my help, so ask for it."

Her heart sprinted with the upfront way she spoke to the man, but she was tired of playing games. She was just downright tired. She wanted to go home, take a hot bath, and climb into bed. The quicker she could get this dinner over with, the better.

Roger opened his mouth to speak, but then closed it. He inhaled deeply and looked her in the eyes. "All right. I obviously can't beat around the bush with you, so I'll just say it. I'm dying."

Allison took a deep breath and closed her eyes. She wouldn't normally invade a person like she was about to do, but for some reason, she felt the need to prove herself to this man. She focused in on him, reading the flow of energy through his body. There would be a block at the source of his problem, and she found it in his head.

She opened her eyes and held his gaze. "You have a brain tumor."

His doubt rolled off him in waves. "That's a lucky guess."

"It wasn't a guess; it's what I do. I'm an energy worker, a healer. Would you like for me to help you?"

He chuckled. "I think I'm beyond help. The doctors have given me less than a year."

"On conventional treatments, maybe. But I'd like to give it a try, if you'll let me."

Roger pursed his lips as he looked her over. "Thanks

for the offer, but it's my time to go. What I was hoping for... I was hoping you would talk to Logan for me. I want to make things right with him before... I don't want him to have any regrets after I'm gone."

She stared into Roger's eyes and thought about her own parents. What she would have given to talk to them one more time. To heal the gaping hole their deaths left in her heart. She would never have closure, and she didn't want Logan to go through that kind of pain.

"I'll talk to him, but I think you need to try again too. You've taken the first step, so let it sink in with him. He might be more receptive next time."

"Thank you, Allison. I appreciate your help."

"You're welcome."

CHAPTER TWENTY-THREE

"Tell me why Logan has been in the hospital for two days, and I'm just now finding out about it." Tina's voice over the line sounded more than a little aggravated.

Allison cradled the phone against her shoulder as she put on her shoes. "Sorry about that. Things have been kinda crazy around here."

"I heard. What happened?"

"Boy, good news travels fast." Allison slipped her purse over her shoulder and headed out the door. "Where do I begin?" She told her about finding Logan passed out in his house and getting him to the hospital.

"Jesus, Allie. That must have been so scary."

"It was, but he's okay now. I'm on my way to pick him up. I would have called you last night, but his dad showed up at the hospital." She got in her car and pulled out onto East Jefferson Avenue toward the hospital.

"That was nice of him. He came all the way from New York?"

"Yeah, but I don't think it was such a good thing. Logan and his dad have issues."

"Issues, huh?"

"Yeah, so anyway, after visiting hours ended, he offered to take me home. Then he asked if he could take me to dinner to show his appreciation for me saving his son. He kept calling him 'my son' like it was some kind of ownership right."

"How'd that go?"

"It was interesting, to say the least. I don't know. I have to talk to Logan about it. I was so exhausted by the time I got home, I crashed."

"Wow. Okay, you're excused for not calling me. I just hated having to hear about it from Logan. Guys are so bad with details."

"Wait… You heard about it from Logan? When did you talk to him?"

"Right before I called you. He asked me to put his house on the market."

"On the market?" She put the phone on speaker and set it in the cupholder.

"He didn't tell you he was selling it?"

"He mentioned it, but I didn't think he was serious."

"Huh. Well, he said after what happened to you, he had to get rid of it. He's selling it for you, Allie. Isn't that romantic?"

Allison pulled into the hospital parking lot and cut the engine. "No, it's not romantic. It's crazy. He doesn't need to sell his house for me. I'm going to clear out the ghost. I have to."

"No, you don't. If he sells the house, you won't have to worry about it anymore. You said yourself the ghost was attached to the property."

She sighed and rubbed her forehead. "It is. But I *need* to clear it out. Not for him… For me. I have to prove to myself that I can do it."

"I understand your need to conquer your fears. I really do, but maybe you need to do it somewhere you're not so emotionally invested."

"That's *why* I need to do this. It's personal now. I'm not going to let a spirit get the best of me. Not again." She grabbed the phone and climbed out of the car. The cool autumn air nipped at her ears as she darted across the parking lot and entered the hospital lobby. "Are you still there?"

"Yeah, I'm here. When are you going to do it?"

"Today. I've got all my supplies in the car. I'm ready this time; I can protect myself."

"I want to be there when you do it. You know, for moral support."

"Thanks, but it needs to be just Logan and me. I think we can do it together."

Tina blew out a hard breath. "Okay, but you better call me right before *and* after you do it. I mean it, Allison."

"Yes, ma'am. I'm at the hospital now."

"Okay. Go get your man, and be safe."

"I will. Thanks."

Allison slipped the phone into her pocket and padded down the hallway to Logan's room, where she found him sitting on the bed, dressed in jeans and a light blue button-up. He grinned and swept her into a hug.

"I missed you." He brushed her hair away from her face and kissed her.

"Mmm… I missed you too. Are you ready to go?"

"Yep. I'm all checked out." With one hand on the

small of her back, he stroked her cheek with the other and looked into her eyes. His gaze was intense, and his eyes smoldered with so much passion, her knees went weak.

"If you keep looking at me like that, you might have to check *me* in. I think I forgot how to breathe."

"Then we better get you home." He swung his bag over his shoulder without breaking his hold on her.

"I was thinking we could go have breakfast. Have a nice cup of coffee, maybe treat ourselves to a pastry. You deserve it." Hopefully she could butter him up with good food before she broke the news about the ghost. He probably wouldn't give in as easily as Tina did.

He smiled. "You know me too well, woman. Let's go." He scooped her up in his arms and carried her past the nurse's station.

Allison giggled. "Are you sure you should be lifting me in your condition?"

"The doctor gave me the all-clear. I can do whatever I want." He grinned and raised his eyebrows.

"Oh, really? And just what do you want to do?"

"You'll have to wait till after breakfast to find out, won't you?" He lowered her feet to the floor and took her hand as they crossed the parking lot.

They drove to a little café down the road from Allison's apartment, and Logan ordered two huge cinnamon rolls, dripping with icing, and two cups of coffee. Allison grimaced when he set one down in front of her.

"I never eat like this. It's so bad for you." She picked up a fork and took a bite of the pastry, closing her eyes as the sweet, gooey goodness melted on her tongue. "Oh… but it's delicious."

Logan shrugged. "I eat healthy all day. Breakfast is my one time to indulge."

"I can see why you like it so much. This could get addicting." She sipped her coffee and watched Logan enjoy his meal. After she ate half of hers, it felt like a brick sitting in her stomach, but he finished off the entire roll.

She traced her finger around the edge of her coffee cup, hesitating to speak. "Tina told me you called her this morning. She said you want to sell your house."

"I can't have that ghost pushing you around, so I'm getting rid of it. You're way more important to me than the house." He paused, searching her eyes, and shook his head. "You don't want me to sell it. It's not safe for you to be in there."

She sighed and folded her arms on the table. "I appreciate that you want to protect me, but I *need* to clear out that ghost for you."

"No, you don't. It's not worth it."

She reached out and took his hand. "Okay, I don't need to do it for you. I need to do it for me. It's personal. It's about conquering my fears and moving on with my life. Do you understand?"

"I understand how you feel, but that's because I can feel it too. I don't understand *why* you feel that way. Did something happen?"

"Yes, something did happen. It was a long time ago, and I'm just now getting over it." She took a deep breath and rubbed the back of her neck. If she really was going to move on with her life, she'd have to start by reliving that horrible night.

"It was Halloween last year, and I was investigating an abandoned mental hospital with DAPS. The owner wanted to turn the building into condos, and I was supposed to clear out the lingering spirits. Normally, it would have been a simple exercise, but…" She let go of his hand and fisted hers on the table.

"There were so many of them, and the veil between the world of spirits and the living is thinner on Halloween, so they were strong. So strong." She shuddered.

Logan reached across the table and took her hand again. "You don't have to say anything else. I can imagine."

"No. I want you to know." She closed her eyes for a long blink. "They assaulted me. Twenty mentally ill spirits all trying to communicate with me at once. They got inside my head, infected my soul. I might have died, had Gage not pulled me out when he did."

"Oh, Allison." He laced his fingers through hers.

"It took me three months to recover. Those spirits took *three months* from me and left me in fear for another eight. I hadn't talked with another ghost since…until your party."

"I had no idea. I'm so sorry I didn't tell you about Lily."

"It's okay. How could you have known?" She held his gaze. "But I'm ready now. I know what to expect, and I can protect myself. I *need* to do this. Will you help me? Please?"

He let out a heavy sigh. "Jesus, Allison. I don't know. If anything happened to you, I couldn't forgive myself."

She leaned forward and took his other hand in hers. "You won't let anything happen to me. I trust you. Please, Logan. I *need* to do this."

"Okay. We'll do it. If…"

"If?"

"If you promise not to push it too hard. If it gets to be

too much, you'll stop. Let me sell the house and forget about it."

"All right. It's a deal." Excitement bubbled in her chest, and she kissed him on the cheek. "Thank you."

He ran his hand through his hair and cracked his neck. "When do you want to do it?"

"If you're feeling up to it, I'm ready now. I have everything I need in the car."

"Shit." He gaped. "Are you serious?"

"The sooner the better."

"Doesn't it have to be dark?"

She laughed. "Not for your ghost. She's strong. I don't think she's affected by the time of day."

Logan put his elbows on the table and leaned his face in his hands. "Are you sure, Allison? You really want to do this now?"

"I'm sure."

"Okay, then." He shrugged and shook his head. "Let's go."

Thoughts rolled through Logan's head on the drive to his house, but he couldn't seem to verbalize them. He wanted to talk her out of it. To find some way to convince her she didn't need to do it. It wasn't a risk he wanted to take, but he understood how she felt. She needed to conquer her fears, and she'd helped him so much with his own. How could he not help her?

But hell, what if something happened to her? What if the ghost took control again, and he wasn't able to stop her? What if she spiraled into another depression like the one before? He had no idea how to stop something like that from happening. Or worse…what if she jumped out the window? Visions of Allison lying dead in a pool of blood on the concrete flashed in his mind. She'd probably have to crash through the glass to get past him, but it was possible. That window was old, and the pane was thin. Her delicate skin would be sliced to shreds if she did that.

Fuck!

He was doing it again. Allison needed his help, and he could not fail her. He had to get it together. Squeezing his eyes shut, he gripped the passenger door as he tried to force the thoughts out of his head. God, there'd be so much blood if she died that way. Her slender frame would be crushed from the impact. He'd probably be charged with murder. *Shit!* He had to stop. He needed something to count. Something to organize. Anything to get his mind off the sick, twisted shit he was thinking.

"Logan, are you okay?" Allison put her hand on his thigh as the car rolled to a stop in his driveway.

"No, I'm not." Beads of sweat formed on his forehead as his breathing grew shallow and rapid.

She unbuckled her seatbelt and wrapped her arms around him. "It's going to be all right. Take some deep breaths for me."

He did as he was told, dragging in a shaky breath and blowing it out slowly.

"That's good." Allison's voice was warm and reassuring. "You remember the meditation I taught you?"

"Yeah." He forced a whisper through the thickness of his throat as he nodded and tried to breathe.

"Okay, let's do it now. Visualize the light from the universe filling you up."

He grunted and dropped his head back against the

seat. "How can a bubble protect me, when it's all in my mind?"

"Forget about the bubble. Just think about the light. Let it fill you up. Can you feel it?"

"Yeah."

"Good. Focus on that and breathe."

She rubbed his back, and he imagined the damn light like she told him to. After a moment, his breathing became deeper and more rhythmic. His mind was letting go. Slowly, the morbid thoughts began to slip from his brain, and his body began to relax. Within a few minutes, he felt like he was in control again.

He straightened his spine and turned to Allison. "That's incredible. How do you do that?"

"I didn't do anything this time. It was all you." She smiled and kissed him on the cheek. "Are you okay now?"

"Amazingly enough, I am. You had to have done something. I can't get over an episode that fast."

"Obviously, you can. Other than coaching you on what to do for yourself, I didn't do a thing. I promise." She bit her bottom lip and looked into his eyes. "Have you ever tried to get help for your OCD? Therapy works wonders."

"I don't have OCD."

"Really? So, your episodes don't involve obsessive thoughts that won't go away? How many times have you reorganized your paperback collection? And the way you keep all your food separated… That doesn't provide you with any kind of comfort…a feeling of control?"

"You're too damn perceptive. All right, maybe I might have OCD, and no, I've never gotten help for it. It's embarrassing." He crossed his arms and stared out the window.

"It's nothing to be embarrassed about. It's not like you did anything to catch it. It just happens to some people." She tenderly stroked the back of his neck until he jerked his head toward her.

"You have no idea what it's like to have a meltdown in the middle of a meeting, and then Trent has to cover for me when I run out of the room. It's humiliating. He makes up excuses for me all the time: food poisoning, emergencies, hangovers. I don't even drink, Allison. I don't drink because I can't stand to lose control. Control is the only thing that keeps me from going insane. Jesus! I can't believe I'm telling you this." He took a deep breath and raked his hand through his hair. "Are you thinking twice about staying with me now?"

She put her hand on his cheek and turned his head toward her. "Of course not. I love you, Logan. *All* of you. Every part, okay?"

"I'm damaged goods. I've got issues." He put his hand on hers to hold it to his face. Why the hell was he trying to convince her to leave? It was the last thing he wanted, but maybe it was best for her if she did.

"We're all damaged. Everyone has some kind of issues, and you know what? You just controlled it, didn't you? You started to have an episode, and you stopped it."

"With your help."

"So? You're still learning, and I'll always be here to help you. Always. Because I love you."

"I love you too." More than she could even begin to imagine. How did he get so damn lucky? He took her face in his hands and kissed her. "What would I do without you?"

"I hope we never have to find out." She rested her

forehead against his. "Are you okay? We can do this another time if you're not ready."

"Are *you* ready?"

"I already told you I am."

He nodded. "Then, enough about me. Let's go bust a ghost."

CHAPTER TWENTY-FOUR

"What's the salt for?" Logan sat on the top step and watched Allison take supplies out of her bag. She had candles and crystals too. He'd never seen her use anything but her mind to do her psychic work, and he picked up a crystal to examine it.

She smiled and took it from his hand. "It's a symbol. We're going to create a circle of protection, kind of like the bubble method I taught you. The salt is symbolic of that circle, and the spirit won't be able to cross it. As long as we stay inside the circle, she can't hurt us."

"And she won't be able to get inside your head again like last time?"

She lit the candles and set the crystal near the window at the top of the stairs. "Not as long as we don't break the circle. Pouring the salt is like a ritual. It helps to strengthen it." She took his hand and led him a few steps away from the stairs.

"Do we have to do it right here? By the window?" he asked.

"Stand still." She poured a ring of salt around them and then took his hands. "It's where her energy is strongest, because this is where she spent her last living moments. We have the best chance of helping her cross over here."

He held her gaze. Her hands were dry and warm, while his went slick with sweat. "I'm scared."

"I am too, but I know we can do this. Are you ready?"

"As ready as I'm going to be." But he wasn't. He wanted to sweep her in his arms and carry her out of the house, to get her away from it all and start over. But she needed this, and he needed to help her.

She took a deep breath and closed her eyes, so he followed her lead. A prickling sensation ran over his skin as his energy joined with hers, and his entire body relaxed into a meditative state. Fast and powerful, it felt like a sudden wave crashing over them, leaving behind nothing but serenity as it retreated to the ocean.

"We have created a circle of protection," Allison said. "Nothing uninvited may enter. We call on the spirit of Lily. You may not enter our circle, but please come forward and show yourself to us. We're here to help you, Lily. My name is Allison, and this is Logan. We want to help you."

The air grew cold as the energy in the room shifted, becoming heavy and thick as Lily made her presence known. Even with his eyes closed, he could feel a static charge forming outside their circle.

Allison squeezed his hands as she spoke. "She's here, Logan. Open your eyes and look. Do you see her by the window?"

He hesitated. He really didn't want to see her, but he

turned toward the window and opened his eyes. "It's her." He expected to see a wispy spirit-like presence, but Lily looked solid. She looked *alive*.

"Have you seen her before?"

"Yeah… Well, no. I've seen her in my head. She looks just like I imagined her."

"That's because you didn't imagine her. You saw her with your mind's eye. Are you ready to help her cross over?"

He took a deep breath and nodded. "Let's do this."

"Look at the crystal. I want you to imagine a beam of light passing through it and up into the universe. That's the portal. We're going to help Lily go through the portal, so she can cross over to the spirit world."

He looked at the crystal and imagined the light. Focusing his mind was so much easier with Allison's help. Her energy flowed through him, warm and kind and loving, as they created the portal together.

"Alex, no!" Blood ran down Lily's face as tears poured from her eyes, splashing to the floor, leaving pink puddles around her bare feet.

He squeezed Allison's hands tighter. "She looks so real."

"She's not. She's just energy, and we have to help her pass… Lily? Do you see the portal we created for you? If you will step into the light, you'll be free from this world. You can be where you belong."

"No," Lily whispered. "I won't leave you, Alex."

"He isn't Alex." Allison's voice was stern. "His name is Logan, and he's mine. You can't have him, so there's no reason for you to stay. Alex is gone. Logan lives here now, and you have to leave his house."

Lily sobbed into her hands. "But I love you, Alex. I'm your wife. Don't you love me?"

"No." Logan's voice was strong and sharp. "I don't love you. I love Allison." The energy in the room shifted again. The hairs on his arms stood on end as Lily drew in more power and threw open the window. She climbed on the ledge and turned to look at Logan.

"I love you, Alex."

"No! She's going to jump!" He rushed toward Lily to stop her.

"Logan, she's a ghost. It doesn't matter." But it was too late. The circle was broken, and Lily took her chance to get rid of the other woman. With a heavy shove, Lily sent Allison tumbling down the stairs. She flipped over backward as she rolled down, and her head hit the marble floor below with a loud *whack*.

"Allison!" Logan raced down the stairs and pulled her limp body into his arms. "Oh my God. Allison? Allison, wake up! Come back to me, baby. Please."

Tears rolled down his cheeks as he held her to his chest. This was his fault. She trusted him to protect her, and he failed her. He broke the circle. He caused the accident. He was a fucking idiot! Trying to stop a ghost from jumping out the window. What the hell was he thinking?

"I'm so sorry." He pulled out his phone and dialed 911.

"An ambulance is coming, baby. Just hold on." He leaned down to kiss her, and her eyelids fluttered open. "Allison! Talk to me."

"Logan?" She reached up and touched his face, confusion clouding her eyes. "What happened?"

"It's all my fault. I broke the circle. I was stupid. I'm sorry."

"It's okay. I thought she was real once too." She snuggled into his arms and closed her eyes.

He sat her upright and pulled her into his lap. "Wake up, baby. You can't go to sleep right now. An ambulance is coming. We'll get you to the hospital and get you checked out."

"I don't need to go to the hospital. I'm fine. Here, just help me stand up." She struggled to get to her feet, but he held her tight.

"We'll let the doctor decide if you're fine or not."

"No, Logan. Please. I can't afford to go to the hospital. I don't have insurance. I'm fine, really."

"You're not fine. You fell down the stairs, and you were knocked unconscious. Don't worry about the money; I'll pay your doctor bills. It was my fault, and I am so sorry."

"You can stop apologizing. I don't blame you. It was an accident."

"An accident that could have been avoided if I'd listened to you and stayed inside the goddamn circle. I will never forgive myself."

The doorbell rang, and he slid Allison out of his lap, leaning her against the wall. "That's the EMT. Stay right here while I let them in. Don't move." He jumped to his feet and jogged to the front door. "She's in here."

The same EMT who'd helped Logan the day before rushed in carrying a big orange medical bag. "You two are having some bad luck lately." He pulled out a small flashlight and shined it into each of Allison's eyes. "Do you want to tell me what happened?"

"I lost my footing and fell down the stairs."

"Are you in any pain? Did you hit your head?" The EMT counted her pulse as he looked at his watch. Then he took her blood pressure.

"I'm a little sore, but I'll be fine."

"She hit her head," Logan said. "And she was unconscious for a couple of minutes."

"Well, Ms. Gray, since you were unconscious, I'm going to recommend you go to the hospital to get checked out. You may have a concussion." The EMT shoved his instruments into his bag and rose to his feet. "I've got a wheelchair in the ambulance; let me get it, and I'll take you there."

Allison sighed and shook her head. "Can't Logan drive me? I don't think I need to ride in the ambulance."

"Go with the EMT." Logan rested a hand on her shoulder, giving it a squeeze. "If you pass out on the way, I won't be able to help you."

She closed her eyes and leaned her head back against the wall. She sure didn't want to spend the entire day in the hospital, but Logan wasn't going to let up until she got checked out. When she opened her eyes, he was staring at her, his hands clenched into fists. Anger rolled off him like a thick, burning wave.

"Are you mad at me?"

A pained looked flashed across his face, and he knelt beside her. "I'm not mad at you." He brushed her hair away from her face and cradled her chin in his hand. "I'm mad at myself for letting this happen. You could have been killed."

"But I wasn't. I'm fine." She got to her feet and swayed as her head spun.

He put his arm around her waist. "You don't seem fine to me. I'm selling the house."

"No, you're not."

"I'm not putting you through this again. The house is gone."

The EMT came in with the wheelchair, and Allison sighed. "We can argue about this later. Will you follow us in your car? I don't plan on being there long."

"Okay, but we're not going to argue about it later because there's nothing to argue about." He slipped his hand beneath her knees and cradled her in his arms before settling her in the chair. "Give me two minutes to run upstairs and pack a bag."

"What do you need your bag for?"

"We're not coming back here, and you're not spending the night alone when you have a concussion."

"I *might* have a concussion." She reached for his hand as the EMT wheeled her onto the porch. "And thank you for taking care of me."

"You're welcome." Logan kissed her on the cheek. "I'll be right behind you."

As he ran inside, the EMT loaded her into the ambulance and wrapped a blood pressure cuff around her arm. He put the familiar claw monitor on her finger and fiddled with a few of the gadgets on the wall. "What's he like?"

"Pardon?"

"Logan Mitchell. I've read about him in the papers. He seems like a cool guy, but what's he really like? Most celebrities put on a show for the cameras."

She laughed and winced when a sharp pain shot through her head. "I wouldn't call him a celebrity."

"He's famous enough that people recognize him. That makes him a celebrity in my book."

"Hmm… I guess it kind of does."

"Is he really as cool as the papers make him out to be? Always giving money to charities and stuff?"

"I don't really read the papers, but *I* think he's amazing."

The EMT chuckled and shook his head. "He really seems to care about you too."

She lifted herself onto her elbows. "Why do you sound surprised?"

"I don't know." He shrugged. "I guess Detroit's Most Eligible Bachelor isn't so eligible anymore."

"Most eligible? What are you talking about?"

He raised his eyebrows. "You don't know?"

She shook her head.

"Three weeks ago, *Detroit City Magazine* named him this year's Most Eligible Bachelor. They did a whole write-up on him, interviewed him and everything. I guess I was surprised because when they asked him what he was looking for in a woman, he said he wasn't looking to settle down."

"I guess I should read more." Pressure mounted in the back of her eyes. Why on earth would she cry about something so silly? Maybe she really did have a concussion. She tried to blink back the tears, but it was no use. They rolled down her cheeks, and she wiped them off with her sleeve.

The EMT looked at her with sympathy in his eyes. "Oh, man. Don't listen to me; I'm just babbling. He really does care about you. I meant that. You can tell by the way he looks at you. Don't cry."

She sniffled. "It's okay. I don't know why I'm crying; it's no big deal. Do you happen to have a copy of that magazine?"

"I think I might." He knocked on the window to the cab of the ambulance, and a blonde woman slid open the glass. "Hey, Jenny. Do you still have that *Detroit City Magazine* up there?"

"It's right here."

"Do you mind if I give it to our patient?"

"Sure. I'm finished reading it anyway." She passed it through the window and then slid it shut.

The EMT handed it to Allison. "It's all yours."

"Thanks." She gave him a half-smile and looked at the cover. Logan stared back at her, wearing a huge grin and an expensive suit. She closed her eyes and sucked in a shaky breath. She didn't want to read the article, but she had to. She had to see it for herself and find out what else he told the magazine about his personal life.

The EMT slipped the blood pressure cuff off her arm. "Here we are. My partner and I are going to take you in on the stretcher, and the nurses will take you from there. I hope you have a better day tomorrow, and don't take that article too seriously. People always put on a show for the media."

She watched the lights in the ceiling go by as they wheeled her into the emergency room. Why was she so upset? She knew what Logan's reputation was like. She knew what everyone else thought of him. So why did it bother her so much that he was named Detroit's Most Eligible Bachelor? He was hot, rich, and single. Those were the only criteria she knew of, and she knew all those things about Logan before she even met him.

It wasn't the title that bothered her. It was what he said in the interview.

He wasn't looking to settle down with anyone. He told her that himself, didn't he? And she'd told him the same thing. But saying it and putting it in writing were two different things. He told the world he didn't want a girlfriend. Had he really changed his mind, or was he just swept up in the passion?

Logan darted across the parking lot and into the emergency room. He followed a nurse down the hallway until she stopped and pulled back a curtain.

"Well, this is where she's supposed to be." She picked up Allison's chart on the wall. "Oh, she's getting a CT scan. You can wait here. She'll be back in a few."

"Thanks." He sat in a green vinyl chair and wrung his hands. There was no doubt in his mind now, he had to get rid of the house. He could find another place. It probably wouldn't be as big, but that would be okay. Cozy might be nice. Maybe he could even convince Allison to move in with him. For her to be there with him every night, to wake up in her arms every morning, that would be pure heaven. He pulled his phone out of his pocket and dialed Tina's number.

"Hi, Logan. Did you get rid of the ghost?"

"No. That's why I'm calling. There was an accident, and Allison fell down the stairs. The ghost pushed her."

"Is she all right? Where is she? I'll be right there."

"No, no. She's okay. We're at the hospital, and she's getting a CT scan to see if she has a concussion. She was up and talking before we got here. You don't need to come down."

"Are you sure? Maybe I better come anyway."

"I'm here. She'll be okay."

"I'm so used to being Allison's only family, it's kind of weird that she has you to take care of her now."

"Yeah." And he was doing a hell of a job at it too. In less than a week he'd already dumped her and given her a concussion.

"I need you to get my house on the market ASAP. I'm not letting Allison back in there again. It's too dangerous."

Tina paused for a beat. "Does she know about this?"

"She knows."

"And did she agree to it?"

He closed his eyes. "Not yet, but I can be very convincing."

"And she can be very stubborn. I don't think she's going to back down on this one. It's personal for her, especially if the spirit physically harmed her. And when she sets her mind to something, she finishes it."

"She's not finishing this one. I'm not letting her get hurt again."

"I wouldn't be so sure about that, but I'll go ahead and look into listing it for you."

"That's all I'm asking."

"Okay. Tell her to call me as soon as she finds out about the concussion."

"Will do. Thanks, Tina."

"My pleasure. And thanks for letting me know about Allison. Sometimes she forgets to call me."

Allison clutched the rolled-up magazine to her chest as she watched the ceiling tiles slide over her head once more. She had to wait outside the radiology room for half an hour before her CT scan, so she had plenty of time to read the entire article about Logan. She tightened her grip on the magazine. He was probably waiting for her in the curtained-off room. What in the world would she say to him?

She'd read the line over and over again. "I'm not interested in settling down with a woman," he'd said. "My job is fulfilling, and that's all I need."

Did he really feel that way?

And then there were the pictures. The one on the cover was innocent enough, but inside the article, he was featured wearing nothing but a pair of jeans with the button undone. It was no wonder why women threw themselves at him like they did. Maybe she'd been wrong about Logan. Maybe he wasn't as scared and lonely as she first thought.

The orderly pulled back the curtain and wheeled Allison into her room. Logan jumped to his feet as soon as he saw her, but she couldn't look at him. She declined his help getting into her bed and did it herself. With the magazine still rolled up tight, a tear slid down her cheek.

"Why are you crying? Are you in pain?" He tried to take her hand, but she jerked it out of his grasp. "Allison, what's wrong?"

She choked back a sob and threw the magazine at his chest before she leaned her head back and squeezed her eyes shut.

"Shit. Is this the first time you've seen this?" He tossed it onto a table and raked his hand through his hair.

She nodded, still not trusting her voice.

He cursed under his breath and sat on the edge of the bed. "I agreed to do this before I met you. I don't... It's not me. You know that."

She took a shaky breath and opened her eyes. "It sure looks like you. Bare-chested and everything. I thought... Well, I don't know what I thought, but I didn't think you would agree to something like this."

"It's not like it's porn."

"I know it's not porn." She exhaled an exasperated breath. "Why did you do it? You said you didn't care about making a name for yourself or what anybody else thought. You wonder why everyone's after your money? It's because you go around flaunting it...*and* your body."

She rolled onto her side away from him. She was torn. Part of her loved him and wanted nothing more than to be in his arms, but the other part of her said maybe she really didn't know him as well as she thought. Maybe her own emotions had clouded her judgment.

She could always read him. Just tear down the walls and let his psyche soak into her. Then she'd know the truth. But he didn't want her to. Now she knew why.

"Christ, Allison. It was a PR move. That's all. When the magazine approached me about it, I told them no. I didn't want to do it. You know me; I'm not after that kind of attention. But after I talked about it with Trent and my PR people, we decided it would be good for business. I didn't do it for attention. I did it for business, I swear."

"Yeah? What kind of business are you in that you have to take your clothes off in front of the entire city?"

He fisted his hands at his sides. "That part was stupid. I admit it, and if I could take it back, I would. Honestly, I regretted doing the whole thing when I saw what kind of attention I was getting from it." He put his hand on her shoulder. "Come on, Allison. You know me."

She turned to face him. "Do I, Logan? Because I'm not so sure. I read that article. You said you didn't want to settle down with a woman. Your job is fulfilling enough for you. Can you really change your mind that fast?"

"Yes, I can. I didn't know you then. Allison, that's not me. That's the façade. That's the part you saw right through. The shell I put on to protect myself. It doesn't matter what was said in the article. You know the real me, and you know I'm in love with you."

"No, I don't." She pointed to the magazine on the table. "That's who you've been all your life. We live in two different worlds, and I don't want to be with someone who has to change for me."

He closed his eyes and rubbed his forehead. "Allison, please don't do this. I don't have to change for you. I'm not trying to change. I'm finally being myself, because with you, I don't have to pretend anymore."

The doctor walked into the room, and Logan wiped at his eyes.

"Good news, Ms. Gray. You don't appear to have a concussion. I'm going to release you, but I want you to come back if you start feeling dizzy or if you get a headache or vision problems, okay?"

"Thank you." She sat up in the bed, swinging her legs over the side as the doctor nodded and left the room. "I want to believe you, Logan."

He took her hand and laced his fingers through hers. "You should. I'm sorry I did that magazine article. I'm sorry I told the entire city I didn't want a girlfriend. Believe me, if I'd known you then, I never would have stepped foot in that photography studio. What else can I do to convince you? You are the best thing that has ever happened to me, and I can't live without you."

"Logan…"

"Read me. I want you to know how I feel. I want you to know everything about me. Please."

She pressed her lips into a thin line and shook her head. "Whenever people find out what I do, they *always* ask me to read them. Whether they believe in my ability or not, they're curious to see what I can pick up. But you never were. You refused my offer for a reading, and it's because you didn't want me to see this side of you, isn't it?"

"No. Allison, you know why I didn't ask you to do it before. I didn't want you to find out about all my issues. My OCD, the ghost, everything. I'm fucked up, but you know everything now. I've got nothing to hide from you. Please, just do it."

A tear slid down her cheek as she cradled his face in her hands. She took a deep breath, closed her eyes, and dropped the wall between them. Focusing only on Logan, she let the rest of the world slip away as his emotions cascaded through her body. She felt his pain at the thought of losing her, his discontent with the life he was leading, and his longing to be loved unconditionally. She felt his love for her—complete and utter devotion.

A sob bubbled up from her chest, forming a lump in her throat. This man loved her, and she'd been prepared to throw it all away over a magazine article. She was the idiot, not him.

"Well," he said. "What do you think?"

She opened her mouth to speak, but she couldn't form an appropriate apology. No words existed to tell him how sorry she was, so instead, she kissed him. She wrapped her arms around his neck as she rose to her feet, reveling in the warmth of his welcoming embrace.

Closing her eyes, she leaned her forehead against his. "I love you, Logan. I'm so sorry."

He trailed his fingers down her cheek and tucked a piece of hair behind her ear. "Please don't ever doubt me again."

"I won't. I promise."

CHAPTER TWENTY-FIVE

Thunder rumbled in the dark sky as the hospital doors slid open, and rain fell in sheets across the parking lot. With Allison clinging to his arm, Logan darted through the downpour to his car. His jeans squeaked on the leather seat as he slid into the driver's seat, and Allison's pale pink sweater clung to her curves, the floral design of her bra showing through the thin material. Christ, she looked good wet.

She ran her fingers through her dripping hair and smiled at him. "I guess we're going back to my place?"

"We're certainly not going back to mine." He took her hand across the console. "Are you sure you feel well enough to go home?"

"I'm a little sore, but it's nothing a hot shower won't fix."

He kissed her cheek and drove her home, parking as close to the building as he could before they ran for the stairs, the frigid rain pelting them from above. Allison shivered when she unlocked her door, and he followed her inside the apartment.

"I must look like a drowned rat." She slipped off her shoes and set them under an end table.

"No." He dropped his bag on the floor and ran his hands up her arms, taking her face in his palms. "You look incredibly sexy." She shivered again as he wrapped his arms around her. "But we probably should get you out of these clothes."

"Good idea." She led him across the living room and through the short hallway into the bathroom. "We don't want to get the carpet all wet."

"No, we don't."

Stopping in front of the shower, she gazed into his eyes, her tongue slipping out to moisten her lips as she slid her hands beneath his shirt. His stomach tightened with the contact, and blood pooled in his groin.

"Do you feel well enough for this?" He brushed a dripping strand of hair from her forehead.

"I feel like this is exactly what I need."

With her consent, he slid his hands down her sides and peeled the shirt over her head. Goose bumps rose on her skin as his fingers glided along the edge of her bra.

"You're so beautiful, Allison." He cradled the back of her head in his hand and pressed his lips to hers. This was how it was supposed to be. Allison belonged in his arms, and damn it, he planned to keep her there.

He kissed her greedily, marveling at the way her body fit so perfectly against his. He unhooked her bra and slid it off her shoulders as he trailed his lips across her delicate skin. Kissing his way down her chest, he teased her nipples with his tongue, hardening them into pearls, and she let out a soft moan as he unbuttoned her jeans and worked the wet denim over her hips. She stepped out of her pants, and he inhaled deeply as he took in her naked form. She was exquisite, and she was shivering.

"You're still cold." He pulled her into an embrace. "Let's get you warmed up."

Reaching behind her, she turned on the hot water. "Let's get warmed up in the shower." She stepped back into the stall and gave him a wicked grin.

He froze.

Showering was a ritual. Something he only did alone. Damn his fucking peculiarities. He was going to ruin the moment because of his issues. "You go ahead. I'll watch." He could handle watching, though his own clothes felt cold and nasty, like a layer of raw meat draped over his skin. He trembled with the need to tear them off, but he couldn't make himself move.

Her brow furrowed. "What's wrong?"

"I have this thing about my showers." He fisted his hands at his sides. "I can't."

"It's not your shower. It's mine." She opened her arms, and he longed to step into them.

"I know, but…"

"Breathe for me, Logan."

He shook his head. "What?"

"Take a deep breath."

"Okay." He inhaled deeply as she grabbed the front of his shirt and tugged him into the stall. Hot water streamed over his head, and she pushed him against the wall, pressing her naked body to his.

"Keep breathing." She took his hands and slid them around her waist while she kissed his neck.

His heart sprinted, his hands trembling as she moved her mouth down his body, licking and kissing with each button she opened. He barely felt her. His hands hardly registered the sensation of her soft skin in his grasp.

What the fuck was his problem?

He inhaled deeply and closed his eyes. He could do this. He *had* to do this. For Allison. For himself. He moved his hands over her slick, wet body, focusing on the moment. On the incredibly sexy woman who slipped his shirt over his shoulders and threw it on the bathroom floor.

"Are you still with me, Logan?" She held his gaze, dropping to her knees to unbutton his jeans. "Do you want me to stop?"

God, no. "I'm okay."

She never took her eyes off his as she slid down the zipper and pulled his pants to the floor before tossing the rest of his clothes out of the shower. Still holding his gaze, she wrapped her hand around his length and flicked out her tongue to taste him.

Oh, yeah. He could do this.

The warmth of her tongue gliding along his shaft made his knees weak, and when she took him into her mouth, he had to lean against the wall to steady himself. She held his gaze as she sucked him, and he forgot all about the routine his showers required. Only he and Allison existed in that moment; the only sensations he felt were the water raining down on him and her mouth wrapped around him.

"Allison."

She released her hold and pressed her body to his as she slid up to meet his mouth. She was warm and wet and soft, and he needed to be inside her. Right now.

"How do you feel?" she asked.

"Like the luckiest man alive." He held her shoulders

and gently pushed her against the opposite wall, lifting her left leg over his hip. Using his hand as a guide, he pushed inside her, sheathing himself with her warmth. She gasped when he entered her, and he took her open mouth with his, drinking in the taste of her.

She roamed her hands over his body as he made love to her, gripping him harder with each thrust of his hips. "Logan." His name was a whisper on her lips, coaxing him to increase his rhythm as she clutched his shoulders, burying her face in his neck as she climaxed.

The only sounds he heard were Allison's moans and his own pulse pounding in his ears as he found his own release. He leaned against her, breathless, panting, trailing kisses up her neck to find her mouth once more.

When he'd caught his breath, he picked her up, wrapping her other leg around his waist and carrying her out of the shower.

She rested her hands on his cheeks and pressed her forehead to his. "What was that thing you had about showers?"

He lowered her to the ground and took a towel off the rack, patting her dry as he spoke, "I think I'm over it."

"I'm still cold, and it seems a shame to get another set of clothes dirty. Do you want to come warm me up in bed?"

"Do you even have to ask?" He scooped her up and carried her to the bedroom. Laying her down, he climbed in next to her, pulling her into his arms. "Mmm…I've missed this."

She laughed. "It's only been a day."

He kissed her forehead. "True, but I thought I was going to lose you there for a minute, so it feels like it's been forever."

"I'm so sorry for overreacting. I don't know what I was thinking."

"Don't apologize. If I saw a picture of you with your shirt off in a magazine, I'd probably overreact too."

"It is a very nice picture."

"I can get you a copy."

"Why do I need a picture when I have the real thing right here?" She ran her hand down his stomach and then climbed on top of him, covering his body with hers.

"Mmm…that's a very good point."

Allison propped her head on her hand and rested her other one on Logan's chest. Pale moonlight spilled through the open drapes, washing the room in a soft silver glow, the light dancing across his skin to accentuate the perfection of his features. His gaze was intense, holding her eyes while he absently glided his fingers up and down her hip.

"What are you thinking about?" she asked.

He took a slow, deep breath and closed his eyes for a long blink. "I was feeling you. I've been practicing turning it off, but for some reason, I can't shut you out. You're always present, even when I'm not focusing on you."

"That's because we're so in tune with each other, I think. I've never been able to completely shut you out either."

"What are you feeling from me now?"

She closed her eyes and focused on him, letting her walls slide away, allowing him in. She felt his love, pure and unconditional, but she also felt a twist of uncertainty. Of fear. "You're unsure about us. What's bothering you?"

He raised a shoulder and cast his eyes downward. "We've gotten so close so fast. I'm afraid of losing you."

She lifted his chin and brushed his lips with hers. "You're not going to lose me. I promise. In fact…" She grinned and climbed on top of him. "You couldn't get rid of me if you tried. You are *mine*."

He slid his fingers into her hair and pulled her face to his. "Yes, I am," he whispered against her mouth. As he kissed her, she remained open to his emotions, felt his desire swelling inside him, and for a moment it felt like her own. She was one with him, unable to tell where her emotions ended and his began.

She needed him, and she needed to show him how deep that need went. Sitting up, she straddled his groin, running her hands along the ridges of his muscles. She couldn't get enough of this man, and she wanted to touch, to taste every inch of him. She bent down and explored his body with her lips, her tongue.

She worked her way down and back up again before lying on top of him and whispering in his ear, "I love you, Logan." So much emotion. His. Hers. She couldn't contain it. She didn't try. A tear slid down her cheek, and he rolled on top of her, kissing it away.

"I love you too. Forever." He made love to her again.

Logan lay on his back with Allison snuggled into his side, and his lids drifted shut. He had just slipped below the surface of slumber when Allison moved, pulling him back to coherence.

"There's something I need to talk to you about," she said.

He opened his eyes. "Uh-oh. That doesn't sound good."

Her brow furrowed as she propped her head on her hand. "It's about your dad."

He took a deep breath and held it for a moment. Why was she bringing him up now? "What about him."

"That night you were in the hospital, and you asked him to leave…he waited for me."

He raised a brow. "Did he?"

"He took me out to dinner. He said he wanted to thank me for saving you, but I knew there was more to it than that."

Of course his father would use Allison to get to him. No surprise there. The man was a selfish prick, and he always would be. "What did he say to you?"

She blew out a hard breath and looked him in the eyes. "He's dying. He has a brain tumor, and the doctors have given him less than a year."

A knot twisted in his gut. "Are you sure? Was he telling the truth?"

"Yes, I read him. I found the tumor myself, before he even told me what it was. He really is trying to mend his ways. He wants to make things right with you before he dies."

He sucked in a sharp breath. "I don't know if he can make things right. Did you know I was ten years old when he started taking me to meetings with him? Of course, I thought it was cool getting to go to work with my dad all the time. He'd even pull me out of school if he had a big deal happening. He used me to feel out the other side and let him know what their breaking point was so he could rip them off as much as possible."

He rolled onto his back and stared at the ceiling. "I

didn't realize what I was doing at first. I didn't know how many people I was helping him hurt. How many jobs people were losing. Hell, it took me nearly twenty years to figure that out."

"I'd give anything to have some closure with my father. Just one more day to say all the things I need to say. Even if you tell him what you just told me, it might help. Think about it?"

He searched inside for some shred of emotion about his father's failing health, but all he found was numbness. He *did* care, didn't he?

Logan hated the man for so long, but he was his father. He should at least hear him out. Give him a chance. "I will, but not now… Right now, all I want to think about is you."

CHAPTER TWENTY-SIX

Logan lay in bed watching the peaceful rise and fall of Allison's chest as she dreamed. He'd spent nearly every night with her the past three weeks, and he still couldn't get enough of her. Ignoring the ghost had been easy enough now that he knew what was happening in his house, and the nights he spent at home were mostly uneventful since Lily had nothing to be jealous about. Allison hadn't stepped foot inside the place since her fall.

Now, the morning sun bathed the room in an orange glow, and the rays reflected off her shiny blonde hair, giving it a soft, warm tone. She was so beautiful, so serene, lying there naked underneath the soft lavender duvet. This was a sight he could get used to. Waking up with Allison every morning would be pure heaven, and he was ready for it to start now.

Her eyelids fluttered open, and she smiled. "Hi there."

"Good morning. How did you sleep?" He brushed a strand of hair from her forehead.

"Wonderfully. You?"

"Perfect."

"Mmm…" She curled into his arms and laid her head on his chest. "Do you have to go to work today?"

"It's Sunday. I don't have to go anywhere."

"Good." She raised her head and kissed his cheek.

He never dreamed he'd utter the words he was about to say, and his heart pounded in anticipation of her answer. "There's something I want to talk to you about."

"Uh-oh." She grinned and wrapped her arm around his waist.

"I was thinking about what to do after I sell my house, and…"

She let out a heavy sigh. "I'm going to get rid of your ghost. *We're* going to get rid of her. You don't have to sell your house."

"But what if I want to? What if I want…"

"Then you can do it after we clear out the ghost. These past few weeks with you have been wonderful, but I'm ready to fight back now."

What if I want to find a place with you? He gritted his teeth. She wasn't going to let up, and she wasn't going to give him the chance to ask her the question that was burning on his tongue. "All right. How are we going to keep you safe while we're there?"

She looked at him through narrowed eyes. "You mean you'll do it? Just like that?"

"Just like that." What choice did he have?

"Wow. I expected I'd have to argue with you about it."

He put his hand on her cheek and kissed her. "I don't want to argue with you. This is something you need to do, so I'm going to help you. What's the plan?"

She grinned and sat up in the bed, excitement bubbling all around her. "What we need is someone to ground us. I thought I could use you last time, but we're too connected. Rather than you grounding me, I think I charged up your abilities, which is why Lily seemed so real to you. We need someone who's not as sensitive to ground us."

He sat up and leaned against the headboard, resting his head against the wall. "That's why you held on to Gage so tightly that night, isn't it? He's who you use to stay grounded. You need him."

The thought of Allison needing another man had his insides twisting in jealousy. It was irrational. He knew that, but he couldn't stand that another man could give her something he couldn't. She must have sensed his mood, because she slid her arms around his chest and rested her head on his shoulder.

"It doesn't have to be Gage. Yes, he is who I usually use, but that's how our team is set up. We're not doing this with DAPS, so we don't have to include him."

"Who can we use, then?"

She grinned. "Are you jealous?"

He shrugged. "A little bit. You know he's crazy about you."

"And you know I'm crazy about you. You have nothing to worry about, okay?"

"I know."

"Good. I think we're going to need two people. One for you and one for me, so I was thinking about Tina and Trent. She texted me last night to say she was on a date with him."

He laughed. Good for Trent. "Do you think they're up yet?"

"Knowing Tina, they're probably still up. I can always call her and find out."

"Why don't you do that, and I'll wash up and get dressed?"

He'd made it through a few showers with Allison now, but only because she distracted him each time. He needed his morning routine if he was going to be at his best today, and he definitely needed to be at his best if they were going to deal with the ghost again.

Allison pushed out her bottom lip and climbed on top of him. "Are you sure you don't want me to help you? Our showers together are awfully fun."

He slid his arms around her waist and kissed her. "They're mind-blowing, but I need to actually get clean this time. It's one of my routines."

"I understand." She kissed him on each cheek, then on the forehead before she slid off his lap. "Go get clean. Because after we get rid of this ghost, we're going to get *very* dirty." She crawled out of bed and walked naked across her apartment.

Damn.

She had to be the sexiest woman alive, and she was his. Rolling out of bed, he followed her to the living room to get his bag. She fished her phone out of her purse and turned to face him, a scant inch or two separating them. Electricity danced between them as he looked into her eyes.

"You better get in the shower, or we'll never leave the apartment." She ran her finger down his stomach, stopping just below his navel before she turned and walked back to the bedroom, placing the phone against her ear.

Oh, hell. She was right. He peeled his eyes away from her swaying hips and headed to the bathroom.

"Hey, girl. It's Allie. Did I wake you?" Allison wrapped herself in a lavender robe and sat on the edge of her bed.

Tina took a deep, sleepy breath. "It's nine o'clock in the morning. Shouldn't you be having sex or something?"

"I've been doing that all night." And she'd be doing it all day, too, if she didn't set her plan into action. Having Logan dripping wet in a hot, steamy shower was more than tempting, but she had to resolve this ghost issue. If she could get this taken care of, she'd be ready to get on with her life with Logan.

"Anyway, do you think I could convince you and Trent to get out of bed long enough to help me get rid of Logan's ghost?"

"I'm not with Trent, and you know I'll help you. What do you need me to do?"

That didn't sound like her bestie at all. "What do you mean you're not with Trent? Didn't you go out with him last night?"

Tina sighed. "I did, but I didn't go back to his place when he invited me."

"Oh? Not your type after all?"

"No, he's very much my type. So much it scares me."

"Wow." Allison laughed. "That sounds familiar."

"I don't want to talk about it. What do you need me to do?"

"Be at my apartment in an hour. I'll explain then. Oh, and Trent's coming too, just so you know." The water shut off in the bathroom, and her heart raced as the door clicked open.

"Great." Tina's voice sounded wary.

Logan walked to the doorway, wearing nothing but a green towel wrapped around his waist, and Allison swallowed. "Better make that two hours. Something just came up." She hung up the phone and slunk toward him, running her hands up his bare chest, linking them behind his neck. "Something is coming up, isn't it?"

His mouth tilted at one corner as he pressed against her, letting her feel exactly what was up.

"Oh, goodie!"

"So, they'll be here in an hour? How'd you convince them to get out of bed?" Logan slipped on his jeans. His legs still felt boneless from his romp with Allison. He pulled a dark green sweater out of his bag and put it on as Allison walked around the room naked, gathering her clothes. She was so confident. Not at all the fragile flower he first took her for. She was smart and witty and so, *so* beautiful.

"Tina's not with Trent. She didn't spend the night with him, so they're coming separately."

He chuckled. "Really? That must've been her doing, because he's been hot for her for a while."

"I think she likes him too much. Don't tell him I said that, though."

He held up three fingers in a "scouts' honor" salute, and his phone buzzed on the nightstand with a message from Trent.

"Damn. His car broke down, so we'll have to pick him up." He tugged Allison's naked body to his. "Or do you want to ghost hunt another time and spend the rest of today in bed?"

She placed her hand on his chest and grinned. "As tempting as that is, I really want to get this over with so we can move forward with our lives."

Moving forward was exactly what he wanted to do

with her, and he was just about to say so when she pulled from his embrace.

"I need to get in the shower before Tina gets here. Go get Trent, and we'll meet you at your house in say… an hour and a half?"

"All right. I'll see you soon."

He stepped through the door, twisting the inner lock and closing it behind him before glancing at his watch. An hour and a half gave him plenty of time to make a quick pit stop before heading to Trent's.

By the time he made it to the house, his buddy was already up and dressed, sipping coffee on his sofa.

"Hey, man." Logan walked through the kitchen and poured himself a cup before returning to the living room.

"How's it going with Allison?" Trent asked.

Logan sat on the recliner and chuckled before he took a sip from his mug.

"That good, huh?" He flashed a knowing smile.

"Yeah. Where's Tina?"

Now it was Trent's turn to chuckle. "That woman…" He shook his head and set his cup down. "I think she's playing hard to get."

Logan raised his eyebrows and waited for him to continue.

"That's okay, though. The ones who are hard to get are usually the ones worth getting."

He nodded. "I hear you. So, listen, man. Allison is dead set on getting rid of that ghost; are you really up for helping us?"

"Of course, but I don't know what I can do. I don't have a psychic bone in my body."

"That's exactly why Allison wants you to help. She thinks you can ground us."

"Ground you?"

"She can explain it better than I can. We're meeting them at my place in half an hour."

"Them?"

"Tina's coming too."

A smile spread across Trent's face. "Well, why didn't you say so? Let's do it."

Tina strode into Allison's living room and perched on the edge of the sofa. "How are things on Lover's Lane?"

Allison grinned. "Never better. You should consider taking a stroll down it yourself."

"Maybe someday. Are you ready?"

"Logan is picking up Trent. Why don't you drive so you can be the one to take him home?"

Tina sighed and rolled her eyes. "That's actually a good idea. I have no reason to be scared of the man, right?"

"Right."

Allison rode in the passenger seat as Tina drove across the bridge that led to Grayhaven Island and Logan's estate. Now that she knew the man who owned it, the mansion didn't seem quite as obnoxious as the first time she saw it. The front lawn had been recently tended, the leaves that once crunched under her feet swept neatly away. The white stucco finish and Spanish tile roof gave the place an almost quaint appearance, and the stone steps that led up to the front porch weren't as intimidating as before.

They pulled into Logan's driveway and parked next to his Mercedes. Tina grabbed Allison's hand before she got out of the car. "Tell me exactly what I'm going to be doing. I've never done one of these with you before, and it's a little freaky."

She patted Tina's hand. "All you have to do is be there. Logan and I will do the rest."

Tina's eyes grew wide. "Oh. My. God. Logan's psychic too, isn't he?"

Allison lowered her voice. "A little bit, yeah. He's just coming to terms with his abilities, so don't bring it up unless he does. It'd probably be bad for business if it got around, you know?"

Tina used her finger to cross her heart. "Absolutely. I won't say a word. And Trent? Is he?"

Allison opened her door and swung her legs out of the car. "He's here to ground us…just like you."

CHAPTER TWENTY-SEVEN

"She's here. I can feel it." Logan rubbed his arm where the hairs stood on end. "She's watching us."

"Huh. I don't feel a thing." Trent relaxed on the couch as Logan paced a short track in the living room. "How can you tell?"

"There's a buzzing electrical feel in the air. I never noticed it before, but it's unmistakable now. I don't know. Maybe I'm just more aware of it."

"Or maybe it's your imagination."

He sat on the edge of a chair and rested his elbows on his knees. "No, it's definitely not. Allison has opened my eyes to a lot of things. A lot of control I didn't know I had. It's liberating."

"As long as you're happy, man." The bell rang, and Trent's gaze cut to the front door.

Logan jumped to his feet, a knot forming in the pit of his stomach as he reached for the knob. The last two times Allison tried to clear out the ghost had ended badly, and he was going to do everything in his power to keep her safe this time. His heart couldn't take it if he lost her again.

He swung open the door and immediately swept Allison into a firm embrace. "I missed you."

"I missed you too, but we should probably get started before Lily gets jealous."

"I swear I won't let you get hurt this time. No matter what happens, I will stay by your side. I promise." He pulled her close and held her in his arms until a slap on the shoulder from Trent interrupted them.

"You ready to do this, man?" Trent asked.

"I know I want to get it over with." Tina stood next to Trent, a nervous smile stretching across her face. "I'm a little freaked out, to be honest."

Trent grinned and wrapped his arm around Tina's shoulders. "I'll keep you safe. Don't worry."

Allison looked at Logan and laughed, while he rolled his eyes. It was little more than a month ago when he and Allison were in that awkward, unsure stage. Now he could honestly say he'd never been more sure of anything in his life.

Allison pulled away from his embrace, but he caught her by the hand. She glanced at their entwined fingers and then at him with a questioning look in her eyes.

"I'm not letting you go this time."

She opened her mouth to protest but closed it again and nodded. "Okay. Let's go. Do you still have my supplies?"

"They're already up there." He led her up the stairs, with Tina and Trent close behind. He felt the unease in the air, and it was hard to tell exactly to whom it belonged. If he really tried to focus on each individual, he could sort out the emotions, but his focus was only on

Allison, the hard edge of her determination slicing through the apprehension.

When they reached the top of the stairs, Allison positioned them in a circle with herself between Logan and Tina. She set the crystal by the window and poured a circle of salt around her friends. Trent watched her with speculation as he rubbed his hand on Tina's back.

"God, Allie. I've never seen you take so many steps before you did your thing. Is this going to be dangerous?" Tina's unease flooded Logan's senses, making it harder for him to focus on Allison. He closed his eyes and imagined a bubble around her and himself, and he filled the bubble with warm light. As he opened his eyes, only Allison's energy buzzed around him, a vibrating electrical current running between them, connecting them.

Allison must have felt it too, because she squeezed his hand and gave him a knowing smile. "I'm not going anywhere, Logan, but if we're going to be this close, you might want to take Trent's hand too. You're going to need a grounding force. And, Tina, it won't be dangerous at all, as long as everyone stays inside the circle."

The four friends joined hands, and Logan finally understood what Allison meant about grounding. He felt the pull of the different energies, and he struggled to find a balance between the two. From the right, where he held Allison's hand, the energy felt alive and electric. It buzzed and swirled, pulling him toward that other realm, the place where Allison found her strength and her calm. On his left, Trent's energy was solid and unwavering. It held him there, firmly on the ground.

Allison began to let down her walls, and the buzzing energy grew stronger and wilder. He squeezed her hand, and a soft smile tugged at the corners of her mouth.

Trent looked at their joined hands, and then he looked at Logan. "This is intense."

"I told you she's amazing." Logan gazed at the incredible woman to his right and smiled. "I'm ready when you are."

Allison nodded, took a deep breath, and closed her eyes. "We have created a circle of protection. Inside, no spirits may enter. No one may do us harm. We call on the spirit of Lily. You may not enter our circle, but we ask you to come forward and show yourself to us."

Logan opened his eyes and looked toward the window, where he saw the same vision of Lily in her long white gown, blood running down her forehead. She looked every bit as real as the time before, but this time he knew she was only energy. And Trent's grounding force kept him planted in place. He would not break the circle this time.

Tina gasped. "It's so cold. Is that the ghost? Is she here?"

"It's okay," Allison said. "She can't come into our circle."

"Jesus, Allie. I had no idea you could do this. I mean, I knew you talked to spirits, but I had no idea."

Trent's eyes grew wide. "Is this that static feeling you were talking about earlier?"

Logan chuckled. "It's a lot stronger, but yeah. Do you believe in ghosts, now?"

"Uh…yeah, I'd have to say I do."

"Alex, why are you doing this?" Tears rolled down Lily's blood-streaked cheeks and splashed on the floor.

"Look at the crystal," Allison said. "Imagine a beam of light rising up into the universe. We're creating a portal for Lily to pass."

Everyone stared at the crystal, and Logan saw the light, not just in his mind's eye, but with his plain sight as well. The golden illumination shimmered as it rose through the ceiling.

"Step into the light, Lily. You don't belong in this world anymore." Allison's voice was calm and reassuring.

Lily's jaw trembled. "Alex, I'm your wife. Don't you love me?"

Logan took a deep breath and shook his head. He knew what she was going to do, and he was prepared this time. "No, Lily. You're not my wife."

He felt the pull of energy as Lily gathered her strength and threw open the window.

"Holy shit." Trent's voice held a hint of terror, but his body was frozen in place. "Is she trying to jump out the window?"

"She's only energy," Logan said. "She's already dead."

"Don't jump, Lily," Allison said. "Don't go through this pain again. You can be free from all your heartache if you'll just step into the light."

"But Alex…" Lily sobbed and held out a hand to Logan.

His heart ached for her. For the love she had for her husband, even in death. "I'm not Alex. Lily, you have to go. It's time to move on."

Lily stepped down from the ledge, and Allison squeezed his hand. The spirit glided slowly toward them and stopped near a large ceramic vase. She ran her fingers across the silk flowers and gazed into his eyes.

"What do you want me to do, Alex?" She walked past the light toward Logan but stopped when she reached the edge of the circle. "What do you want me to do?"

"I want you to step into the light. You'll find peace there."

"It's where you're supposed to be," Allison said.

Lily's gaze snapped to Allison, and feral anger burned in her eyes. "You! You're the reason he's doing this. Get out of my house!" she screamed.

"This isn't your house. It's Logan's."

Emptiness pooled around them as Lily drew in every ounce of energy she could obtain. She glared at Allison and picked up the vase.

"Lily, what are you doing? No!" Logan's feet fought to carry him to the spirit. To keep her from hurting Allison, but his mind held him firmly in place. Allison said they were safe in the circle.

"Get. Out. Of. My. House." Lily reared back like she planned to throw the vase, and Logan's heart nearly stopped. If the circle didn't work—

He yanked from Trent and Allison's grasp and threw himself at Lily, but his body passed right through hers. Icy electricity clawed its way through his insides as her energy ripped out of him, and he plowed into the wall.

Allison screamed. The vase shattered.

He'd broken the circle. Again.

He pushed from the sheetrock and turned to find the woman he loved on the floor, wrapped in Trent's arms. A stream of blood flowed down her forearm, and her eyes grew wide with fear.

"Allison." He stepped between her and the spirit.

"She's fine. She blocked it with her arm." Trent helped her to her feet, and she poured another ring of salt around them.

"Get back inside the circle, Logan." Allison held out her hand to him. "She's too strong."

He shifted his gaze to the spirit. Longing and sadness radiated from her form, and fresh tears streamed down her face as she sobbed. "I'm sorry, Alex."

"Logan, she can hurt you out there." Allison's voice was insistent. The connection he forged with her still held strong, and he could feel her fear, her need to have him by her side. "Wait." Her energy shifted. "Stay where you are."

He looked at her quizzically.

"If she won't listen to Logan," Allison said, "maybe she'll listen to Alex."

Of course. The ghost hadn't asked Logan what he wanted her to do. No, she'd asked Alex. "Don't be sorry, Lily. I'm the one who should apologize." He stepped toward the spirit.

"Alex?" She wiped the bloody tears from her face.

"I'm sorry, Lily. Can you ever forgive me?"

Her lower lip trembled. "But all those women."

"They meant nothing to me. You're the only one I want."

"Oh, Alex. I love you." She threw herself toward him, and he reached out his arms to catch her. But her essence passed through his body, grating against his senses, lighting his nerves on fire.

He shuddered, inhaling sharply, and turned to face her. "I love you too, Lily."

The spirit looked at her hands. "Why can't I touch you?" She reached for his arm, but her energy passed through him again.

"It's time for you to move on. We made this portal just for you. Step inside, and you'll be free."

The spirit looked at the portal and then at Logan. He held out his hand, and she hovered hers above it. "Are you coming with me?"

"It's not my time yet, but I'll be there soon."

Her gaze cut between him and the light as if she was unsure what to do. This spirit wasn't evil. She didn't need to be forced out of his house. All she needed was to be loved.

"Go ahead. It's what I want you to do."

She looked at him, her gaze traveling down his body and back up again, and whispered, "I love you, Alex."

She stepped into the light.

Allison exhaled a slow breath as the weight in the room lifted, Lily's unyielding sadness and desperation disintegrating as her energy transcended. Her gaze locked with Logan's, and she smiled.

He sauntered toward her and wrapped his arms around her, grinning at their friends. "She's gone. You can relax now."

"Oh my God." Tina melted into Trent's arms.

"That was awesome!" Trent said. "Allison, that was incredible. And Logan, I thought the ghost was going to take you with her for a minute there."

Allison brushed the hair away from her face and wrapped her arms around Logan's waist.

He squeezed her tighter. "I'm sorry I broke the circle again, but when she reared back to throw that vase… It was instinct. I had to protect you."

"It's okay. You did it. You got rid of the ghost."

"*We* got rid of the ghost. Together."

She couldn't fight the smile tugging her lips. Though the method was unconventional, they'd done it. They'd faced the spirit together and won. Her heart raced with excitement, and tears of relief streamed down her cheeks.

Logan tilted her chin and wiped them away with his thumb. "We need to take care of your arm. You're still bleeding." He lifted her hand to examine the cut and shifted his gaze to the shattered vase on the floor. "And clean up this mess."

"It's nothing a Band-Aid won't fix."

Trent darted down the stairs and returned with a broom and dustpan and swept up the salt and broken glass.

Tina gave her a hug. "The ghost is really gone? You're safe now?"

Allison nodded as Tina's gaze followed Trent back down the stairs.

"In that case, Trent and I will be going. You two probably have some celebrating to do." She hugged Logan. "Take good care of each other."

He caught Allison's gaze and smiled. "We will."

CHAPTER TWENTY-EIGHT

"Come here, woman." Logan swept Allison off her feet, his heart pounding with anticipation as he carried her across the thick burgundy rug lining the hallway. "How's your arm?"

She ran her finger across the bandage. "All better."

"Good." He pushed open the bedroom door and lowered her to her feet. The psychic connection they shared before had been severed, but he could still feel her excitement as she pressed her body to his.

"I've never been in your bedroom before. It's nice." Her gaze never left his as she spoke, and she slid her hands beneath his shirt to caress his skin. "Have I told you how much I love your body?"

As her fingers slipped into the waistband of his jeans, he sucked in a sharp breath. "I don't think you've mentioned it."

"Well, then... maybe I should show you how much I love it. How much I love *you*." She lifted his shirt over his head and folded it neatly before putting it on the dresser. He glanced at the shirt and looked at her quizzically.

"I don't want you to be distracted by a mess on your floor, because right now, you are all mine." She popped the button on his jeans and slid down the zipper, letting his pants fall to the floor. He stepped out of them and snatched them up before she could grab them. "I'll take care of these."

She grinned as he folded the garment and laid it next to his shirt. Then she went for his underwear.

"Mmm…that's much better." She ran her hands up his chest and pushed him to the bed. Then she took off her own clothes and stacked them next to his. There was something about the way she folded those clothes, standing there naked. Christ, she was sexy.

She glided toward him, slipping into his arms and pressing her body to his. "Can you make that connection again? The way you did earlier? I'll help you."

He sucked in a shaky breath and closed his eyes. The feel of her body pressed to his was almost unbearable; he needed her so badly. But he tried. He imagined the bubble around the two of them, and he filled the bubble with light. Then he felt her reach out and complete the connection, the vibrating energy forming a psychic link between them.

He opened his eyes and drank her in. She was part of him, her own energy swirling through his until he couldn't tell where his consciousness ended and hers began.

Laying her on the bed, he climbed on top of her, running his hands down her sensuous curves. He felt her, feeling his touch. As if they were one being, every sensation of pleasure he provided her became his own.

He made love to her, feeling her pleasurable ache as he

filled her completely. He felt the burst of electricity shooting through her core as he moved inside her.

Body to body, mouth to mouth, they moved in unison, the smoothness of their rhythm penetrating every nerve, setting his soul ablaze. She moaned softly, the vibration of her voice rolling through him as if it were his own. He gave himself to her, complete and utter devotion, and as her mutual emotions swirled into his consciousness, he lost control. They climaxed together, wave after wave of ecstasy crashing through their bodies, and he felt it all. Her orgasm and his own.

Breathless, he collapsed on top of her and took her mouth in a tender kiss. He slid onto his side, their legs in a tangle, and pulled her into his arms. "Allison, that was…"

"Incredible." She rested her hand on his face and stroked his cheek with her thumb.

"That doesn't even begin to describe what we just did. You are the most amazing woman I have ever met."

They lay in each other's arms, their psychic link still buzzing between them. He felt her love and contentment and knew she felt his too.

"Do you have any plans for next weekend?" he asked.

"I was planning to be with you." She traced the outline of his mouth with her finger then placed a soft kiss on his lips.

"Will you go to New York with me? My sister called, and she wants me to bring you out to meet the family."

"I would love to meet your family." Her eyes brightened, a spark of joy emanating from her chest.

"And, if you don't mind, Lisa wants to steal you away for a few hours of shopping with my mom. Girl bonding time, she said."

"That sounds like fun. What will you do while I'm gone?"

He exhaled sharply. "I'm going to talk to my dad."

She pulled him into a tight embrace. "You won't regret it."

"I know." God, he loved this woman. She made him a better man. He needed to make her his forever, and it needed to happen now. He sat up and swung his legs over the side of the bed.

"Allison, you know how you said we could talk about selling my house after we got rid of the ghost?"

"I don't understand why you want to sell it. It's a great house."

"It is a great house, and I like living here."

Gathering the sheets into her lap, she moved to lean against the headboard. "So why not stay if you're happy here?"

He swallowed hard and turned toward her. "Do you think you could be happy here?"

She tilted her head. "Could I be happy living here?"

He nodded.

A soft smile tugged at her lips. "Are you asking me to move in with you?"

"No. Absolutely not." He shot to his feet and rummaged through his pants pocket. "That wouldn't be good enough."

Climbing into bed, he snuggled next to her, wrapping his arm around her. With his other hand, he offered her a black velvet box. "Allison, will you marry me?"

Her breath hitched as she reached a trembling hand toward the box. He flipped it open and pulled out a sparkling diamond ring.

"Oh, Logan."

His heart pounded as he slipped it on her finger. "What do you think?"

"Yes! Of course I'll marry you." She threw her arms around him and showered him with kisses, elation and love pouring off her, swirling with his own happiness to create the most magical sensation he'd ever felt.

Allison knew him better than anyone, his strengths and his weaknesses—and he had more than his fair share of those. Yet here she was, loving him in spite of them all…or maybe because of them all. Either way, he was the luckiest man alive.

He stroked his fingers down her cheek and tucked her hair behind her ear. "Are you sure you can put up with me? I've got issues."

She grinned. "I'm sure I can keep you in line."

"You think so?"

She climbed into his lap and pushed him to the bed. "Oh, I know so."

He laughed. "I'm going to love watching you try."

ALSO BY BY CARRIE PULKINEN

New Orleans Nocturnes Series

License to Bite

Shift Happens

Life's a Witch

Santa Got Run Over by a Vampire

Finders Reapers

Swipe Right to Bite

Batshift Crazy

Collection One: Books 1-3

Collection Two: Books 4-7

Crescent City Wolf Pack Series

Werewolves Only

Beneath a Blue Moon

Bound by Blood

A Deal with Death

A Song to Remember

Shifting Fate

Collection One: Books 1-3

Collection Two: Books 4-6

Haunted Ever After Series

Love at First Haunt

Second Chance Spirit

Third Time's a Ghost

Love and Ghosts

Love and Omens

Love and Curses

Collection One: Books 1 - 3

Collection Two: Books 4 - 6

Stand Alone Books

Flipping the Bird

Sign Steal Deliver

Azrael

Lilith

The Rest of Forever

Soul Catchers

Bewitching the Vampire

ABOUT THE AUTHOR

Carrie Pulkinen is a paranormal romance author who has always been fascinated with things that go bump in the night. Of course, when you grow up next door to a cemetery, the dead (and the undead) are hard to ignore. Pair that with her passion for writing and her love of a good happily-ever-after, and becoming a paranormal romance author seems like the only logical career choice.

Before she decided to turn her love of the written word into a career, Carrie spent the first part of her professional life as a high school journalism and yearbook teacher. She loves good chocolate and bad puns, and in her free time, she likes to read, drink wine, and travel with her family.

Connect with Carrie online:
www.CarriePulkinen.com

Printed in Dunstable, United Kingdom